D0921236

THE
NAKED
TRUTH

#1 *NEW YORK TIMES* BESTSELLING AUTHOR
VI KEELAND

THE NAKED TRUTH
Edited by: Jessica Royer Ocken
Proofreading by: Elaine York, Eda Price
Cover model: Simone Bredariol - D'men - www.dmanagementgroup.com
Photo credits: Mondadori Portfolio/Paolo Stella, ARteProduction/Jonathan Segade
Cover designer: Sommer Stein, Perfect Pear Creative
Formatting by Elaine York, Allusion Graphics, LLC

THE
NAKED
TRUTH

It takes strength to forgive.

When you fall in love with a
strong woman and screw up, she will forgive
you...after she is done kicking your ass.

Chapter 1

Layla

"I'm sorry. I forgot to call you. I'm not going to be able to go to lunch today." I sighed and waved at the papers strewn across my desk. "Pittman asked me to do a presentation for a new client."

"Old Man Pittman or Joe asked you?"

"Old Man Pittman. Well, *asked* isn't really the right word. He opened my door without knocking while I was on a conference call, made me put my client on hold mid-sentence, and then barked something about *three o'clock in the executive conference room* and walked out. I had to call his secretary Liz to get the details."

"That's great. You're finally getting back in the good graces of the named partners. I knew you'd work your way there." Oliver came around my desk and kissed the top of my head on his way out. "I'll bring you back the fresh tuna tacos you love."

"You're the best."

I'd been seeing Oliver Blake for about a month now, even though we'd been friends for nearly five years. He was a junior partner in the copyright division of my law firm, and I wasn't exaggerating—he seriously was the best.

When I was sick last weekend, he stopped by with chicken soup. If I was down, he reminded me of all the good things in my life. He'd been my biggest supporter even before we started dating—encouraging me to ride out the storm here at Latham & Pittman after I nearly got disbarred and fired a couple of years back. Smart, handsome, and with a great job—he was the dream man a girl would love to bring home to meet her parents. And totally the opposite of the jerks I'm usually attracted to.

Last week he'd mentioned that his lease was up in a few months and hinted that he'd love to have me help him look for a bigger place—since he hoped I'd be spending more time there in the future. Smart, handsome, a great job, *and*...not afraid of commitment.

I made a mental note to check his closets for hidden skeletons the next time I went to his apartment, and then went back to studying my presentation.

I'd watched the senior partners give the client pitch a few times, but this was the first time I'd be giving it myself. And I hated not having more than a few hours to study the slides and write my own notes. Not to mention, the only thing I knew about the investment firm I'd be pitching was that it was a start-up with a massive bankroll coming in. Probably some hotshot, arrogant trader who left his firm and took a billion dollars of investors with him—just the type of account the senior partners loved.

Old-school investment firms were good clients— steady billing to review contracts, prospectuses, and countless dealings with the SEC—but young, arrogant, new-age investment firms run by yuppies racked up legal bills like they were paying with Monopoly money.

They were sued for harassing employees, discrimination, breaching contracts, securities violations. Hell, even our tax department would get involved because all those young guys thought they were smarter than the IRS.

A couple of hours later, when it was time for my presentation, I rode the elevator up to the top floor and walked through the thick glass doors to the executive-level suites. My firm wasn't cheap—my personal office was spacious, and the furniture was high-end. But the executive floor reeked of money, old money—mahogany reception desk, crystal chandelier, Persian area rugs, and original artwork with perfectly positioned lighting.

It wasn't lost on me that the last time I'd been invited up here was almost two years ago, when I'd been summoned to explain my actions, which had resulted in charges against me by the New York State Bar Association disciplinary committee. It meant something when you were beckoned to the top floor—good or bad—which had me even more curious about why I was making today's presentation.

Sarah Dursh, one of the senior partners, met me in the hallway as I walked to the conference room. "You all ready?"

"As ready as I can feel without knowing much about the client."

Sarah's brow furrowed. "What do you mean you don't know much about the client?"

"I know the basics. But the corporate prospectus wasn't available yet, so I don't know much about the key players. I feel a little unprepared."

"But you've worked with the CEO before." She shook her head. "That's why he requested that you specifically make the presentation."

"I was requested to do the presentation? I didn't realize that. Who requested me?"

Arriving at the glass door to the executive conference room, I could see Archibald Pittman standing on the other side, laughing as he spoke to a man. His back was toward us, so I couldn't immediately see his face.

Nor did I immediately put two and two together when Sarah said, "There he is. That's Mr. Westbrook. He's the one who requested you lead the pitch meeting."

Since I had an armful of files, my laptop, and a venti Starbucks coffee, Sarah opened the door, and I stepped through first. I'd made it exactly two steps when the man Pittman had been talking to turned around. Then everything fell apart.

Literally. I froze.

Sarah, who was right behind me, walked into me, causing the files I held to slip from my hands. I bent to catch them. My coffee bobbled, and I gripped the container, which caused the lid to pop off. When I grabbed for it, the entire venti coffee spilled all over the carpet. The only thing I somehow managed to save from the conference room floor was my laptop.

Before I could collect my things or even right myself to standing, a strong hand found my elbow as I wobbled down at the floor. The man had crouched down directly in front of me, and all I could do was stare.

Yet I couldn't believe my eyes.

Nor could I figure out how to use my big mouth to say a single word, and we were suddenly face to face. The intensity of our connection knocked the wind right out of me. My pulse raced, heart pounded inside of my chest, and I didn't even attempt to pick up my files or splattered coffee.

Keeping hold of my elbow, he held out his other hand for me to take.

"Good to see you again, Freckles."

***

I had no idea how I managed to make it through the beginning of the presentation. I'd originally thought I'd be nervous with Mr. Pittman and the other named partners in the room while I spoke. Then again, I'd had no idea Gray Westbrook would be staring at me from the opposite end of the table. His eyes were penetrating, and his smirk both infuriated and intimidated me.

Even worse, he was more gorgeous than I remembered. His skin was tanned, which made the green in his eyes that much more penetrating. Through his suit, I could tell he'd grown bulkier, that underneath the expensive, tailored clothing was a body just as chiseled as his jaw. And sitting at the head of the table, he exuded a power that hit all my hot buttons. I'd forgotten a man could physically affect me in that way.

I attempted to ignore him and stick to my slides. But he made it damn near impossible. From the moment I'd started, he'd forced me to interact by asking questions. My presentation was approximately thirty slides, and so far he'd interrupted on at least ten. At first it made me nervous, even though his questions were basically softballs. But after I regained my wits, his constant forcing me to respond to him had started to piss me off.

"Our securities division works closely with the SEC, FINRA, DOJ, and New York State Securities Division to monitor and—"

He interrupted me. *Again.* "Who will be heading up my team?"

"As I was going to say, the securities division is comprised of a senior partner who worked at the Department of Justice, litigating securities fraud for eleven..."

While I was speaking, Gray looked at his watch. He then proceeded to interrupt me for what had to be the twentieth time in less than half an hour. "I'm sorry. I have a meeting across town I need to run to."

If eyes shot daggers, the man would have looked like a slice of Lacey Swiss. *What the hell is he doing? Trying to get even for the way things ended?*

I folded my arms over my chest. "Was it unclear that our presentation would take at least an hour?"

Though my eyes never left Gray's, I felt heads swing in my direction. The senior partners were probably having a heart attack right about now.

I didn't give a shit.

Gray's lip quirked. He was enjoying himself. *The asshole.*

"We initially booked an hour, but something urgent has come up that requires my immediate attention."

"Really? When did it come up?"

"*Layla*," Mr. Pittman warned, stopping short of *that'll be enough out of you.* But he didn't need to say it; his tone said it all.

Then he turned his attention to Gray. "I'm sorry, Mr. Westbrook. Of course we understand that you're busy. Perhaps we can reschedule, and I'd be more than happy to finish the presentation and answer any questions you might have."

Gray stood and buttoned his suit jacket. "That won't be necessary."

Mr. Pittman began to talk, but Gray spoke only to me across the table. "Perhaps Layla can finish tonight over dinner."

I squinted. "I have a previous engagement with a client."

Pittman's eyes nearly bulged out of his head. "I'll fill in for whatever you have tonight, Layla. You'll finish your presentation over dinner with Mr. Westbrook."

The big boss wasn't asking; he was telling. I had already pushed my luck as far as it could possibly bend without snapping, so I kept my mouth shut and silently glared at Gray.

The partners all shook hands with our prospective client and made small talk. I had no intention of going down to the other end of the table. Instead, I packed up my laptop and files to busy myself and hoped *Mr. Westbrook* would just disappear.

No such luck.

Gray approached and extended his hand. "Ms. Hutton."

Seeing my bosses watching our exchange over Gray's shoulder, I placed my hand in his, which he then used to pull me closer. I felt his hot breath on my neck as he whispered in my ear.

"You can act like you're pissed off all you want. But your body tells me otherwise. You're as happy to see me as I am you."

I pulled my head back, indignant. "You're crazy."

His eyes dropped to my chest, where my nipples were practically piercing through my sheer blouse. *Fucking traitors.*

Gray smirked. "Logan's, 7PM. I'll make a reservation and send a car for you."

"I'll meet you there."

He shook his head and laughed.

"Missed that attitude, Freckles."

Good, because you're going to get a lot more of it.

Of course I was the only one on time. I checked my phone. Ten after seven. Deciding college rules applied, I vowed to give Gray five more minutes to show up before I ditched and called him a no-show.

"May I get you something to drink while you wait for the rest of your party?" the waiter asked.

I would normally wait to see what the client did and follow his lead on alcohol. But tonight was not the norm.

I rubbed at my stiff neck. "I'll take a vodka cranberry, please."

I hoped it would help calm my nerves and release some of the tension in my jaw before I gave myself a full-blown headache. Taking out my phone, I started to scroll through emails to distract myself while waiting for my drink and dinner companion.

My head whipped up at the sound of Gray's voice behind me. "Sorry I'm late."

My heart unexpectedly fluttered, and I fought against the feeling of excitement. "Are you really? Because I get the sense you don't have any manners after the way you interrupted me a million times today."

He completely ignored my attitude as he took the seat across from me. "Traffic is a bitch getting downtown at this time. Next time we'll have dinner at my place."

"There won't be a next time."

Gray's mouth curved into a smug smile as he snagged my gaze. "Sure there will. There'll be plenty of next times. And eventually you'll stop pretending you don't enjoy my company."

I hated that my body reacted to him. Right from the very start, we'd had a crazy chemistry between us that was difficult to dull.

I sighed. "What are you doing, Gray? Why did you come to my firm?"

He lifted the cloth napkin in front of him and laid it across his lap. "Isn't that obvious? I need new legal representation."

"At my firm? And you'd prefer that representation come from an associate instead of my boss's boss—the head of our securities division? Or even from Pittman, who would gladly hold your hand and provide you whatever legal advice you need from his fifty-plus years of experience?"

"Loyalty is important to me. I want someone I can trust with my business."

"And you've decided that's *me*? An associate with five years experience who just got off probation with the Bar Association for violating attorney-client privilege?"

The waiter arrived with my drink. "Here you go, ma'am." He turned to Gray. "May I get you something to drink? Or would you like to wait until the last of your party joins you this evening?"

"It's just the two of us. I'll have a Macallan, neat, please."

"Coming right up." The waiter walked around to the other side of the table and started to remove the third place setting.

I put my hand out, stopping him. "We actually do have another party coming, so you can leave that."

"Very well." He nodded.

Gray waited until the waiter was out of earshot. "I didn't invite anyone else to dinner."

I sipped my drink and offered a saccharine-sweet fake smile. "I did. Figured an important client like you should have more than one attorney to answer his questions."

Just as I set down my glass, I saw the other man I was waiting for enter the restaurant. He scanned the room, looking for me, so I held up my hand and waved.

"Perfect timing. There's Oliver now."

Gray glanced at the man heading toward us and back to me. Instead of being pissed off, the jerk was amused. "That's cute. You invited a chaperone because you don't trust yourself with me."

Chapter 2

Gray

"So you're Layla's boss?" I sucked back a healthy gulp of the drink our waiter had just brought me.

"No, I'm not her boss. I'm in the copyright division, actually. But I'm a junior partner at Latham & Pittman. I've been with the firm for fifteen years. I can answer just about any question you might have."

I wanted the annoying clutter sitting between Layla and me removed. "Are you insinuating that Layla isn't capable of answering any questions I might have?"

"No, not at all."

"Then why are you here?"

The pencil neck looked to Layla to answer.

"I invited Oliver," she said. "Like I told you, I thought there should be more than one attorney available to answer your questions, considering how valuable your account would be to our firm."

"You thought wrong." I turned back to Oliver. "You can go. I trust that Layla will be able to handle any questions I might have."

Layla spoke through gritted teeth, but managed to keep a level tone. "Oliver is already here. And he brings a lot of value. I'm sure you'll see that by the time we finish dinner."

The waiter appeared holding menus.

I grumbled to myself, "I'm sure I won't."

After we ordered dinner, Layla's chaperone excused himself to go to the bathroom.

As soon as he was out of earshot, I said, "We need to talk, Layla. Alone. Tell him to take a hike."

"What? No!"

I stood. "Fine. I'll take care of it myself."

I ignored Layla shouting after me as I trailed Mr. Junior Partner to the bathroom. Pencil Neck was at the urinal. Apparently his neck wasn't the only thing that resembled a pencil. I stood next to him and reached into my pocket. Peeling ten hundred-dollar bills from my thick billfold, I waited until he zipped his fly. Then I extended the cash.

"Have dinner somewhere else? On me."

Pencil Neck looked down at the cash, up at me, and walked over to the sinks. I waited while he washed his hands.

When he was done, he leaned against the sink and folded his arms across his chest. "I assume we're talking man to man in here, not attorney at Latham & Pittman to potential client, right?"

"Of course." I nodded once. "Man to man."

He smiled. "Good. Then let me tell you, you're wasting your time if you're interested in Ms. Hutton."

"Why is that?"

"Three reasons. One, Layla would never go out with a client. Two, I did my due diligence on you. You might be a client worth a lot of money to the firm, but you're also an ex-con. And three, she's my girlfriend."

My blood started to pump harder. I hadn't expected that last part. Although, if Oliver thought that would scare me away, he had another thing coming. I'd just done three years in prison. Even if I found this guy mildly intimidating—which I didn't in the slightest—he'd never see me sweat.

Instead, I smiled and put a hand on his shoulder. "Let me be honest—you know, man to man—I find none of those *three reasons* a deterrent."

***

At least he was smart enough to take the hint. Oliver—*the boyfriend*—kept his mouth shut during most of dinner, allowing Layla to take the lead. Unlike this afternoon, I let her tell me all about the firm I already knew I was hiring, without interrupting. I didn't really give a fuck about any of the old cronies who would oversee my needs. But sitting across the small table, watching Layla's mouth move while she talked, staring at the light smattering of freckles she tried to conceal, letting my eyes linger on her full lips when she was paying attention and Pencil Dick wasn't, had turned into a fun game: *Make Layla squirm in her seat.*

It had been over a year since I last saw her, and if it were possible, she'd grown even more beautiful. Her dark hair was longer, and she was letting its natural wave show, rather than making it silky straight like she had a year ago. Looking at her, all I saw was what I'd dreamed that straight hair would look like after our bodies spent hours slapping against each other.

That had been a recurring damn dream after she'd cut off all communication with me. It had filled my thoughts on many lonely nights.

Tonight her plump lips were painted a bright red, and the top center dipped low, forming a perfect little V. I wanted to trace them with my tongue. Her long, feminine neck needed sucking and biting. But her eyes were the showstopper. They were a pale greenish-blue that I knew firsthand darkened when she was turned on.

"Are you even listening to me?" Layla blinked twice.

Shit. I hadn't heard a word she'd said. "Of course I am."

She leaned forward and lowered her voice. "Then what did I just say?"

Well damn, her eyes also go dark when she's pissed. I couldn't wait to fuck her when she was angry and see what that looked like.

"You were talking about the firm."

She looked back and forth between my eyes and squinted. "Whatever. I've been doing all the talking this evening anyway. Tell me, *Mr. Westbrook*, what kind of services are you looking for from a firm? This afternoon you mentioned your SEC license appeal and your new business venture. But I don't know anything about your plans since you were too busy to give us that *full hour* earlier today."

Pencil Dick looked back and forth at the two of us. I could see he had no idea what to make of Layla's attitude. Don't get me wrong, I'm sure he was enjoying it, since I'd tried to buy him off, but I got the feeling he had no idea of the history between Layla and me. I decided to test that theory.

"You look familiar, Oliver, yet I can't place it. Have you ever been up to Otisville Federal Correctional Facility?"

It was the first time I'd spoken to him directly since the men's room.

"Me? No, I haven't." He looked to Layla. "But that's where you taught that prisoner appeals program class for a while, isn't it?"

"Yes." She flashed me what I thought might be warning eyes.

Oliver was obviously quick at math, putting two and two together and all. "Is that where you did your sentence?"

I lifted my drink to my lips and smiled. "It is."

He looked at his loving girlfriend, then me, then back to her. "Did you two ever come across each other?"

And his loving girlfriend lied right to his face. "*No.*"

It made my fucking day. I offered Oliver my first genuine smile. I'd thought Pencil Dick would hamper my ability to gauge whether Layla had any interest in trying to figure things out with me. But her lie said more than she would've admitted on her own.

Unless you're pathological, you don't lie without a reason. And there's only one reason you lie to the guy you're dating about another man: so he won't get jealous. Which meant there was something there for him to be jealous about.

I arched a brow and smirked at Layla. She scowled, and her eyes darkened even more.

"Why don't you fill us in on your legal needs, Mr. Westbrook," she said. "What kind of a business are you starting?"

"A venture capitalist firm. We plan to focus on technology and communication investments. So I'll need someone to perform due diligence on the license requirements of potential investments, handle the purchase agreements, draw up loan agreements, and make sure we're not getting into bed with any crooks."

"That last part is interesting." Layla sipped her drink. "And you're planning on applying for your securities license back?"

"I am. But not just yet. I'd like to focus on the new venture for now while I work on a few things that might help improve my application for licensing."

"You know, the chances of the FINRA reinstating your securities license after a felony conviction are very slim," Layla said. "It's an automatic ten-year disqualification."

"Technically I wasn't convicted. I accepted a plea deal rather than risk a trial. At the time, it was the lesser of two evils."

"In the eyes of the law, acceptance of a plea deal is the legal equivalent of a conviction."

"I understand the consequences of accepting the deal. However, I've read you can get special permission for licensing notwithstanding disqualification."

"The rules say you can. But it's not easy. We've applied for a few and never had one go through."

"Well, then, I see lots of *firsts* for us in the future." I raised my glass to her.

After dinner was over, the three of us walked outside to the valet together. I took my time digging in my pocket for the ticket stub that would retrieve my car. Lucky for me, the first car to arrive belonged to Oliver, and another car that wasn't mine or Layla's pulled up right behind it, which meant he couldn't linger.

He stalled, trying to wait it out, probably hoping Layla's car would pull up so he wouldn't be leaving the two of us alone. But it didn't.

When a couple got into the car behind him, I lifted my chin to point at it. "Looks like you're blocking a car that's ready to leave."

He looked at Layla, then back to me.

I smiled and said, "Don't worry. I'll make sure she gets into her car safely."

If the shoe were on the other foot, no way would I leave my woman alone outside a restaurant with an ex-felon who'd already made it clear he had a non-business interest in her—potential large client or not.

Although he looked conflicted, Oliver's decision came down on the wrong side of manhood.

"I'll see you in the office tomorrow." He squeezed Layla's shoulder, then extended his hand to me. *Soft shake...pussy.* "It was nice meeting you. I hope you'll be joining Latham & Pittman."

My answer was a firm handshake. "Goodnight."

Layla and I watched in silence as her interference drove away.

"Oliver is my boyfriend," she said in a warning tone.

"I know. He mentioned that in the men's room when I tried to pay him off to take a hike. Nice kiss goodbye, by the way."

Her eyes flared. "*You didn't.* God, you're such an asshole!"

My gaze dropped to her lips. "I missed that wicked mouth." *And I can't wait to fuck it*, although I was smart enough to know it wasn't the right time to mention that.

"You're insane. And kissing me goodbye in front of a client would have been completely unprofessional—although it's not surprising *you* wouldn't realize that."

"I think the insane one is your boyfriend, who just drove off and left his woman with a man who clearly expressed an interest in her. And, by the way, I wouldn't give a shit if it was professional or not, I'd be marking my territory."

Layla's hands went to her hips. "He *trusts* me. And what are you? A dog? *Marking your territory*. Do you piss on fire hydrants, too?"

"He trusts you? That must be why he didn't see your lie when you told him we'd never met before."

I took a step closer, right into her personal space. Instead of backing up, she tilted her head to look up at me. I fucking loved that she refused to back down.

"There is no reason for him to know about us. You know why? Because there was never an *us*."

"Tell yourself whatever you need to."

"God, you are so arrogant."

I stroked her hair. "You changed your hair. I like it wavy like this. It's sexy. But you're covering up those beautiful freckles on your nose again."

She slapped my hand away. "Are you even listening to me?"

"Yes. He trusts you. No us. I'm an arrogant asshole."

She growled at me. It was fucking adorable.

"Your keys, Miss."

Neither of us had noticed her car pulling up or the valet dangling the keys while standing next to us.

Grabbing the keys from his hand, she strutted toward her car. The valet ran back to open the door. Layla began to get in and then stopped and spoke over the hood of her car. "Hire another firm, Gray. Whatever you think is going to happen between us, *isn't*."

Chapter 3

Layla

"These are gorgeous."

Becca, the receptionist who was also my friend and frequent lunch partner, walked into my office carrying a huge bouquet of yellow roses. There had to be two dozen. She set them down on the desk and sighed. "I wish I could find a guy like Oliver. That man is crazy about you."

I smiled. Although I had a nagging feeling they might not be from him. I hoped I was wrong.

"Lunch today?" she asked.

"Definitely. Around one?"

"I'll buzz you then. If I don't, you won't come up for air until it's dark outside."

She was right. I had a tendency to jump into a project and lose track of time.

Becca was just walking out of my office as Oliver walked in.

"Why don't you have a brother, Oliver?" she teased.

He smiled. Then his eyes landed on the enormous delivery on my desk, and his playful smile wilted.

Shit. He didn't *send them.*

"Secret admirer I need to be worried about?"

"Uh... Becca just brought them in. I thought you sent them."

He shook his head. "Wish I had."

While Oliver and I had been dating for almost a month, we'd never had *the talk*—more because it was unnecessary than anything else. Neither one of us had *time* to date someone else. Hell, we grabbed lunches when we could, but in four weeks, we'd only been on a couple official dates together. We both worked ten-hour days, six days a week. So I'd never bothered to consider that Oliver might be dating other women, and it looked like he hadn't thought that a possibility for me either, *until now*.

He didn't ask, but he also stood there waiting, his eyes occasionally flickering to the unopened card stapled to the outside of the clear cellophane wrap. Things grew awkward.

I silently willed the phone to ring, but of course it didn't. Eventually, I detached the card while my brain deliberated on how to handle this if the flowers were indeed from Gray. Oliver watched as I slipped the tiny card from its pink envelope.

Reading it, I forced my perfected courtroom fake smile. "My friend. I helped her with some legal work, and she sent them to say thank you."

Oliver looked relieved. I folded the card into the palm of my hand, which had already started to sweat.

"So what brings you slumming down to my floor?" I asked him. "Come to see how the other half lives?"

Oliver's office was two floors above mine. It had been recently renovated, and even though my floor was nice by law firm standards, his was luxurious.

"Thought I'd say good morning and tell you about a little chat I had with our prospective client last night."

Shit. I was digging a big hole of lies, and they all had to do with Gray Westbrook. I wasn't even entirely sure why I had started this mess by pretending I didn't know him. But the lies just kept coming.

"Oh?" Technically, this wasn't a lie—it was an omission to pretend I didn't know Gray had tried to chase him off in the men's room. Although omission or lie—whatever I called it—it still felt wrong.

"He's interested in more than legal advice from you. Jackass actually thought he could hand me a wad of cash and I'd take a hike before dinner."

"What did you say?"

"Told him you'd never date a client or an ex-con."

"I see..."

"Anyway, it was the first pitch the named partners had you on, so I know it would be good if you landed the account. But the selfish side of me hopes he goes elsewhere so he isn't hitting on you."

"I can handle myself."

"I know you can. That's one of the things I think is so sexy about you. You have balls bigger than most men I know. But this guy just got out of prison."

"Federal prison for insider trading. He's not a rapist."

"Yeah. But I hate the idea of you around some guy with no morals or ethics."

"If I didn't spend time with people who lacked morals and ethics, I'd have very few clients. You do know I work for the securities side of the firm, not the artsy and upstanding copyright department like you?"

"Sad." Oliver grinned. "But true. I gotta run—have a ten o'clock I need to prep for. Dinner this week?"

"Sure. Sounds good."

I asked Oliver to shut my door on the way out, feigning a conference call I needed to jump on. Once I was alone, I sat back in my chair, unfolded the crinkled card in my hand, and read it again.

Freckles,

I missed you. Take a chance and give me a second one.

X

Gray

I hated everything about what this man had done in the last twenty-four hours. He'd shown up without warning at my firm and insisted I give the presentation, demanded in front of the partners that I attend a dinner—a dinner where he was rude to Oliver, made me lie about not knowing him, and had the gall to send me flowers. But most of all... I hated that I had butterflies in my stomach when he was around.

The smell of roses permeated the air. Even though I hadn't removed the cellophane or taken the vase out of the cardboard protective wrap at the bottom, a sweet floral fragrance wafted through my office. I'd caught myself staring at the arrangement on more than one occasion while my mind wandered. It distracted me while I tried to finish reading a stock purchase offering. I'd spent the entire morning and three hours after lunch attempting to finish going over the damn thing, when it should have taken me an hour in total.

Frustrated, I ripped my reading glasses from my face, tossed them on the desk, and sat back, glowering at the damn roses on the corner of my desk.

"You know, you're a lot like him." I'd definitely lost my mind, considering I was now talking to an unopened bouquet of flowers. "So pretty and smelling good. But give in and pick one up, and I'll get pricked by a thorn."

It was clear I wasn't going to accomplish anything with the damn things taunting me on my desk. Blowing out a deep breath, I stood, picked up the bouquet, walked over to my garbage can, and tossed what was likely two hundred dollars worth of flowers in the trash.

Maybe it was symbolic, or maybe I was just *that nuts*, but I was able to concentrate after that. In less than a half hour, I'd finally finished up what I'd been working on and walked out to my paralegal to have her type up my handwritten notes.

I'd returned to my office and was rummaging through my file cabinet when someone knocked on my open door. I looked up to see Old Man Pittman in the doorway. I shut the cabinet.

"Mr. Pittman. How can I help you?"

It was the second time in two days he'd come down from the ivory tower to speak to me. I knew whatever he wanted had to be related to a certain potential client. For the first time, it dawned on me that the blow I'd dealt to Gray's ego might've caused him to bad-mouth me to my bosses. I wouldn't survive at this firm if the senior partners thought I'd intentionally sabotaged a large potential account. The shaky ground from my suspension had only recently started to steady.

"We thought we'd give you the good news, Layla." Pittman flashed a rare smile.

"Good news?"

"Yes."

He took a few steps into my office, and for the first time, I noticed he wasn't alone. Gray strutted in like he owned the place. He flashed a wicked smile.

Pittman motioned to him. "Mr. Westbrook has just signed on with us. He said you were very persuasive at dinner."

I fought against the headiness I felt. "Oh. That's... that's fantastic news."

Pittman patted Gray on the back. "You've made the right choice. Layla here will take very good care of you."

The fucker's eyes gleamed. "That's what I'm counting on."

"Well, I'll leave the two of you to talk." Pittman looked at me. "I know you'll need coverage for the Barag deposition. I'll have Charles sit in for you. Mr. Westbrook is a VIP client, so we'll need to rearrange some things to see that you're available when he needs you."

"The Barag deposition? It's tomorrow."

"Don't worry. If Charles can't get up to speed, we'll reschedule it. Mr. Westbrook's trip takes priority."

"Trip?"

"You'll be accompanying him to Greensboro."

I stayed quiet with a practiced smile plastered on my face until I closed the door behind Pittman. He'd left with dollar signs in his eyes, none the wiser about my wanting to strangle the new VIP.

Folding my arms across my chest as I turned to face Gray, I hissed, "What kind of game do you think you're playing?"

"What? I need new counsel."

"I thought I made it clear last night that I wasn't interested in representing you when I said, *'Hire another firm.'* What part of that was vague?"

"I'm a good client. Your firm credits you for landing the business. It's good for you."

Defiant, I jutted my chin out. "You have no idea what's good for me. *You* are not good for me."

I held my breath as he walked toward me. The nerve endings on my skin came alive even though I hadn't been touched. But there was no way in hell I was backing down or letting him see the effect he had on me. Gray got right into my personal space.

I expected the deep vibrato of his intimidating voice to put me in my place. Instead, he caught me off guard when he spoke softly.

"I'm sorry I lied to you, Layla."

I'd hardened when it came to this man. I couldn't do soft.

"Whatever happened more than a year ago was a mistake," I said. "But the mistake wasn't in your lie. The mistake was getting involved with you."

The slightest twitch of his eye was the only indication that he'd felt my strike.

"We need to be in Greensboro at noon to meet with my new partners," he said. "It's best to have your input while the terms of the partnership are being negotiated so things are already smoothed out when you draft the agreement."

The request in itself wasn't odd. I'd accompanied clients to business-formation negotiations on occasion. What was off, though, was that I was essentially stuck. No doubt Gray was fully aware of the predicament he'd put me in. If I went to the partners now and refused to work on the new account, I'd have to give them an explanation.

And what would I say? "*Remember when I had to do pro bono legal services as part of my sanctions for violating attorney-client privilege? You know, that time you almost fired me? Well, while I was fulfilling my punishment by working at a men's prison, I met Grayson Westbrook and started to fall for him. Sometimes we'd sneak into the stacks of the library and make out. Everything was great—until he lied to me. What's that? You think I should've seen that coming? But how was I supposed to know getting involved with a prisoner arrested for insider trading was a bad idea?*"

I shot him an annoyed glare. "I'll have my assistant make my arrangements and email them over to you."

A slow grin spread across his handsome face. I wanted to smack it the hell off.

"Great. Let her know I prefer the Langham."

"A hotel? I thought the meeting was at noon?"

"It is. But some of the investors are from out of town—they're also flying in. They'll expect to have dinner."

"So have dinner with them. You don't need me for that."

"Dinner will be a continuation of our business discussion."

I squared my shoulders. "Then you'll take notes and let me know if anything changes after the *actual* business meeting during the day. I'll be flying home on an evening flight."

To my surprise, Gray gave in. He nodded, took a step back, and extended his hand. "Glad to have you on my team, counselor."

My eyes dropped to his hand. A memory I hadn't thought about in ages flashed before my eyes. The first time he'd kissed me, he'd cupped my face with his big hands, and I'd nearly melted. I hated that it now made me feel vulnerable and afraid to even touch him. It was a bad idea to let the past have power over me.

Hoping I didn't tremble, I put my hand in his. A spark zapped right through me. It was akin to sticking my finger in an electrical socket. Abruptly, I slipped my hand from Gray's and walked around him toward my desk.

"Email me the names of your partners so I can do a quick search with the SEC and our investigator."

"That's not necessary."

With the desk now acting as a barrier, I lifted a file and gave it my attention while speaking. "Let's get one thing clear. If I'm your counsel, things are going to be done my way and with proper due diligence."

I didn't look up but heard amusement in his voice. "Yes, ma'am."

"Leave your contact information with my paralegal on the way out. Have a pleasant day."

A minute later, the door clicked open, so I chanced a glance up. Of course I found Gray waiting for my attention. He pointed his eyes down to my trash bin full of roses.

"Allergic?"

I couldn't hide the smirk. "Yeah. That's it."

Gray's eye's crinkled at the sides, and he winked. "Next time I'll send candy."

"Next time send them to your wife."

Chapter 4

Layla

2 years earlier

"You'll need to change your shoes."

"Shoes?" I looked down at my feet. The red Brian Atwood strappy sandals didn't exactly go with the look of my conservative lawyer suit. But if I was forced to work here on a Saturday, I needed something to help me feel human. And they certainly weren't so off that I'd need to change them. I looked back up at the corrections officer. "What's wrong with my shoes?"

"No open-toe shoes allowed in a federal correctional facility."

You've got to be kidding me.

"No one told me. I drove four hours at five o'clock this morning to get here. It's my first day of volunteering."

She smirked. "What'd you do wrong?"

"Wrong?"

"Lawyers who *volunteer* up here on the weekend are usually not really volunteers."

"Oh."

The corrections officer raised a brow—she was waiting for an actual answer.

I sighed. "Two hundred hours of community service for violating attorney-client privilege."

She whistled. "Two hundred hours. Sanctions dished out here are easier than that."

"Oh yeah? What happens when someone gets in trouble here?"

"Snitches get stitches."

Great. Just great.

She handed me back my identification. "So you have an extra pair of shoes or what?"

"I don't. Is there a store around here where I can grab a pair of pumps or something?"

"Twenty miles up the road is a Walmart."

I looked at my watch. "I'm supposed to start in thirty minutes."

"Better get a move on then."

I was inside a prison. Not in the type of visitor room you might see on TV—one where the visitor is on one side of thick safety glass, and the parties need to lift a phone to hear each other—but inside an actual prison where men walked around freely. Unlike the neighboring, higher-security prison, the Otisville minimum-security prison camp where I'd be teaching classes every Saturday for the next few months felt sort of like a college. The perimeter of the facility had no fencing. Inmates didn't even live in locked cells. Instead, they had dormitory-style housing and lockers. If I hadn't known it was a prison when I walked in, I wouldn't have looked twice at the men walking around in leisurely khakis and button-downs. Most could have passed for professors. They seemed to be mostly older men, clean cut, and with an air about them that said their other homes were penthouses.

"How many people does this facility house?" I asked the guard walking me to the library.

"Goes up and down on any given day, but usually a little over a hundred."

We walked through a door and down a long, windowed corridor. The men outside were smiling and seemed to be enjoying themselves.

"Is that...a bocce court?"

He chuckled. "Yep. Got a baseball field better than my kid's high school, too. They don't call these camps Club Fed for nothing."

The place was way nicer than I'd expected, but the library—the library was pretty damn insane. Two dozen stacks held more books than my local public library had housed growing up. There were large tables with wooden chairs that reminded me of the ones I'd sat at until late at night in law school. A glass wall separated a large classroom with a flat-screen computer monitor at every desk.

"Jeez." I looked around.

"Not what you expected, I take it."

"Not at all."

The guard pointed toward the classroom. "The library will be closed to anyone who isn't registered to take your classes. So you can use the classroom or the library, whatever you want. I think there are fourteen guys registered in the class that starts today, not including Westbrook. So you'll have plenty of room."

VIKEELAND

"Westbrook?"

"He coordinates all the classes going on right now."

"Oh. Okay."

"Speak of the devil." The guard lifted his chin. "Here comes our resident pretty boy now."

I turned to find a tall, dark-haired man coming toward us. Walking with another man, he kept his head down until he reached the doorway to the library. When he lifted it, the view made my heart do a little two-step dance. "Pretty boy" didn't do the man justice. He was gorgeous. Ridiculously so. The type of rugged, dark, masculine looks that probably made him completely arrogant and full of himself. *My weakness.*

Our eyes caught, and a slow, cocky smile spread across his face. It was then that the big guns came out—the most prominent, deepest dimples I'd ever seen.

Yep. He's definitely full of himself.

Although...maybe this punishment wouldn't be so bad after all.

The guard made the introduction. "Westbrook, this is Layla Hutton. She'll be teaching the inmate pro-se appeals class."

He extended his hand with a nod. "Nice to meet you. Grayson Westbrook. Guards here only call people by their last name. Civilians call me Gray." His eyes did a quick sweep over me. "I'll have to stick close by. A lot of these men haven't seen a woman as beautiful as you in..." He shook his head. "Hell, this might be a first for most."

The guard chuckled. "Yeah. That's why you'll be sticking close by, Westbrook." He turned to me. "Like I said, this is a minimum-security camp. Our doors aren't locked, and prisoners are basically on the honor system. No violent offenders in here. They decide to leave, they get brought back eventually, and then they're not guests at this nice facility anymore. You feel okay if I leave you with Casanova here for a bit while I go grab a bite to eat? We have limited staff and usually leave lawyers and regular contractors on their own if they're comfortable." He pointed to cameras on the walls and ceiling. "We'll always have eyes on you and be a shout away. And the library door will be locked since it's closed today."

"Umm...sure." I was actually pretty nervous, although some of that was alleviated when the gorgeous program coordinator flashed his dimples again.

After the guard disappeared, Gray walked me to the adjoining classroom. "So...you draw the short straw at your firm for pro bono work or get yourself in trouble and this is part of your punishment?"

I guess most attorneys didn't volunteer to drive to the middle of nowhere and teach convicted criminals how to overturn their appeals out of the goodness of their hearts. "Punishment. Today is the first day of my prison sentence."

"It could be worse. You could actually be a resident here instead of being forced to work here for a while."

"True."

"What did you do that got you into trouble?"

"Don't you know it's not polite to ask a woman her age, weight, or why she almost got disbarred?"

He smiled. God, he needed to stop doing that. "Sorry."

"It's fine."

Gray turned on the laptop at the front of the classroom. "This has Wi-Fi, but it's limited. If you need a site that isn't accessible, just let me know, and I'll get you access."

"Okay. Great."

"Class doesn't start for another two hours or so. I'll hang around next door in the library so you can get yourself set up. If you need anything, just tap on the glass."

I spent the next half hour making sure I had access to all of the research resources I would review during my first presentation. Then I went over the slides I'd prepared.

Gray had taken a seat in a chair in the library and was reading a book—wearing glasses he hadn't worn earlier. They must've been for reading. Since I had overly prepared to teach the class today (as usual), I had plenty of time to kill. And... I was curious to see what the bespectacled Adonis looked like up close. So I went next door to the library side.

"*Quicksand,* huh?"

Gray had been engrossed in his book and didn't hear me come in.

"Is it fiction or non-fiction?" I asked.

He looked up. The thick-rimmed, square glasses he wore really worked for him—worked for me. The sharpness of their shape complemented his angular jaw. He slipped them from his face, and I found myself debating whether I liked him better with or without while he spoke.

"Non-fiction. It's a memoir written after the author received a lung cancer diagnosis. It's sort of his look back while he was still here."

"That sounds depressing."

"It does. But it's actually not. It's funny. He looks back at the shit he took seriously with a whole new perspective at the end. And he realizes some of the most important days he ever had were just ordinary ones spent with the right people."

I took a seat at the table across from him, and our eyes met. He shut the book. I'd just met the man, knew nothing about him other than he worked at a prison, but I had the strangest feeling that today was one of those important days. It was crazy.

We smiled at each other in silence, our off-the-charts chemistry rising to an incendiary level, until the guard opened the library door.

"Just checking in on you. All good?"

I waved. "Everything is fine. Thank you."

"I'll be back later, before your students arrive."

"Okay."

Gray hadn't taken his eyes off of me during the exchange with the guard. He didn't even pretend to look elsewhere while I settled back into my seat. It made me feel like a teenager being watched by the cute boy next to me in math class—sort of a nervous excitement. But my way of dealing with nerves was always head-on. Even in high school, I'd turn to the boy and smile back until he backed down or made his move. It was no different now.

"You're staring at me," I said.

His smile widened. "You're beautiful. Does it bother you that I'm appreciating that?"

I held his gaze. "No. You're not so bad yourself. Will it bother you if I stare?"

The gleam in his eyes sparkled a little brighter. "By all means, stare away."

We spent the next few minutes just looking at each other. It was the oddest interaction I'd ever had with a man I'd just met.

"Tell me something about you, Layla Hutton. Other than your age, weight, or reason for near disbarment, of course."

"I'm twenty-nine, weigh a hundred and eighteen pounds, and I found out a client was abusing his wife, so I broke confidentiality and reported it to the police."

He smiled and rubbed his chin. "Sounds like you should have gotten a medal for that last part, not nearly suspended."

"Yeah, well...that's how I feel. But the disciplinary committee and the partners at the law firm where I work have a different way of thinking."

I sighed. It actually felt good to meet someone and get all of that off my chest right away.

"You know what?" I said. "This is the way it should always be. You meet a man. He tells you he thinks you're attractive. You tell him it's mutual. Then you air your dirty laundry. If he still looks at you the same way, you continue. If not, you walk away. Life's too short to waste time."

"I agree. Tell me, how am I looking at you after you've aired your dirty laundry?"

I studied him. He arched a brow when I leaned in closer to get a good look at what he was thinking inside that handsome head of his. What I found gave me goosebumps. The eyes really are the windows to the soul.

I sat back in my chair. "You're looking at me like you'd like to see me naked."

Gray threw his head back in laughter. "Very good."

I lifted my chin. "Your turn. Tell me your dirty laundry."

His dark eyes shadowed and his expression turned serious. "I'm thirty-one, weigh two hundred and five the last time I checked, and..." He paused and leaned forward, his elbows resting on the table as he looked directly into my eyes. "And I was sent to prison for insider trading that I didn't commit."

My smile wilted before the last part even registered in my brain. I was confused. "You've been to prison?"

"I'm the program coordinator, Layla. It's my job. My *inmate* job." Gray leaned closer and searched my eyes. "How are you looking at me now?"

Chapter 5

Layla

I'd been trying to cut back to one cup of coffee, but this morning a double dose was definitely necessary. I'd tossed and turned all night, not able to switch off the rambling thoughts in my head long enough to relax and drift off. Thank goodness for concealer.

I stared out the bedroom window of my third-floor apartment, sipping my coffee. I had a half hour before the car would pick me up for the airport, and all I needed to do was get dressed, which left me yet more time to think.

A black town car slowed, then pulled up at the curb of my building. I glanced over at the clock next to my bed to see if I'd lost track of the time. Six thirty. The car service had arrived really early. Of course, I could've made the driver wait until seven, the time I'd scheduled, but that wasn't my style. I chugged the remainder of my coffee and headed to the closet to get the dress I'd picked out to wear today, but I stopped when my buzzer buzzed. Drivers normally just idled until I came outside, rather than parking and letting me know they were here.

I hit the intercom. "Hello?"

"Morning, beautiful."

I froze. Gray's voice was deep and distinct. It couldn't be mistaken for anyone else's.

"What are you doing here?"

"We're here to pick you up to go to the airport."

"We?"

"Me and my driver."

"I have my own car coming. I'll meet you at the airport."

"I canceled your car."

"You *what*?"

"We need time to go over some things before the meeting. Besides, there's no point in taking two cars to go to the same place. Your secretary gave me your itinerary, so I called your service and told them the car was no longer needed."

"You can't do that."

"I'm here instead of your car, aren't I?"

I looked up and counted to ten. Gray was trying to do more than share a car to the airport. He wanted to throw me off my game. I did it to opponents occasionally to make them feel unbalanced. I'd randomly change up the topic of my questioning mid-stream, scramble my witness order—anything that might make them feel unsettled allowed a bit of vulnerability to creep in.

I had no intention of becoming a pawn in whatever games Gray thought he could play with me.

I pressed the buzzer after a long pause. "I'll be down in a few."

"I need to use your bathroom."

"No!"

"It's either that or find an alley somewhere."

"Get looking for an alley." I released the intercom button and went to get dressed. From the other room, I heard his voice reply in the distance, but I couldn't make out what he'd said. It didn't matter. He was most certainly not coming up to my apartment.

By nature, I was a people pleaser. So without thinking, I rushed to get dressed so I wouldn't keep the driver and Gray waiting. When I caught myself, I slowed down, spending a few extra minutes fixing my hair and adding another coat of mascara. But that only made me more annoyed with myself, because I felt like I was putting extra effort into my appearance for my travel companion.

I needed to stop overthinking and treat Gray like any other client.

I loaded my bag with the few files I had, added some legal pads and pens, and took a deep breath before heading downstairs. Gray stood just outside the front door of my building, leaning against the railing.

"Find an alley?" I snipped.

"Nope. Thought better of it. I'm out on probation. Getting tossed back inside for indecent exposure isn't in my plans."

"There's a coffee shop at the corner."

"Tried. Owner said it was out of order."

I rolled my eyes and groaned before turning to go back upstairs. "Come on. Bathroom *only*."

In the elevator, I stared straight ahead, even when I caught his eyes on me through my peripheral vision. Although, staring at the shiny silver doors that reflected back almost as well as a mirror didn't do much to help me avoid looking at Gray. He was dressed in a Brioni custom-fit, five-thousand-dollar suit, and the tailor had done one hell of a job. It showed off his slim waist, hugged his broad shoulders, and made him look effortlessly elegant. Some women liked a bad boy look—all James Dean in a leather jacket. But a well-fitted suit pushed every one of my hot buttons.

Admiring the package presented before me almost made me forget his true colors. *Almost.*

The doors slid open, and I rushed out of the car, anxious to breathe air that wasn't shared with Gray Westbrook. Unlocking my apartment, I held the door open and pointed.

"Down the hall, first door on the right. *No lingering.*"

I wrenched my gaze away from him as he walked, not wanting to notice that the tailor had done as good of a job on the back as he had the front.

While I waited impatiently, holding the front door open, a cell phone rang from somewhere. I glanced around the kitchen before realizing it was coming from the bathroom.

A few minutes later, Gray strode down the hall. The ringing started again as he reached where I stood at the door. He slipped his phone from his pocket and held up one finger.

"What's up?" he answered. "Is everything okay?"

He sounded concerned. Through the receiver, I heard a woman talking, but I couldn't make out what she said. So I listened to one side of the conversation.

"I'm never too busy for you. What's going on?"

His eyes shut as the woman spoke again.

"Are you hurt? What happened?"

The anxiety in his voice settled in my chest as he listened again.

He dragged a hand through his hair. "Who was driving?"

Another pause.

Gray shook his head. "Where are you? Are the police there yet?"

More muffled sounds through the phone.

"I'll be right there. Don't talk to anyone, Etta. Not a word."

He swiped to end the call and looked up at me. "Change of plans."

"What happened?"

"A family friend had an accident. She's seventy-seven and had her license taken away last year by the doctor. She still drives anyway. I need to get to Queens."

"Let's go."

———

Gray stared off out the window as we made our way to Queens.

"Everything is going to be okay. They'll just give her a ticket for driving without a license."

He nodded.

"What's her name? Did you say Etta? I remember you mentioning her a few times."

"Short for Henrietta. But don't call her that. She hates it. Etta might be in her seventies, but she's still scary as shit."

I started to laugh until I realized he wasn't joking. "Who is she?"

"She was my dad's housekeeper for almost thirty-five years. When I was little, she used to watch me, too—basically raised me since my father was never around."

"Oh. Wow. And she lives in Queens?"

"Yeah. In one of the rental buildings my father owned. He didn't do right by most women, but he took care of Etta."

Two police cars were parked diagonally in the street, surrounding the accident when we pulled up. EMTs lifted an older gentleman on a stretcher into the back of an ambulance.

Gray jumped out of the car almost before we came to a full stop and ran right over to Etta's car. I followed behind as fast as I could. The driver's side door was open, and she sat behind the wheel with her legs sticking out of the car. An officer stood next to her, writing something in his little notepad.

"Etta. Are you okay?"

"I'm fine, Zippy. I didn't want to have to call you. I just wasn't sure if I was going to need some assistance with the police."

Zippy?

Gray knelt down and looked Etta over. He seemed to be assessing her health.

"Was she given medical attention?" he asked the officer.

"Paramedics checked her out. Everything was fine, and she didn't want to go to the hospital."

"Does anything hurt?" he asked her.

"Nothing that didn't hurt before."

"You should go to the hospital anyway, Etta. Just as a precaution."

She waved him away. "Nonsense. People my age go into the hospital for a few stitches and wind up dead a week later from a staph infection they picked up."

"Did you hit your head or anything?"

"It was a light tap. My Henry used to do more damage hitting my noggin against the headboard back in the day. The man was a lion."

The officer's eyebrows jumped, and he shook his head with a chuckle.

Etta's eyes lifted to me. "Speaking of headboard banging, who have we here?"

"This is Layla Hutton. She's…"

I stepped forward. "I'm Gray's attorney."

Etta's eyes twinkled. "Layla. It's so nice to finally meet you, dear." She turned to Gray. "And she's a hell of a lot better looking than the moron who told you to take that bad deal."

"Yes, she is," Gray said. "What happened with the accident, Etta?"

"I was on my way home from picking up a new *TV Guide*. I think the postman's stealing mine."

Gray interrupted. "At six thirty in the morning?"

"When you get to be my age, God stops requiring sleep so you don't have to waste what little time you have left."

Gray took a deep breath and closed his eyes for a moment. I could tell he was frustrated and upset, but he did his best not to show it. "Go on. Tell me about the accident."

"Not much to tell. I stopped at the stop sign on the corner, and some geezer who should've had his license taken away rear-ended me."

The cop stopped writing in his notepad and pointed his pen at Etta. "He had a license, Mrs. Bell. Unlike you."

"Whatever." Etta rolled her eyes.

I turned my attention to the officer. "Could we talk for a minute?"

The policeman tilted his head toward his patrol car. "Sure. Just let me call in that the ambulance is about to take off."

It took me ten minutes to talk the officer out of issuing Etta a citation. I had to tell him she had trouble remembering she no longer had a license and promise I'd take the keys away as soon as I got her home.

I walked back to the car with the police report in my hand. "He's gonna let it slide this time. But you have to get a license or stop driving, Mrs. Bell."

"Call me Etta. And I had a license more years than that idiot was alive. And the eye doctor who ratted me out to the DMV, too, for that matter. I think if a person is going to take away your license or give you a ticket, they should at least have the decency to be over thirty."

Gray shook his head. "Thank you for taking care of that. Looks like her car is still drivable. It's just a dent in the back bumper. Why don't I drive Etta home, and you can follow with my driver."

"Sure." I glanced at the time on my phone. "We aren't going to make our flight."

"I'll call the airline and see if we can get on the next one when we get to Etta's."

As I settled back into the car by myself and let the driver know what was going on, I realized there was no livery or car-for-hire license information displayed in the back. "Umm...excuse me, do you work for a car service?"

"No, I work for Mr. Westbrook. Name's Al, ma'am."

Gray had only been released two weeks ago. I'd checked. "Hi, Al. How long have you worked for Mr. Westbrook?"

The driver caught my eyes in the rearview mirror. He was older with silver hair, probably in his sixties. "Off and on for eight years now."

"Off and on?"

"Yes, ma'am. While Mr. Westbrook was...out of town...I did some freelance driving. But now that he's back, I'm back."

I don't know why, but I found that interesting. Gray had been in prison for three years, out for barely two weeks, and he was already saving his old nanny from a ticket and rehiring his driver.

Etta's house was only a few blocks from the accident. The driver pulled to the curb while Gray parked in the driveway. I got out to see what I could do to help.

Turned out, Etta didn't need much help. She got her car door open and had climbed out before Gray could shut off the engine and run around to help her.

We walked into her house together.

"Have a cup of tea with me, Layla," she said.

Gray closed the front door behind us. "What? I'm not invited for tea?"

"You're invited *to make* the tea. You stopped being a guest in my home when you were in diapers. Now mind your manners and go put on the kettle. Rustle us up something to have with our tea. I think there's some biscotti in the cabinet to the left of the refrigerator."

Gray looked from Etta to me and then back to Etta. "Fine."

I found it amusing how such a large, dominant presence like Gray was easily transformed into something totally different by this woman. Their interactions were interesting, to say the least.

Etta walked over to a chair that sat across from a couch. "Come, dear. Sit. We don't have much time."

Something told me she didn't mean time was limited because Gray and I had to get going for work. Curiously, I took a seat across from her.

She smiled warmly at me before beginning to speak. "Let's get the obvious out of the way. Gray can be a real asshole."

My eyebrows jumped. "Wow." I laughed. "I'm not sure what I expected you to say, but it certainly wasn't that."

"I passed the age where you stop to think about whether it's appropriate to say something or not a long time ago."

"I appreciate that. I'm actually pretty direct myself."

"I know. That's one of the things that first attracted Zippy to you."

I'd suspected by her reaction when we were introduced that she knew something about me, and something about my history with Gray.

"Gray told you about me?"

She opened the drawer on the end table next to her and lifted out a thick batch of rubber-banded envelopes. "You were in every letter since the day he walked into that library and saw you. Can't visit a prisoner unless they put you on their visitor list. The little shit wouldn't add my name; he didn't want me to see him in that light. But he wrote every week."

"I didn't know. That's very sweet."

"That's what I wanted to talk to you about. Grayson *is* sweet. He's made some poor choices, didn't have the best role models in life, but he's not the man you think he is."

"Not to be disrespectful, Etta, but how do you know who I think he is?"

She nodded with a smile. "I was married for more than forty years before my Henry passed away." She looked over to a framed wedding picture on the wall, and her eyes softened. "He was a charming man. Could talk the pants off of any woman. This woman included. We met at The Plaza Hotel—literally walked into each other in the lobby. He was new in town, and the two of us hit it off pretty well. He'd told me he'd never had a serious girlfriend before. About a month or so after we became inseparable, I found out he'd been married. I'd say that was about as serious of a girlfriend as you could get, wouldn't you?"

"Absolutely."

"Anyway, to make a long story short, I stopped seeing Henry after finding out he'd lied to me. Later, I came to find out Henry had been in a car accident with his wife. He was at the wheel, and she'd died in the wreck. They'd only been married a few weeks. He held himself responsible for it, even though the accident wasn't his fault. Unable to shake the memories in the small town they'd lived in, he'd relocated to New York, where he'd grown up, and left everything behind. It was too painful for him to talk about, so he just pretended it never happened."

"That's so sad."

"It is, isn't it? The best thing I ever did was give Henry a chance and hear him out. He'd lied to me. But sometimes people tell lies for reasons other than keeping the truth from us. Sometimes those lies are to protect themselves."

"I don't know, Etta. Gray's wife didn't die. I can't imagine what reason he could have to justify a lie like that. It wasn't like we had a normal relationship. We couldn't go out to dinner or the movies. All we had were long talks and truth. That's why it really hurt when I found out he was married. I spent all day on Saturdays visiting him for a year after my six-month teaching assignment was over. He had every opportunity to talk to me." I took a deep breath. "Besides, I've moved on. It honestly took me a really long time to do it. But I did. And now I'm dating a great guy."

She reached over and patted my knee. "Okay, sweetheart. I don't want to upset you. I just wanted you to know that I've known the man all of his life. And he's as loyal as they come. In fact, that's what got him into trouble. You're as lovely as he's said you were in his letters. I hope you're happy, dear."

Gray walked in carrying two cups of tea and saw our serious faces. "Oh, Jesus. Don't believe any of the crap Etta tells you."

Etta scolded him for his use of the word *crap*, but I saw the light in her eyes when he spoke. She loved the man fiercely.

We sat and had tea with Etta before Gray reluctantly said we had to get going. He hugged her goodbye and said he'd be back to check in on her over the weekend.

When it was time for me to say goodbye, she pulled me into an embrace. "It was wonderful to finally meet you, Layla."

"You too, Etta."

"Gray, would you mind getting my *TV Guide* out of the car before you go?"

Once we were alone again, she squeezed my hand. "I see the way he looks at you. He cares for you a great deal. I'm happy for you that you've moved on. But I know my Zippy; he's strong willed. He won't move on if he thinks he has the slightest chance of making things right with you. He's just lost three years of his life that he didn't deserve to lose. If you have it in your heart, just hear him out. Let him finally tell you his story. Seeing that you're not interested after you know everything might help him move on, too. He's lost enough time."

Chapter 6
Layla

"Thank you for this morning," Gray said as we took our seats on the plane—next to each other, in first class.

I assumed that was another detail on my itinerary Gray had chosen to fix, because the seat assignment my assistant had provided was in row twenty-three. I didn't complain about this change at least.

"Anytime. Etta's great. She cares about you a great deal."

"She's more like a parent to me than the one I had. Most of my teachers in grade school thought she *was* my mother after my mom died. Etta was the only one who showed up for parent-teacher conferences and chorus concerts. My father never did."

I felt myself going soft, slipping back to the type of heart-to-heart conversations we'd spent more than a year having. I didn't want to be mean when he spoke so nicely of a woman who was obviously important to him, but I also didn't want him to use this situation to get back in with me.

Offering a sympathetic smile, I turned to look out the window. Gray might be a lot of things, but at the top of the list was perceptive. He took the hint, and we were both silent for the rest of boarding and take off. I'd brought my headphones and had planned to put them on to avoid small talk with Gray, but after this morning, it felt ruder than I wanted to be.

Fifteen minutes after we hit our cruising altitude, he shifted in his seat to look at me. "Now that your choices are jumping thirty-five thousand feet or listening to me, I want to explain myself."

We were in row two, so I could see the door of the plane. I eyed it. "Give me a minute; I'm weighing my choices."

He smiled before his face grew serious. "I'm not going to tiptoe around what I need to say. I've been waiting a long time to get it off my chest."

Our gazes caught, and he read my silence as safe to proceed.

"I was married. Briefly. But technically, I didn't lie to you when you asked me. I had the marriage annulled. Which means it never existed."

I felt a sudden, overwhelming wave of nausea. On a few occasions, I'd considered going back and calling him out on catching him in his lie, but I'd been so hurt and felt so stupid for falling for a guy who was in prison.

It had been a year of bad choices for me, and I'd gotten to a point where I doubted all of my decisions. If Gray had been a regular guy I was dating, and I'd found out he was married, I'd have marched to his house to call him out on his lies. But with Gray, deep down I think I was a little afraid to give him the chance to explain. My heart had fallen fast and hard, yet my head was still screaming it was a bad idea.

"She signed in as your wife on the visitor log."

"I can't explain that other than to say when I'd made my list of visitors, things were very different, and she was still my wife."

"Why wouldn't you have just told me that you were married, and the marriage had been annulled, when I asked if you'd ever been married? You also told me you'd never been in a serious relationship before. I think marriage qualifies as pretty serious."

Gray raked his fingers through his hair. "I was afraid to."

"Why? Being divorced or having a marriage annulled wouldn't have scared me away. But being lied to and being made to feel like I was being played for over a year...that was awful."

"I know. I got that message when you sent back my letters unopened and stopped visiting."

"I don't understand. Why were you afraid to tell me all this?"

"Because you'd ask questions, and I didn't want to explain what an idiot I was. I knew you were skittish about what was happening between us to begin with. Let's face it, you met me while I was in prison. The deck was stacked against me already."

I looked out the window for a few moments as thoughts spun through my head. *Do I believe him? Does it matter if I do?* What if he'd been honest with me a year ago? Where would we be today? *What about Oliver?*

A part of me didn't want to hear Gray's story. The woman in me didn't want to give him a chance to come clean. I would never trust him again anyway. He'd broken more than my trust; he'd broken my heart.

But the lawyer in me needed to get to the bottom of what had happened. And if I was going to be working with him, we needed to move past this mess. Otherwise, there would be something hanging over us forever. Etta seemed to think it would help Gray move on if he could tell his story and see that it didn't change things between us. Maybe we both needed him to finally do that.

It couldn't put any *more* strain on our relationship to listen and accept his apology.

I took a deep breath, put on my game face, shifted in my seat, and gave Gray my full attention. "Start from the beginning."

Gray studied me for a moment and then nodded. "Max and I started the investment company together."

"You told me about him. You said your partner set you up."

He shook his head and closed his eyes. "Max isn't a him. You assumed that, and I let you to avoid telling you the truth. Max is a woman. She was my partner, and my wife for a period of time."

"The partner who set you up was your wife?"

Gray looked down. "Yeah. I saw none of it coming."

"How long were you married?"

"Enough time to royally fuck up my life." He paused. "Two years after we started the firm, we were managing upwards of a half-billion dollars in investments already. When we closed the biggest account we'd ever landed, Max and I took a trip down to the Dominican Republic to celebrate. We were both workaholics. We spent twelve hours a day together, but things between us were strictly business until that trip."

"Okay."

"We celebrated for a long weekend, and shit happened between us. The night before we left to come back, we got drunk and wound up getting married. It was a spur-of-the-moment thing, or at least I thought it was at the time." Gray shook his head. "I had no idea it was the beginning of a set up that would literally steal years from my life."

"And you got it annulled when you came home?"

"No. That's what I *should've* done. But instead, I started to warm to the idea of being married. I worked long days and didn't have the time or desire to put into a relationship. Whenever I'd go out with a woman, I'd be upfront about not wanting a commitment. They'd say they were good with it, but that always changed after a few dates. Being with Max made it easy."

"Did you love her?"

"I don't know. I thought I did. Not so much as a wife, but as a partner and friend, at least."

"How long did you stay married?"

"Almost two years."

"You'd told me your partner set you up, and you took a plea deal because the evidence was so strong against you that you could've gotten ten years more than the deal they offered you. So you knew it was her and just couldn't prove it?"

Gray blew out a deep breath. "I took the deal *for* her. It's a long story. But she made it seem like one of the guys who worked for us had set *both* of us up. We were *both* being investigated. I was indicted first. Hers was supposedly on its way. I took the deal because our lawyer said there was a good chance we'd both get more than ten years. I would've risked it for me. I was fucking innocent. But I couldn't let Max—*my wife*—go to prison. My lawyer was able to negotiate a deal where I'd do a few years if I took the blame for the entire thing. Max got immunity from prosecution." He shook his head. "Betrayal doesn't come from your enemies. It comes from the people you care about."

My eyes widened. "So you took a plea deal to keep the person who set you up from going to jail?"

He smiled sadly. "How's that for irony?"

Emotion surged inside me. Sadness. Guilt. Anger. Pity. Surprise. *Fear*. I was afraid to believe him, even though somewhere deep down, I knew he was telling me the truth.

"You could have told me…"

"I was embarrassed. And you were nervous about getting too close to me to begin with. I didn't want to scare you away with any of this shit—an ex-wife, how gullible I was. I just wanted to move on with my life and not look back anymore."

"When did you realize it was Max who had set you up?"

"About a month after I started my sentence, a buddy of mine came to visit. He'd been on the subway and happened to see Max, only she didn't see him. She was too busy sucking face with Aiden Warren."

"So you got suspicious because she was cheating?"

"Aiden Warren was the guy who we thought set us up."

My eyes widened again. "Shit. So the two of them set you up together?"

"More than ten million in profits from insider trades went into and out of an account with my name on it—none of it was ever found or recovered. I had my buddy hire an investigator and dig on Aiden. Apparently the two of them had been a couple since before I hired him as an employee."

"Can you prove all of this? Did you consult with your lawyer about getting the guilty plea withdrawn?"

"My lawyer said it's tough to get any guilty plea overturned once you've been sentenced—even tougher after the sentence has been served. We have some evidence, and I'm still working on it, but I'm not even sure I want to waste time fighting that battle."

"But getting it overturned means you wouldn't have the uphill battle to get your Series 7 license back."

"I know." He nodded. "I had thirty-nine months to do nothing but think about my life. I was born with money. My father ran a successful investment firm, and I was on track to follow in his footsteps. Always working. Never home. No amount of money ever being enough. I married a woman because it was convenient with my job. My father didn't pick women he worked with. After my mother died, he picked women who didn't care if he was home and were happy spending his money. But eventually they got bored being alone, and he'd get divorced again. He was married five times by the time he was fifty. He died alone of a heart attack at fifty-nine while I was serving my last month in prison."

"I'm sorry."

Gray gave me a sad smile. "Thank you. Those years in Otisville made me realize I don't want to wind up like him. The market burns people out anyway—I was halfway there. My father left me enough money to pay restitution and still start my own company. I have a chance to start over. I'm going to take it."

"Wow. It sounds like you've really done a lot of soul searching."

"It's amazing what years of having nothing to do but replay your life over and over in your head will do—makes you realize what's important."

My chest ached for him. If everything he said was true, which my gut thought it was, then he'd lost three years of his life, his business, his father, and had suffered the ultimate betrayal by the woman he'd married and obviously trusted. Yet he didn't sound bitter. While the saying is *when life hands you lemons...make lemonade*, I'm pretty sure I'd be using the lemons to peg people in the head if I were in his shoes.

I'd leaned on the armrest between us. Gray reached over and gently stroked my arm.

"I'm sorry I hurt you, Layla. I know it will take time for you to trust me. But I'm going to earn that back."

I didn't know how to respond, so I chose not to. Although removing my arm from the armrest probably said more than any words would have.

Regret clouded his eyes. "Do you love this Oliver guy?"

"He's a good guy. We're good together."

He searched my face. "Didn't hear the word *love*."

"It doesn't matter." I waved my hand back and forth between the two of us. "We're not going to happen, Gray."

A slow smile stretched across his handsome face. "Yes, we are. You can fight it all you want." He leaned his face to mine.

Our noses were practically touching. My body tingled feeling his hot breath on my skin.

"In fact, I want you to fight it. Fight it tooth and nail. It will make it that much better for both of us when you finally give in."

Chapter 7

Gray

It was impossible to concentrate all day.

Half the time, I stared across the table at Layla while she spoke, not hearing a goddamn word but knowing that each time she made the *th* sound, I'd get a glimpse of her wet, pink tongue as it peeked out between her bright red, painted lips and pearly white teeth. When she half smiled, it was always on the left, and the slightest little crow's feet dented her porcelain skin.

Luckily, one of my two partners had the ability to focus. Franklin Marks had been a lifelong associate of my father's and was in his mid-sixties. Joining with me to start this venture capitalist firm was a hobby for him. He already had more money than the next two generations of Marks' kids could burn through. Franklin brought years of experience in finance to the table—the kind that didn't get taught in Ivy League MBA programs. He was on the conservative side, but that was okay because he'd help balance out Jason, my other partner.

Jason and I had been friends since we were kids. I trusted him with my life. Over the years, we'd invested together in some small projects for fun. But he had a tendency to take risks, in business and his personal life. He worked hard and played even harder. Which was why I pulled him aside after our meeting to tell him the attorney he'd been salivating over all day was off limits.

I'd mostly planned the meeting today as an excuse to travel with Layla—get her alone for a while. I'd even blown off dinner with my partners tonight, just to have a few more hours on a flight home together. But the trip had turned out to be productive. Layla now had everything she needed to finalize the agreements we needed drawn up, and Franklin was so impressed with how she managed the three of us all day, he told her he'd be giving her a call for some other work.

In the car on the way back to the airport, my phone buzzed. I lifted it to find the best fucking text I'd ever received. Unable to contain my smile, I showed Layla the message from American Airlines.

"Flight got canceled."

"What? No!" She grabbed the phone from my hand to verify the authenticity of my news. "They rebooked us on a flight tomorrow? We need to call. There must be a flight tonight we can catch."

I shook my head. "When I pushed back our plans because of the accident this morning, my assistant said it was the last flight of the day."

"That's impossible."

"We're flying from Greensboro, not Atlanta. There aren't flights in and out every three minutes all day and night."

She got out her own cell and went online to double check. While she made her futile attempt to escape my company, I took the opportunity to look for a nearby hotel with a good restaurant—preferably something romantic.

I'd stayed at the O. Henry Hotel before. It was pretty nice, and I remembered passing an adjoining restaurant. Calling it up on my phone, I checked out the photos. The hotel looked as nice as I remembered, and better yet, the restaurant looked quiet, with a nice ambiance. Layla was still searching when I booked us two suites.

She huffed. "I can't believe there really isn't another flight out tonight."

"I booked us rooms at a hotel I've stayed at before." I left off that I'd requested they be next to each other.

"I don't even have a change of clothes or a toothbrush."

"There's a shopping village across the street, an outdoor mall with chain stores, and a restaurant at the hotel."

She scowled at me. "Can you at least pretend you're not happy about this? Your smile is really pissing me off."

"Promised myself if I got you to speak to me again, there'd never be another lie. So I'm not even hiding that I'm fucking thrilled we're stuck here."

I told the driver to take us to the O. Henry Hotel, and Layla called her office to let them know about the change of plans. When we pulled up out front, it was already pretty late, and the shops were going to be closing soon.

"We should run over to the stores before they close."

"Okay."

The first store we stumbled upon happened to be a Victoria's Secret. It felt like I'd dated this woman for over a year, yet I had no idea what type of lingerie she favored. If I'd held out hope that I would get to find out soon, that thought was quickly squashed.

She stopped in front of the store. "Why don't you go get whatever you need? I don't need help in here."

"Are you sure? You might need a second opinion when you're in the fitting room."

She pointed toward a Gap. "Go."

I smiled. "I'll check us in after I grab a few things and meet you over at the hotel."

She opened the door to the store. "I can check myself in."

I spoke to her back as she walked away. "My favorite color is red..."

At least she didn't give me the finger. *Progress*.

———

I knew she was named Layla because her mother had been a huge Clapton fan. I knew that in the third grade she'd gotten into a fight with a boy, punched him, and broken his nose. Yet I'd never seen her in a pair of jeans or shared a decent meal with her. I sat at the restaurant bar, enjoying the view of her shapely hips gliding back and forth, clad in tight denim as she walked toward me.

"Don't look at me like that."

I sipped the scotch and soda I'd ordered. Another thing I'd missed. "Look at you like what?"

"*You know.*"

"Like I'd rather eat *you* for dinner than anything on the menu at this place?"

The hostess walked over to tell me our table was ready, curtailing whatever wicked response Layla had been about to dish out. That disappointed me.

I stood and held out my hand. "After you."

She squinted. "Fine. But don't look at my ass."

Like there was a snowball's chance in hell of that happening.

Once we were seated, Layla ordered wine, and I declined a second drink. Three years without alcohol made my tolerance low, and I wanted my mind to stay crystal clear while spending time with this woman.

I gazed across the table at her. She felt like a stranger in many ways now. Yet stranger or not, I felt more connected to her than anyone else in my life. A tether existed between us, and while she tried to sever it, I planned to keep pulling.

"So...your new partners seem nice," she offered.

"Yes. Certainly better than the last one." Knowing my alone time with her was limited, my mind only had one track: "So how long have you been seeing Pencil Neck?"

She furrowed her brow, so I clarified. Though I thought it perfectly clear to whom I was referring. "The attorney you work with. Doesn't your firm have a policy against dating fellow employees?"

"You know his name is Oliver. And it's none of your business how long I've been seeing him or what policies my firm has."

The waitress brought Layla's wine and took our dinner order. Watching Layla lift the glass to her lips and following her slender throat as she swallowed was an extraordinary sight.

She caught the look on my face and shifted in her seat.

"You're right," I said. "The less details I know, the better. So long as you aren't fucking him."

"I'll sleep with whoever I want."

"Have you slept with anyone since we started dating?"

She scoffed. "Dating? Is that what you're calling my mandatory community service that forced me to work with you?"

"No. But that's what I call the three hours we spent together each week before you 'clocked in' for your mandatory community service. And all day Saturdays that we spent together when you didn't have to come anymore. And the long letters we exchanged every week. Of course it wasn't ideal—I didn't get to wine you and dine you or feel you up at the end of the evening—but I still considered it dating."

"That makes one of us."

I knew she was lying. She'd been right there with me. But it was easier to move on if she didn't admit the truth.

"Tell me about your job. How are things for you now? When we stopped..." I smirked. "...dating, you were on shaky ground. I take it things worked out well since you're still there?"

"I billed nearly three thousand hours last year—higher than any other associate by at least two hundred hours. I made it financially foolish for them to get rid of me."

I did some quick math. "Three thousand hours is sixty hours a week of billing. Factor in lunch and commute, a couple of bathroom breaks, and you must've been working twelve hours a day, seven days a week."

"I was. I've cut back to six days this year so I won't get burned out."

"At least that left you little time to date."

She rolled her eyes before gulping the remainder of her wine. Finishing the glass seemed to relax her a little. Conversation became less adversarial.

"So, you've been out for what, two weeks now?"

"Fifteen days. I needed to get some things in order before I showed up at your firm. I was out of town for a week taking care of some stuff for my father."

"I'm sorry again about your loss. That must've been hard on you."

"My father and I had a strained relationship. But his last wishes were honorable. He had five wives but wanted to be buried with my mother."

"She'd died when you were little, right?"

"Yes. Breast cancer at thirty-eight. She was buried out in California with her mother and sister, both of whom died before forty from the same thing."

"Wow."

"She was a florist—actually met my father when he came in to send his girlfriend flowers." I shook my head. "Should've been a red flag right there for her."

"So you had him buried beside your mom?"

"She's probably gonna kick my ass for it someday, but yes. Made those arrangements while I was still locked up."

Layla smiled.

"I was only nine when she died. But they'd been living apart for a few years already. Although she never did divorce him. She said he was the love of her life, and that when you found your one true love, you couldn't replace them, because you'd given your heart away."

"Wow. And I guess he felt the same way since he had four other wives, yet wanted to be buried with her?"

"Guess so. They couldn't be together, but they never stopped loving each other."

Our eyes locked, but Layla quickly looked away.

"So you went out to California to visit their resting place?" she asked.

"Yes. And plant a giant garden."

Her forehead crinkled. "A garden?"

I laughed at the crap I'd spent my first full week as a free man doing. "When they first got married, she wanted a house in the suburbs. He wanted to be near his office and live in the penthouse he already owned. They agreed that they would stay in the city for a few years and then move to Westchester or Long Island. She had a huge plan for a garden in the backyard when that happened, with all her favorite flowers and trees. I remember her working on it all the time. It was on big, blueprint-size drafting paper, with all kinds of details. She worked on it once or twice a week for years, constantly adding things and redesigning it. After we moved out of my father's penthouse, I never saw those plans again. She got sick pretty soon after they split."

"So you planted a garden for her?"

"Not just any garden, *her garden*. My father's attorney had those old blueprints with his will and legal papers. He'd kept her plans all these years and left directions to hire someone to plant the garden where they were buried."

"That's oddly romantic."

"Took me a week to find all the stuff she wanted planted. My neck is still sunburned from digging that thing."

"You planted it yourself?"

I nodded. "The plan was for me and my mother to make it together. We never had the chance. It was the least I could do. And as much as I despised my father for a lot of things, I hope my parents are reunited and enjoying the garden together."

The waitress interrupted when she brought our dinner. After she left, Layla was looking at me funny.

"What?" I said.

"Nothing." She shook her head. "Just eat and don't make me like any more of the things that come out of your mouth."

I smirked. "I think you'd like the things I can *do* with my mouth even more."

Chapter 8

Layla

I had been quiet since we arrived at the airport. While we waited in the lounge for boarding to begin, I busied myself on my laptop with emails. I could work twenty-four seven and never work myself out of things to do at my firm. But today, if I was being honest, my head stayed down with my nose buried in work because I didn't want to talk to Gray.

Last night, we'd made plans to meet for breakfast before our flight. But after hours of staying awake, fixating on the man I'd gotten a glimpse of last night, feeling like I'd been lulled into seeing the man I'd gotten to know two years ago—a man who had crushed me—I needed to use my head and not my heart to put things into proper perspective.

Conveniently, I had a headache this morning and didn't join him for breakfast. I didn't need any more personal alone time with Gray. I'd just gotten my life back on the right track, and the last thing I wanted was to reopen old wounds.

After hearing him out, though, I felt bad. I really did. But it had taken me almost a year to move on, and we hadn't even been physical. The connection we'd shared was unlike anything I'd ever experienced, and his lie—technicality or not—coupled with his crazy past and the fact that he was now a client, was all just too much.

I didn't have a good track record with picking the right guy. Neither did my mother. And I was determined not to become her—a woman who spent her life with a man who was never really hers—no matter how much I felt the temptation gnawing at me.

When our fight home reached cruising altitude, I took out my laptop in an attempt to ignore Gray. He gently reached over and closed it.

"It's going to get expensive if I have to lock you up at thirty-five thousand feet every time I want to talk to you," he said.

"Sorry. I'm catching up on some things I didn't get to last night. Did you want to discuss your partnership agreement?"

He shook his head.

I took a deep breath and exhaled audibly. "Gray, you're starting a new company. You have your life back. You should move on. I'm sure all you'd have to do is snap your fingers to get a date. Did you even notice the way the flight attendant was looking at you when she came over to give us the hot towels? She's attractive. Why don't you ask her out?"

He shot me an annoyed scowl. "Do you go out with all the decent-looking men who are interested in you?"

"No. But I *am* seeing someone."

"He's not right for you."

"And you know this based on one dinner where you disrespected him, and he was forced to remain polite to you because of his job?"

"No. I know it because he's not me."

We embarked on a long stare-off. I got the feeling that nothing I'd said on this trip had deterred him in the least. "I've moved on, Gray. You need to accept that if we're going to be working together."

"And if you weren't seeing the Pencil Dick?"

"I thought his name was Pencil Neck?"

"I followed him to the men's room. Trust me, the thin neck is representative of the entire anatomy."

"You're such a jerk."

"You're not defending his honor to say I'm wrong. Which means only one of us has had the unfortunate experience of seeing his little dick, or you know it's true and the subject is indefensible."

"I think you've lost your mind. I'm not discussing another man's genitals with you."

"That's good. Because I'd much rather we discuss mine."

I couldn't help but laugh. "Seriously, Gray. How about we don't discuss anyone's dick, and instead you tell me what else I can do for you, other than draft the partnership agreement?"

"You can't ask me that question—what else I want you to do for me—and expect a legitimate answer."

"I'll watch my phrasing in the future."

Gray's playful face morphed into something more serious. "There's actually one thing you can do for me."

"What's that?"

"Let's start clean. No bringing up the past or anything."

Totally not what I had expected he would say. "Okay. I think that's a great idea. We've rehashed it and put it to bed. I think moving forward with a clean slate, if we're going to be working together, is a good thing to do." I tilted my head. "Although, I'm a bit surprised you would suggest that since you've spent most of the last twenty-four hours trying to make me remember what happened between us in the past."

My left hand had been sitting on the armrest between our seats. Gray covered it with his and looked up into my eyes. "I just wanted to explain myself. Clarify the facts. But I'm willing to start from scratch to win you back."

"Gray…"

"I'll give you a little space now. I know you need it." He caught my gaze. "But there won't be any more lies or even omitted facts. That being said, we're not over. We're just getting started. Because what we had was real, and *real* doesn't go away, no matter how much you want it to."

Chapter 9

Layla

2 years earlier

"Tell me something about you that no one else knows."

Gray scratched at the scruff on his chin. We'd been sitting at the library table for hours, supposedly prepping for the class I had to teach in an hour, which is how we'd been getting away with spending so much time together on Saturdays for the last eight weeks.

"I don't eat watermelon," he said.

I squinted. "How is that top secret?"

"It's not. But no one knows the *reason* I don't eat it."

I leaned my elbows on the table. "Go on..."

Gray pointed to me in warning. "No laughing."

"I'm not sure I can make that promise."

He shook his head with an easy smile. "In nursery school, my teacher read us *Jack and the Beanstalk*. I guess that somehow led me to think giant things could grow from seeds, if planted in the right place. At home, we'd had this round watermelon sitting on the kitchen counter for a while, and one day my mom decided to cut it open.

She said it was seedless, and I didn't see any of the regular black seeds, so I dug in. On my third piece, I told my mom I liked the round watermelons better than the oval ones she usually bought because they were crunchier."

"It was crunchy? Your watermelon was bad?"

"No, there were little white seeds inside that were soft, but the edges had a crunch to them, I unknowingly chewed up the seeds. My mom pulled them out of a piece and showed me. She said they were harmless. But I had it stuck in my head that a giant watermelon was going to grow in my stomach, and I'd wind up exploding. Every night I went to bed and pushed out my stomach to see if it was growing. And I was so sure it was going to happen, I thought I saw my stomach getting bigger."

I covered my mouth and laughed. "Oh my God. And you stopped eating watermelon after that?"

He nodded. "Going on twenty-five years watermelon-free now."

"That's crazy."

He pointed. "And there's the reason no one knows why I don't eat watermelon."

I watched as Gray's eyes roamed my face, flickering to my lips, then climbing their way back up to meet my eyes. "You have freckles on your nose," he said. "But you try to cover them up."

I raised my hand to my face. "Apparently I'm not doing a very good job."

"I like them. They remind me you're real. Sometimes after you leave, I start to wonder if I've imagined you."

For some reason, that caused my heart to swell.

A guard interrupted by popping his head in for his occasional check. "Everything okay in here?"

I waved and nodded. "All good. Thanks, Marcus."

"Be back in half an hour for the start of class."

My face fell. The few hours alone with Gray each Saturday had become the highlight of my week. But they seemed to go faster and faster lately. By the time I'd relaxed enough to again convince myself I wasn't crazy for starting to fall for a man who lived in a federal prison, it felt like it was time to begin class. I'd started to arrive three hours early every week, feigning the need to prep for the course with Gray. But the two of us really just sat across from each other and learned everything we could in the time we had. It was like a date—I spent extra time getting ready beforehand, felt the adrenaline rush when he walked into the room, and wanted to know more and more about him. The hardest part, though, was trying to ignore our physical connection. It was always present, and last week, we'd ventured into new territory when Gray *described* the kiss he wanted to give me. I never knew just *talking* about being physical could be so erotic.

"Your turn," Gray said.

My mind had jumped the tracks. "For what?"

Gray's eyes dropped to my lips, and the corner of his mouth twitched like he knew where I'd gone in my head. "Your turn to tell me something no one else knows."

When I didn't immediately respond, I looked back up and found Gray's hint of a smile had grown into a full-blown grin. I shook my head in an attempt to clear it.

"Ummm..." I thought of something not even my best friend knew about, but might be too crazy to share. "I have a *yeahway* notebook."

His brows drew together. "A what?"

"A yeahway notebook. Well, actually, it's more like seven yeahway notebooks now."

"What exactly is a yeahway notebook?"

"It's a list of things I analyze to decide yeahway or no way. Don't knock the name. I started it when I was seven. I'd asked my dad if we could get a dog, and he said a dog needed a lot of exercise, had to be cleaned up after, and was expensive. I said they were good as watchdogs and would teach me responsibility. He laughed and told me it was a nice try, but the pros outweighed the cons. So that night, I took out a fresh notebook, opened to the first page, and drew a line down the middle. I wrote out all the pros and cons I could think of, and then took another shot at my dad. Of course I'd come up with twenty-five pros and only ten cons."

Gray smiled. "The lawyer in you came out early, I see."

"Yeah. My list didn't change his mind, but my mom did, so we ended up getting the dog anyway. And I found I liked writing out the pros and cons of things. Sort of helped me organize my thoughts."

"What other type of stuff do you make lists for?"

"Anything. *Everything*. Should I kiss Danny Zucker in eighth grade? Should I go away to college? Is it worth spending fourteen hundred dollars on a pair of leather boots."

Gray's eyes glinted. "Did you kiss Danny Zucker?"

I held up my left hand and started to tick off the pros. "He was popular. He had nice lips. He had experience kissing." I held up my right hand and ticked off the cons. "His experience included swapping spit with..." I wrinkled up my nose. "Amanda Ardsley." I ticked off more cons. "Everyone knew all the girls he'd kissed before, so people would probably know I did it, too. Germs. Braces." I ticked up my last finger on my right hand and deadpanned. "Halitosis."

Gray threw his head back in laughter. "I take it poor Danny lost out."

I grinned. "He did."

"Did you go away to college?"

"I did. That was probably my most uneven list. The cons had that I'd miss my mom and friends. And that I was afraid. The pros took up a front and back."

"Boots?" he said.

"I'll wear them for you next week."

I really loved the little crow's feet around his eyes when his full face smiled.

"And you've kept all the notebooks where you do these pros and cons lists?"

"Yep. Seven full notebooks dating back close to twenty years. They've sort of become my own peculiar version of a diary."

"Do you still do it? Make lists?"

I bit my bottom lip and debated telling him the one I'd started working on last week. "On occasion. I find it soothing for some reason."

His eyes roamed my face. The man had an uncanny ability to read me. It unnerved me almost as much as I found it fascinating. When our eyes met, I knew he had the answer before he'd even asked the question.

"Have you made one for getting involved with me?"

Class had ended ten minutes ago, but I still had a few people waiting to talk to me one on one. The more I taught them about the appeals process and researching case precedents, the more it sparked questions on the viability of overturning their own cases.

A guard I had seen once or twice, but never spoken to, stopped by the classroom.

"Time's up, boys," he said from the door.

My eyes flashed to Gray's. He walked over to the guard, and the two of them spoke for a few minutes. Their eyes occasionally flickered up to where I stood. When they were done, Gray walked back to the front of the room and spoke to the stragglers hanging around.

"Kirkland's gotta clear the room before the end of his shift. You guys are going to have to ask your questions next week."

Without much complaint, the last of the students walked to the door. Dealing with the majority of the guys housed here felt no different than dealing with people at work. These men were white collar, many of them educated better than I was.

The guard yelled back to Gray with a warning tone. "You got ten minutes, Westbrook. That's it. Then I need to take her for sign out."

I waited until the door clicked closed to ask any questions. "What's going on?"

"Fourth stack from the library door. It's a blind spot for the cameras." Gray lifted his chin. "Take that book with you that you used for class like you need to put it away."

"But that's from my firm's library. I brought it with me."

He looked me in the eyes. "Trust me. I'll meet you over there in two minutes."

By the way his black pupils pushed away almost all the green in his eyes, I suspected I knew what was about to happen. And even though just thirty seconds ago I had felt completely normal, my entire body immediately changed in anticipation. I nodded and walked to the adjoining library, counting the stacks as I went. The skin on my face burned, yet my fingers and toes seemed to go cold and lose their feeling. My head spun while I tried to walk normally on wobbly legs and act natural, knowing that cameras had eyes everywhere.

Unsure what to do with myself when I arrived at the fourth stack, I tried to look busy by fingering through the book titles on the spine. If someone had shown up, held a gun to my head, and told me to read the words, though, I would've been dead. I was too wired to see straight.

I smelled Gray before I saw him. He had a clean, fresh, yet masculine smell. My back was to him as he walked up the aisle behind me, and one of his big hands gripped my hip as the other pushed my hair to the side. I gasped. If I'd been on a roller coaster, inching its way up to the top, this moment hovered at the summit—my blood pumped faster, full of adrenaline-laced fear and anticipation, waiting for the hair-raising nosedive down.

His low voice tickled my neck. "Stop me now, Layla, if you don't want this."

The coaster car rocked back and forth at the precipice. "What about the cameras?" My voice was so husky and breathless, I barely recognized it.

"Trust me," he said.

Trust me.

As crazy as it was, I did. And maybe I didn't even care about the consequences, if there were any. I wanted to touch this man more than anything I'd ever wanted. I turned, and Gray's heated gaze caught mine. He looked into my eyes, seeming to give me one last chance to stop him. Unable to speak, I gave him the slightest nod as my chest heaved up and down.

Before I could prepare myself for what I'd just agreed to, Gray grabbed my face with both hands and backed me up against the bookshelf behind me. His head dipped down, and he planted his lips over my mouth.

The jolt from feeling his body press up against mine made me forget anything else existed. He licked my lips, urging me to open, and groaned into my mouth as his tongue found mine. I whimpered in response. Never in my life had I felt such hunger, felt so deeply desired. A heavy throb between my legs had me pushing into him, but I still couldn't get close enough.

As if he sensed what I needed, Gray reached his hands around to my ass and tugged my thighs, guiding me to wrap my legs around him so he could press deeper. He crushed his erection against my aching clit and ground up and down. The friction had me so turned on that I thought it was possible he could finish me off with just more grinding.

My fingers laced through his silky hair, pulling and tugging at the soft strands. He groaned again, and the sound caused a ripple from our joined lips straight down to between my legs. One of the hands at my ass moved up to my neck and tightened as his thumb tilted my head more to one side and he deepened the kiss.

The feeling of weightlessness hit my belly, and I began to fall. My roller coaster car rocked back and forth one last time before careening down the long slope. As we panted and clawed at each other, I lifted my imaginary hands into the air and enjoyed the crazy, scary, wonderful ride down.

When our kiss broke, I was mesmerized by the effect this man had on me. Gray's hands came back to my face as he cupped my cheeks, stroking gently with his thumb while trailing feather-soft kisses from one end of my lips to the other.

His voice was gruff. "This is real."

I swallowed, not understanding what he meant at the time.

The creak of the door opening and the guard's loud voice made me jump. "Time's up, Westbrook!"

Gray leaned his forehead against mine. "I gotta go. Remember what I just said when you start doubting yourself by Tuesday."

Chapter 10

Gray

2 years earlier

"**M**y commissary account balance somehow went from zero to the max of two hundred and ninety bucks," Rip, my bunkmate, announced. "You wouldn't happen to know anything about that, would you?"

I was glad my back was facing him. I continued to fold the laundry I'd just finished on top of my bunk. "How the hell would I know where the money in your account came from?" I lied.

I'd written a letter to Etta and asked her to fill his account a few weeks ago. She had access to all of my personal funds out in the real world. I'd been wondering if he'd gotten it.

"Maybe my Katie did it?"

I felt bad for giving him hope that his daughter had come around. But he wouldn't take the money from me, and I knew he had a stack of letters he'd written her, but couldn't afford to buy any postage. Rip and I had been bunkmates since the day I arrived. He'd already been here a few months, so he showed me the ropes.

"Maybe. But at least now you can pick up some of the gourmet foods you like so much," I teased. "Ramen Noodles, prunes, Pop-Tarts."

"Not everyone grew up eating caviar off a silver spoon, pretty boy."

I chuckled. "What's on your agenda today after dialysis?"

"Probably watch some TV. They've got a John Wayne movie marathon playing in the activity room this afternoon."

"Ah. So a good long nap, then?"

He tossed a towel at my back.

Rip's real name was Arthur Winkle. But he'd been nicknamed Rip because of his penchant to catnap. *Rip Van Winkle*. The guy nodded out in the middle of conversations, during dinner, and *inevitably* during TV time. He always denied being asleep, claiming to be "resting his eyes." Whenever the inmates gathered to watch something, they all groaned when Rip joined them because he'd be snoring up a storm within ten minutes of the show starting.

"What time is your lady friend coming today?" he asked.

"Ten."

Rip knew all about Layla and me. Mostly because I didn't shut the fuck up about her, ever. Weekdays were basically a countdown to the weekend. And while Saturdays were always incredible, Sundays sucked because it was so long until I'd see her again. Her six months of community service only had another two weeks left, and I'd hesitated to bring it up because it felt wrong to ask her to keep driving here every week just to visit me, yet the thought of not seeing her for more than a year until I got out killed me.

"I think I'm going to write a letter to Katie and thank her for the money, then mail all these backlogged letters." Rip wrote his daughter every week, like clockwork. She had never written back to him once.

"Sounds like a plan." I looked at the time—ten to ten—then scooped up the apple I'd saved from lunch yesterday to butter up the teacher. "Better head down to class."

"Tell me something you hated about your childhood."

I sat back in my chair and folded my hands behind my head. *Tell me something* had become a weekly ritual for Layla and me. Each week one of us would ask a random question of the other. The experience of wanting to know everything about a woman was foreign to me.

Don't get me wrong—I wasn't the kind of guy who went on a date and only talked about myself. I'd had conversations, but most of them were surface—talk about jobs, vacations, that type of current stuff. I'd never wanted to know about a woman's childhood. It had never even dawned on me to ask that kind of a question.

But I wanted to know everything and anything about Layla—namely, *what made this woman tick.*

"Thursdays. I hated Thursdays growing up."

I arched a brow. "Big test day at school?"

"Nope. It was the day my father left every week."

She'd mentioned that she didn't speak to her father anymore, but shied away from elaborating. We only had a few hours together each week, and I didn't want to use them to pry into shit that might be bad memories if she wasn't ready to share.

"Every week? Did he split his time for work or something?"

"He split his time between his families."

"He had an ex-wife and kids?"

She looked down and shook her head. "No, he had a wife and kids. We got him from Monday night through Thursday morning. His wife and kids had the other four days out on the west coast."

"Jesus. So your mom was his mistress?"

"Yep."

"How long did that last?"

"More than twenty years. Until my mom died."

"That's fucked up. And she knew he was married?"

"Yep. And his wife knew he had a girlfriend. Everyone except me seemed to be okay with the arrangement. And I didn't start to think anything was wrong with it until I was a teenager—because oddly, my dad was a great dad to me. Even though he was only around for a few days each week, he spent more time with me than any of my friends' dads who were around all the time spent with them. Dad just had two families, and we didn't talk about it. But once I got a little older, I couldn't comprehend being able to love two people and need two families."

"Did he grow up Mormon?"

"Nope. Catholic."

I shook my head. "Well, I can see why you'd hate Thursdays."

Layla blew out a deep breath. "You're the only person who knows that besides my best friend since childhood."

I held her gaze. "I'm honored you shared it."

She smiled, then relaxed back into her chair. "My turn."

"Pretty sure anything I share after that is going to seem boring."

"Well, I think we could use something less depressing after that share. Let me think." She tapped her finger to her lips.

God, I wanted to suck on those things so bad.

"Tell me the last lie you told."

"Easy. I lied to my bunkmate a few hours ago."

"Rip?"

"Yeah. I stuck some money in his commissary account and said I didn't. He won't take handouts."

She smiled. "That's sweet."

"Except now I got his hopes up that his daughter did it."

"They're on bad terms?"

"Hasn't spoken to him since he got arrested. Never came to visit once. No one has, as far as I know. His wife passed away a few years before his arrest."

"That's sad."

"Yeah. He's a good guy, too. Most of the guys in here are here because of greed. He's in because he's selfless."

"You said he was making and selling Social Security cards. He's in for federal counterfeiting, right?"

"Yeah. Owned a printing shop for forty years. Had a really sick granddaughter with medical costs, so he started making them for some guy who sold passports, licenses, and all kinds of fake documents. He sent her the money anonymously because he wouldn't have had the money to give her by any legal means."

"Oh, wow. And his daughter doesn't talk to him because of that?"

I nodded. "Families do crazy stuff when the shit hits the fan."

"Tell me about it."

I suddenly felt her bare foot on my calf. She'd slipped out of her shoe and lifted my pant leg—one of the few touches we could enjoy without the camera. I loved the way her eyes twinkled when she said or did something she shouldn't be doing. My eyes fell to her nose. I'd noticed it while she was talking, but hadn't said anything.

"You didn't cover up your freckles today. Did you do that for me?"

She smirked. "Maybe. Do you like it?"

"I love it. They're sexy as hell, but the fact that you did that for me is more of a turn-on than anything."

She rubbed her toes higher on my calf, and I groaned. "You're going to give me a hard-on from a fucking foot on my leg."

The light in her eyes danced. "Well, we have another hour before class starts. Might as well make it a good one."

I squinted, unsure what she had up her sleeve.

"Remember when we played that little game where you described how you would kiss me?"

"Yeah, Freckles. Not much I forget about your visits."

"Well, how about we play that again, but I describe how I would kiss you *below the belt*?"

Chapter 11
Layla

"I need a drink like you wouldn't believe."

"And here I thought you came to visit me because of my winning personality."

My best friend Quinn owned a bar less than four blocks from my office. O'Malley's was a local pub that her dad had owned as far back as I could remember. After he decided to move to Florida a few years ago, Quinn kept it running while he had it up for sale. Six months later, she'd discovered what her dad had loved doing his whole life and decided to keep the place herself.

For the most part, it was an old man's day bar. But it was the perfect place to come hang out after work—no young guys to assume a woman sitting alone at the bar was looking to get laid. It was a good thing I was a workaholic, or I could've easily spent all my time in this place and become a different type of -*holic* instead.

Quinn pulled two shot glasses from the rack and reached down below the bar for a bottle of something. Seeing no label, I knew what she was trying to feed me.

I covered the tiny glass with my hand. "No way. I had a headache for a week after drinking that stuff."

"It's a new batch."

"You made it?"

Quinn smiled proudly. "Sure did."

"Then no thanks."

After watching one too many episodes of *Moonshiners*, Quinn had decided she could make her own liquor. She could—only it was undrinkable and tasted like nail polish.

Quinn pouted and poured herself one before reaching for the private stash of my wine that she kept behind the bar. "Busy day at the office, honey? Wait, let's start with the good stuff. Have you ended your drought and slept with the new guy you're dating yet? What was his name again?"

I traced the rim of my wine glass with my finger. "Oliver. And, no. But we have a date tonight. He's meeting me here in an hour."

She arched a brow. "You don't sound too excited about that."

Quinn *knew* me. We'd been inseparable since February 2nd of fourth grade. That was the day I'd been sent down to the principal's office to bring the new girl to class. She'd had on mismatched socks and carried a bullfrog in her cracked lunchbox—her peanut butter and jelly had been squished at the bottom of her backpack in a brown paper bag.

I sighed. "I am. Maybe not as excited as I should be, but I do enjoy spending time with Oliver."

Quinn put her elbows on the bar and rested her head atop her hands. "Spit it out. What's going on? You were all excited about the first date you had with this guy a month ago. Wait...let me guess. Halitosis? Talks about his mother all the time? Stuffed animals in the back window of his car?"

I laughed. "Nothing like that. It's just...well...I sort of took on a new client."

Quinn's eyes lit up. She'd married her high school sweetheart at nineteen, so she lived vicariously through me—not that she'd gotten to hear anything exciting over the last year.

"The client's a *he,* I assume?"

I nodded.

"Well, keep going. What does he look like?"

"He's tall, has the most stunning green eyes—the kind of color that keeps you warm in the winter while you trudge through snow because it reminds you that spring grass will grow again soon."

Quinn's brows drew down and her smile grew quizzical. "That's an awfully elaborate description. Go on."

"Bone structure like a Greek god, lean and muscular body, droolworthy forearms, and he totally reeks of confidence."

Quinn let out a dreamy sigh and closed her eyes. "Veiny forearms?"

"Some. Enough to tell you he works out a lot, but not so much that it looks like putting in an IV would cause a geyser to spout."

She opened her eyes. "I have this theory. People say big feet means big dick. But I think it's all about the forearms. They're basically a visual substitute—thick and veiny forearms, *oh God*. Skinny forearms, *is it over yet?*

I laughed. "I'll have to take one for the team and test that theory."

Quinn's face was suddenly crestfallen. "He's married? Is that the problem?"

"Actually, turns out he's not."

"So why are you meeting Oliver here and not the new guy? What's his name?"

I looked her straight in the eyes. "Grayson."

Her forehead scrunched. "Grayson? Like the asshole?"

I nodded my head slowly and waited, knowing she'd figure it out.

Her eyes grew to saucers. "Your new client is Gray? Prison guy?"

I tipped my wine glass toward her before taking a healthy gulp. "One and the same."

For the next hour, I caught my friend up on the last ten days, since Gray had waltzed back into my life. There was a lot to tell—the presentation, dinner, flowers, our trip—*his marriage*. Luckily she already knew the rest of our history, which also meant she knew how devastated I'd been when I'd discovered he was married and ended things. So I didn't have to explain what my heart felt like now, how conflicted I'd been.

"So what happened after you arrived home from your trip?"

"Nothing." My shoulders slumped. "I haven't heard from him."

Gray had kept to his word about giving me space. In the eight days since we'd been back, I hadn't heard a peep from him, other than a short email exchange after I'd sent over the draft of the partnership agreement I'd written.

And I hated that a part of me missed him.

At least this week had been busy. I'd been at the office late every night because the work on my schedule *before*

Grayson Westbrook stormed back into my life hadn't been reassigned—other than one deposition.

"What are you going to do? Are you going to give him another chance?"

"I can't. I'm over Gray. I've moved on."

Quinn's face screamed bullshit. "Let me ask you something."

"What?"

"How long has it been since you've seen Oliver?"

"You mean since our last date?"

"No. I mean laid eyes on him. Was it today? Four days ago? How long?"

Hmm. Oliver and I worked in the same office, but we were lucky to catch one lunch and talk in the elevator for three minutes some weeks. "Well, yesterday I was out of the office all day for a deposition. So Thursday, I guess." I paused. "Wait. No. He wasn't in on Thursday—he had a conference to go to. It must've been Wednesday. Or maybe Tuesday. We had lunch at the Greek diner one of those days."

Quinn refilled my glass of wine. "And what about Gray? When was the last time you saw him?"

"A week ago Thursday."

"You're sure?"

"I'm positive. Thursday morning about nine thirty to be exact. We landed at the airport. What the heck are you getting at?"

She set the bottle of wine on top of the bar and tapped the cork in. "You're not over Gray. You're still hung up on him."

"What are you talking about?"

"When you know exactly how long it's been since the last time you saw someone, you're not over him."

"That's ridiculous."

"Does he have your cell phone number?"

"Yes. It's on my business card. All my clients have it. But he's never called me on it."

A knowing grin spread on Quinn's face. "Do you check it for missed calls or texts from him before you go to bed?"

I pursed my lips.

She reached over and took my hands. "It's okay, sweetie. You'll figure it out."

Quinn moved down to the other end of the bar to help a customer. When she returned, she asked, "Does Oliver have dirty blond hair and look like a handsome prep school boy all grown up?"

"I guess so."

She looked over my shoulder. "Then I think the man you *are over* is heading toward us."

"Hey." Oliver cupped my cheek for a tender but quick kiss.

Such a sweet guy. I turned back and introduced him to Quinn just as I noticed my phone vibrating with an incoming text on top of the bar. Catching the name flashing *Gray*, I quickly grabbed it and glanced back at Oliver to see if he'd also caught the name. He hadn't.

But while he was smiling and paying attention to Quinn, a quick look at the smirk on her face told me *she had*. I dumped my cell into my purse and silently promised to ignore it during my date tonight.

The three of us made small talk while I finished my wine, and Oliver had a beer. After twenty minutes, he looked down at his watch.

"I'm sorry. I didn't realize your friend worked here. I thought we were just meeting for a quick drink, so I made reservations for eight at Gramercy Tavern."

My friend whistled. "Gramercy Tavern. Fancy. Go. You two have fun. I need to get back to work anyway."

Oliver reached into his pocket and pulled out some cash to cover our drinks. Before he could place it on the bar, Quinn put up her hand.

"Layla doesn't pay here, and neither does her guest."

He smiled warmly. "Thank you."

I leaned over the bar and kissed my friend on her cheek. "I'll see you Thursday night for dinner, right?"

"Yep. It might be mac and cheese, unless Brian gets home from work early. But it's a date. Your goddaughter has big plans to paint your nails. Which means most of your fingers will also be painted. So you might want to get a manicure appointment on the calendar for sometime Friday."

I laughed. "Okay. Thanks for the warning."

Oliver reached over the bar to shake Quinn's hand. "It was nice to meet you."

"Likewise." While his hand was still in hers, she used her other to push up the arm of his sports jacket, exposing his forearm.

Oliver seemed rightly confused, but let her examine his arm anyway.

"Oh." She shook her head. "Sorry. I thought I saw some ink peeking out. I was being nosy."

Always the good sport, Oliver smiled. "Nope. No ink on me."

When my date turned toward the door, I flashed scolding eyes at her. We both knew exactly what she'd been doing. But in case I hadn't caught on, she touched her thumb and pointer together, forming a tiny circle, and mouthed, "Skinny forearms."

The damn message was sucking away at my ability to concentrate. I imagined my cell would be hot if I plucked it from my purse. It was the proverbial heartbeat of my past under the floorboards that only I could hear. And at the same time, the fact that it distracted me also made me angry, which I needed to shake off. Because the more I let someone old take up residency in my heart, the more I felt like I had no room for someone new.

Flanked by the phone taunting me, and the realization that this was my *third official date* with Oliver, I felt on edge.

I wanted to throw myself into the evening and forget anything else but having a good time with this sweet guy. But when I managed to focus on Oliver, all I could think about was that he'd invited me back to his place to watch a movie after dinner—which I assumed was code for sex.

For the most part, I wasn't easy. I'd tried out a one-night stand or two in college and realized quickly it wasn't for me. And although the third date might be a common point for couples to jump into bed, it often took me longer. I needed to get to know the guy and build trust, something that didn't come quickly for me. But I'd known Oliver for years now, so the third date already had the comfort that sometimes only came after six months of dating.

Between the anticipation of what would come later, the daunting text message waiting for me, and the conversation I'd had with Quinn at the bar earlier, an awkwardness settled into the air during dinner. Oliver had to feel it, too. There were lulls in our conversation, and they seemed to be getting longer. Things between us had always come easily. Yet suddenly I felt like I'd opened my brain's junk drawer and begun reaching in to pull out random useless crap.

"So...what musical artist do you think is the most overrated?"

Oliver shot me a questioning look. "Musical artist?"

I sipped the after-dinner cappuccino the waitress had just brought and nodded.

"I guess Blake Shelton."

More silence.

"Seen any good movies lately?"

Oliver set down the coffee he'd just lifted. "Is everything all right, Layla?"

"Yes. Why?" I answered too fast to have given the question any real consideration.

"I don't know. You seem...sort of on edge. Nervous almost. Is everything okay at work?"

"Yes, things are fine."

"It's just...your questions, while they aren't unusual questions per se...like asking me about movies I saw recently...they..." Oliver trailed off. The lines on his face smoothed as a look of recognition came over him. "*Movies*... Are you maybe uncomfortable coming back to my place after dinner?"

Oliver was a damn good attorney. He was used to following a person's train of thought from deposition questioning. We both were. He'd deduced that I was freaked out about tonight. Which...wasn't entirely wrong.

I decided to be honest. Letting out a rush of air, I blurted, "I'm not ready to have sex with you yet."

Oliver sipped his coffee. "I'm not ready to have sex with you yet, either."

My eyes widened. "You're not?"

He grinned sheepishly. "Nah. I'm just kidding. But it's fine. I didn't mean to make you feel any pressure by inviting you back to my place."

"Can I ask you something?"

"What?"

"Was *movie* code for sex?"

He looked me in the eyes. "I'd be lying if I said I didn't hope things would progress there. But I actually did rent a few movies I thought you'd like."

I offered a sad smile. "I'm sorry."

"Don't be. It's fine." He reached across the table and took my hand. "I enjoy your company, Layla. It doesn't matter how long it takes."

I felt more relaxed after that conversation. Even enjoyed the dessert we shared. Outside the restaurant, Oliver gave his valet ticket to the attendant and took my hands. "You want to come back to my place for that movie? And by movie, I actually mean *movie*." He smiled.

I wished my heart were into it. "Can I take a rain check? I'm actually pretty tired."

"Of course." He tried to cover the disappointment, but I still saw it. "Let me at least give you a ride home?"

Oliver lived up in Westchester, and I lived in the city— in the complete opposite direction he would be going. Yet I felt like I'd insulted him enough for one evening.

"Sure. That would be great. Thank you."

I could finally scratch that damn itch. But not before pouring a big glass of merlot, ditching my dress and bra in favor of comfy sweats and a tattered college T-shirt, and putting on some soothing music. Slumping into the couch, I picked up my cell and entered my password to *finally* read the message Gray had sent hours ago. My pathetic heart sped up just seeing his name illuminate.

I tossed back a healthy gulp of wine and settled in to read the long string of messages.

Gray: Hey. Sorry to bother you. Unless you're out on a date. Then I'm not sorry.

A few minutes later another text had come in.

Gray: Maybe I'm taking this honesty thing too far. Let me start over. Etta got herself into trouble with the police again today. A ticket for speeding and driving without a license. She also came clean and told me it was her second one. Which Google said could mean it's a felony now. I told her you didn't do traffic court-type work, but she won't let me call anyone else. Maybe you could talk to her at least? Give me a call.

Shit

I couldn't very well drag Etta's wellbeing into things between Gray and me. That wouldn't be fair. So I had to call him.

At least that's how I justified my finger hovering over his name and debating whether to text him back at eleven o'clock on a Saturday night.

Chapter 12

Gray

My evening had been occupied by the delivery of a new mattress and obsessively checking my phone for texts.

I'd just spent three years cooped up in a place I couldn't leave—without women and eating shitty food. And here I was, alone on a Saturday night eating crappy Chinese food in my apartment all by my lonesome self.

After checking my phone yet again, I tossed it on the couch and blew out a sigh of frustration.

I should be out at some dive bar, meeting a woman who wanted no more than a hard cock between her legs. But instead I was home being loyal to a woman who was most likely out on a fucking date.

Layla Hutton.

A part of me thought maybe my obsession would wear off once I'd gotten to see her again and say my piece after a year of having to remember what she looked like, what she smelled like.

No such luck. The woman was deep under my skin, and I couldn't shake her—unlike the woman whose two-thousand-dollar Breville espresso machine I was currently tossing into a box to send to the local Goodwill store.

I'd expected the condo I owned and shared with Max to be empty when I walked in after a three-year absence. But it was just the opposite. She'd left everything that had been inside when I started my sentence. Even her clothes were still in the closet. Although with the amount of money she'd swindled, I'm sure it was no skin off her nose to start over on her collection of fine goods.

Since my afternoon had been light, I'd decided to go on a cleaning spree—basically getting rid of all her shit. I didn't care if it was new or something I could use. I wanted everything she'd brought into my life gone.

The hallway to my penthouse was now filled with boxes and bags of donations.

Prada shoes.

Hermes bags.

Cartier sunglasses.

Max had expensive taste. I'd probably be donating over fifty grand worth of overpriced crap. But the purge of the remnants of my life with her was worth any price.

Throwing out a KitchenAid mixer she'd bought and never used, I looked around my half-empty apartment. *Out with the old, in with the new.* Other than the new mattress I'd had delivered today, there wasn't much I had the urge to replace right away.

I wasn't sure if Max had picked up the unopened, thirty-year-old bottle of scotch I currently had my eye on, but *hey*, I'd get rid of it tonight—after it was empty.

I took a seat in my favorite beat-up old leather chair, which sat across from a designer couch, and sipped the aged liquor while staring out at the city. My Tribeca condo overlooked lower Manhattan from the living room and had a view of the Hudson River from my bedroom. The city was dark, but the crisp, bright skyline illuminated the evening. The more I stared at it, the more I found myself wondering where Layla was tonight.

I wasn't stupid enough to think winning her back would be quick and easy. But the thought of her out there with some other guy wasn't something I would be able to handle for very long. Even if I couldn't have her, I needed to find a way to make sure no one else did either.

My phone buzzed from where I'd tossed it on the couch. Looking at my watch, it was a little after eleven, so I figured it was likely one of my business partners. They both lived on the west coast and never slept either.

But a little sunshine peeked from the dark horizon when I saw Layla's name on my screen.

Layla: I'm sorry to hear about Etta. Of course I'll help her.

I rattled the ice in my glass, deciding on a response. I'd done well not making contact lately, giving her the room to figure out we weren't done yet on her own. While Etta's situation was not something I'd ever be happy about, just seeing Layla's text response brought me some relief that she hadn't decided to cut me off completely.

Gray: Thank you.

I couldn't stop myself from sending another one.

Gray: It's late. Just get in?

Layla: Yes.

Gray: Date?

I watched the dots jump around, then stop, then start again.

Layla: Not that it's any of your business, but yes. I was out with Oliver.

The thought of her out with another man should have pissed me off, but instead I smiled to myself and tossed back the remainder of my drink.

No sleepover. That's my girl.

I texted back.

Gray: I haven't been getting laid either.

She went radio silent for a full five minutes. Perhaps I'd pushed it too far. Teasing over text isn't the same as in person. I raked my fingers through my hair and texted again.

Gray: Sorry. Was joking around.

Another ten minutes went by, but this time, I watched the dots jump and stop. Jump and stop. Jump and stop. Clearly, something was on her mind, and she had reservations about sharing it with me. I was just about to text again when her response arrived.

Layla: You're ruining my chance of having a nice, normal relationship.

Shit.

I started to text back and then thought better of it. Instead, I hit call. She picked up on the first ring.

"Hey," she breathed out.

One word, and I knew she was feeling more emotional than angry. I needed to tread softly.

"I missed your voice."

"You missed it after a week?" she said. "You didn't hear it for a full year and did just fine."

I lifted my bare feet up onto the coffee table in front of me. "*Ah.* But I did hear your voice. I reread your letters every day. Pretty sure some of them are memorized by now. In my head, I heard your voice saying all the things you wrote in them."

"Perhaps you should dig them out if you still have them. You can use them when you feel the need, rather than call me."

I chuckled. "They were only a substitute because it was physically impossible to have the real thing."

"It's still physically impossible." I heard the smile in her voice.

"Not at all. Just say the word, and I'll be at your door in twenty minutes."

She went quiet for a minute, so I teased, "If you're debating it, I'm going to head over so we don't waste any time on the off chance you land on yes."

I didn't expect the confession that came next. "I haven't had sex since before I met you."

"Why haven't you?"

She was quiet for a few moments while my hopes ran wild. Then, "I didn't want to."

"Because you want to have it with me?"

"No. I don't *want* to have it with you."

"You don't *want to* or you don't *want to want to*. There's a big difference, Freckles."

More silence. "I don't *want to want to*. I don't even want to want to talk to you."

That hurt like hell to hear. But it was understandable that she was afraid. I needed to earn her trust back.

"If it makes you feel any better," I said. "I haven't had sex since I met you either."

From her tone, I pictured her rolling her eyes. "Poor baby. You've been free for three weeks and can't find anyone to fulfill your needs?"

"Don't fool yourself. Ass comes easy for me, too, Layla. But there's only one ass I want, and that's *yours*."

I heard her breathing, so I knew she hadn't hung up. *Fuck it. Might as well go for broke.* I hadn't thought this conversation would be happening anytime soon. Sometimes you need to push open the door and run inside before it gets slammed in your face.

"Have dinner with me? Lunch even. Breakfast? I'll take whatever you're willing to give."

"I don't know, Gray." She went quiet again. "I have to go. Text me Etta's number, and I'll call her in the morning."

"Goodnight, beautiful."

I waited until she hung up to move the phone from my ear. "She didn't say no," I mumbled to myself. *Progress.*

"Hello?"

I rolled onto my back with my cell pressed to my ear. Morning light streamed in from the small space where the blinds were missing a slat. That reminded me, I needed to toss those things, too. The slat had fallen off the first night my new bride and I had returned from the Dominican Republic, when a drunken make-out session had included backing her up against the window.

"Don't tell me you're still in bed, boy. You just wasted three years of your life. You should be up at the ass crack of dawn, raring to do things."

Etta.

I rubbed sleep from my eyes with one hand. "What time is it?"

"It's after seven in the morning."

"Four in the afternoon is after seven in the morning, Etta. How about something more specific?"

She ignored me. "Are you free later?"

"If later means *hours* after seven in the morning, yes."

"My door lock isn't working."

I sat up in bed. "Okay. Give me a few minutes, and I'll head over."

"No. No. I have the top lock on, and my neighborhood is still safe. The girls are coming over to play mahjong today. Why don't you come over about four? I'll make you your favorite meal."

My mouth watered. "Gumbo?"

"And homemade peach cobbler if you stop at the store and pick something up for me."

"I'll rob a store if you'll make me gumbo and peach cobbler, Etta."

"Now now...I think it might be too soon for those type of jokes after getting out of the slammer. Never know who might be listening on the phones these days."

I laughed. "What do you need me to pick up?"

"Some wine. Red."

"You hate wine."

"Well, I'm hankering for some, and I don't know my way around the wine section of a liquor store."

"No problem. I'll pick you up something on the way."

"See you this afternoon."

Since I was up early, I figured Etta was right. There were things I would've given anything to be able to do over the last three years. Yet now that I could, I hadn't made any attempt to appreciate the opportunity I had. So I dragged my lazy ass out of my comfy new bed and started my day with a long run through Central Park. Then I went to the animal shelter. I'd had to give my dog up for adoption when Max moved in because she was allergic.

I still felt guilty about it, even though I'd thoroughly vetted the couple who'd adopted him. In hindsight, I should have gotten rid of Max and kept my dog.

———

"Yeah, buddy. I know how you feel." I stuck my fingers through the cage to pet an odd mix of Basset Hound and... *something*.

"Sir, please do not put your hands into the cage. Some of the dogs get aggressive when they're in cages. If you'd like to meet one of our adoptees, just let one of our volunteers in the blue shirts know."

"Okay. Sorry."

I slipped my fingers from the cage. *Aggressive when you're locked up, huh? I hear that. Looks like you guys don't have a gym around to burn it off. No bocce court either.*

I continued my walk. There were a shitload of cages, each with an information card hanging from the top.

Polly. Age: Two. Breed: Terrier mix. She hovered in the back of the cage. I said hello and moved on.

Buster. Age: Twelve. Pug/Pekingese mix.

"Hey, buddy," I said. He looked unimpressed by my greeting.

Snowy. Age: Eight weeks. Staffie mix.

"You're fucking adorable. Some little girl is going to sucker her dad into bringing you home within days. You don't need me."

Snowy lifted her nose into the air like she knew it.

I walked two more rows of cages, looking for my dog. No one jumped out at me, until I hit the last cage on the bottom of the last row. Unlike all the others, there was no information sign hanging from the cage. When I crouched down to look inside, the dirtiest face greeted me. He was lying on a shoe and lifted his chin in the universal bro language that said *what's up*.

I reciprocated. "What the hell happened to you, buddy?" I thought there might be a springer spaniel underneath all that matted mud.

I stopped a volunteer as she walked by. "What happened to this guy?"

"He just came in today. That's what he looks like *after* the bath. Sad story. He was the pet of an older gentleman who lived alone. He died in the house while he was working on transplanting a bunch of plants, and this little guy couldn't get anyone to listen to his barks for days. Had no food, so he chewed into a bottle of glue and somehow got himself covered in it and then apparently rolled around in some potter's dirt, making mud. It's all caked to his skin and hair now. We didn't want to bother him too much today, since he just came in. Tomorrow we'll shave him and try to get the rest out."

"Can you take him out of the cage for me?"

The woman's brows drew down. "You want me to put that dirty boy into a visitor pen?"

I smiled. "Why not? I just came back from a run. He might be just as put off by what I look and smell like."

Me and Mudface headed to one of the small private rooms where people looking to adopt could play with the dogs and get to know them. The volunteer brought the shoe and set it down beside him.

"What's up with the old shoe?"

"It was his owner's. He growls if any of us try to take it away. But other than that, he's really lovable. We think he's just attached because he misses his owner."

I crouched down and offered my hand for him to sniff. Mudface took one step and leaned in to smell me. Not wanting to scare him, I thought I'd let him take his time. Only Mudface had other thoughts. After about twenty seconds of sniffing, he pulled his head back and tilted it, studying me. Then he suddenly charged at me, knocking me back on my ass, and began to lick my face.

I laughed. "Jesus, dog. Your breath is almost as bad as you look." He continued standing on his hind legs, with one paw on each of my shoulders, to keep licking.

"No." The volunteer who'd brought us in stood and walked over from where she'd been sitting nearby, playing with her phone. She tugged at the dog's collar. "No, Freckles."

I looked up at her. "What did you just say?"

"I'm trying to get him off of you."

"But what did you say?"

"I said, '*No, Freckles*'."

"Freckles?"

"That's his name. If you look closely, buried underneath all that mud and glue, his white nose has a bunch of brown dots." She shrugged. "They look like freckles. Probably why the owner named him that."

I looked closer at the dog. Sure enough, there were spots under that mess. "Freckles, huh?"

He responded by licking me again.

I nodded. "Okay, buddy. If that didn't seal the deal, I don't know what will." I looked up at the volunteer. "I want to adopt Freckles."

I caught myself whistling as I rang Etta's bell. It was a beautiful spring day, tomorrow I'd go pick up my new little buddy at the shelter, Etta was making me gumbo and peach cobbler, and Layla hadn't said no to having lunch or dinner with me. What else could I ask for?

The door opened, and that question was most definitely fucking answered. It had been a damn good day, but the prospect for an even better one had just grown exponentially.

Because it was Layla who opened Etta's door.

Chapter 13

Layla

"What are you doing here?" My tone was more than a little accusatory.

"Etta asked me to come over and fix her door lock," Gray replied.

"She wanted to talk to me about her tickets. Said it was hard for her to get around so well without driving, and asked if I could come by this afternoon." I narrowed my eyes. "You put Etta up to this, didn't you?"

He held up his right hand like he was taking an oath. "I had no idea you would be here. I swear." A look of understanding crossed his face. He set down the bags he was carrying, along with a small toolbox. "Let me look at the lock."

Gray knelt down and jiggled the door handle a few times. The bolt moved in and out. It seemed to work fine. Then he stuck a screwdriver into the strike plate on the other side of the doorjamb, and something popped out.

"What is that?" I said.

He swiped it from the floor and began to unfold it. "Looks like a folded-up empty book of matches kept it from locking properly."

"A folded-up book of matches?"

"Yep. I think we both got played." Gray closed his toolbox and stood, lifting the other bag he'd brought in with him. "She also asked me to bring red wine, even though she's never liked wine. Said she had a *hankering* for it."

"She asked me yesterday on the phone what kind of wine I liked. I said anything red."

"Who's at the door, Layla?" Etta called from upstairs.

If I had any doubt about Gray telling the truth, Etta's tone confirmed she was indeed the orchestrator of this evening. It was a few octaves higher than normal and almost sing-songy. I knew she had on a big grin upstairs all by herself.

Gray shook his head and rolled his eyes. "It's me, Etta. I'm checking out your door." He lowered his voice and spoke to me. "I'm sorry. She means well."

The impenetrable wall I'd built around my heart suffered a hairline fissure that he apologized on her behalf and stuck up for her, rather than calling Etta out for her little white lies. He wouldn't embarrass her. It was sweet. *Damn it.*

"Oh, that's great," Etta called again. "I just made gumbo. Layla agreed to join me for dinner. You should stay, too."

Gray's gaze turned serious, and he kept his voice low. "You good with that?"

My insides were doing a little dance, even if my brain still hadn't joined the party. "Yes, it's fine."

He lifted his toolbox and extended his hand toward the stairs. "After you."

Etta's face lit up when Gray walked into the kitchen. "Zippy. Thank you for coming to my rescue."

Gray smiled and dug the folded matchbook she'd shoved into the door from his pocket. Holding it in the palm of his hand, he said, "Lock's all fixed." He winked at me. "Wind must've blown some debris in, and this got stuck in it."

Etta turned her attention to the oven. "Great. That's wonderful. Now we can all sit and have an early dinner. Did you know gumbo is one of Layla's favorite dishes, too?"

Gray caught my eyes. "I did. She also likes escargot. Although that one I'm gonna have to disagree with."

I was beginning to think he wasn't exaggerating when he said he remembered everything about our time together.

"If I recall correctly," I said. "Gray has SpaghettiOs with little hot dogs on his favorite food list. So I think we'll have to agree to disagree on the best meals."

Etta set a peach cobbler on top of the stove and took off her mitts. "He likes it best when you grill the hot dog and slice it up real thin, then add it to a can of regular SpaghettiOs. Did he ever tell you about the time he made them for his friend Percy while I was out at the grocery store?"

Gray walked over to a drawer and pulled out a wine opener. He took the wine he'd brought from the brown paper bag. "If we're going to be sharing my childhood stories, I think I'm going to need this."

Etta took my arm. "Come, sweetheart. Let's go sit in the living room while Gray brings us some wine. By the way, before we get to the hot dog cooking story and I forget, let me tell you what Gray's little speech issue had him calling his best friend Percy for years."

Gray groaned and clunked the wine bottle down on the table as he mumbled under his breath, "*Fuck.*"

"Poor boy couldn't pronounce his *errr* sound for a long time, so everything came out sounding more like an *uhh*. It was cute, except Percy became a word ladies don't usually say—you know, a baby kitten." She chuckled. "The funny part is, turned out he was right. That Percy grew up to be a big wimp."

Etta and I went to sit in the living room together, and eventually Gray joined us with two glasses of wine and a drink he brought for Etta without having to ask what she wanted. She told me story after story about young Grayson, each more embarrassing than the last, until tears streamed down my face.

"Oh my God." I laughed. "Stop. I can't even sip my wine because I'm afraid it will come out my nose and stain your couch."

Gray shook his head, but he wasn't upset. I got the feeling nothing Etta could say or do would make him truly mad at her.

"I think we should stuff Etta's face with some gumbo now to keep her quiet for a while."

"Oh, Zippy. It's all in good fun. I'm not embarrassing you, am I?"

Her use of his nickname made me realize I still didn't know the origin. I took a drink of my wine, which was my second glass and nearly empty already, before asking. "Where does your nickname for Gray come from, Etta? Why do you call him Zippy?"

Gray's shoulders slouched, and his head hung. "*Shit,*" he muttered.

He seemed to have given up on trying to keep Etta quiet by saying her name in a warning tone and dishing out subtle glances. Instead, he braced for it.

Etta's eyes danced with amusement. "It was the summer between kindergarten and first grade. A real hot one, but Gray wasn't one to stay inside and play in the air conditioning, even when it was ninety-five. So he'd gotten prickly heat." She leaned in and lowered her voice. "On his testicles."

I covered my mouth and tried not to laugh. "Oh my God."

"So that summer became known as *commando summer*. Gray said it was cooler without underwear on, and God knew he was itchy enough down there, so I didn't force the issue. It was all well and good until *the zipper incident*."

The snort I had been attempting to contain snuck out, and then Etta burst out laughing right along with me. She had to tell the rest of the story through fits of laughter.

"He was pulling on a pair of jeans and got the tiniest piece of the skin of his third leg caught." Etta shook her head and cackled. "I put a Band-Aid on it. Didn't bleed too much. Luckily, at that age the blood isn't always rushing south. Think that was the end of commando summer."

Gray was a damn good sport. He looked at the two of us laughing at his expense and leaned forward to fill my wine glass.

"Keep drinking. Maybe you won't remember any of this tomorrow."

I wiped tears from my eyes. "Not a chance, Zippy."

He stood, lifting the now-empty bottle of wine, and stared down at me as he spoke to Etta. "This isn't something I ever really wanted to hear you repeat, Etta, but I've heard you tell this story before, and you're missing a part that I think is essential to restoring my manhood after the last half hour."

Etta's brows drew together and then she grinned. Leaning forward, she whispered. "He probably has a little scar, but by George, the boy had a big cannon for being such a little thing."

I looked up at Gray, who wore a wicked smile on his face. Feeling flushed, I averted my eyes, and since he was standing, they landed face to face with the topic of our conversation. He had on a pair of jeans with a zipper, but it was the bulge that caught my attention.

I stood abruptly and took the empty wine bottle from his hand. "I'll throw this out."

Needing a minute, I stood looking out the kitchen window over Etta's sink. I was so lost in thought that I hadn't heard footsteps entering the kitchen. But I definitely felt the body standing close behind me.

I didn't turn around when Gray started to speak. His voice was low. "When I was in Otisville, I had to eat when I was told, shower at an assigned time, and I couldn't leave the same old gray building for three years. Yet the thing that made me feel imprisoned, more than anything else, was not being able to touch you the way I wanted to when you were near me. And I don't even mean feel you up or anything sexual. I just wanted to put my hand over yours when you fidgeted every week when the guard told you it was time to go, rub my thumb along your arm to get your attention when you'd looked away from me after I said something that hit home, brush the hair off your face when you laughed and a piece got stuck on your long eyelashes." He paused. "I'm free now, but a big part of me still feels like I'm in prison."

I closed my eyes. I remembered wanting nothing more than to have him touch me during all those months when I lived for Saturdays. The truth was, I wanted nothing more than to have him touch me right now. I couldn't deny the attraction was still there. The rise in my temperature when he stood behind me was more than just radiating body heat.

I finally turned around. Gray made no attempt to back up, staying firmly planted in my private space and staring down at me intently. When I chanced looking up, our eyes met, and I allowed myself to get lost for a minute. Out of nowhere, I found myself asking something that had been bothering me since he pushed his way back into my life.

"On the last day I came to visit, I signed in on your sign-in sheet and saw a signature above mine. I couldn't make out the handwriting of the name, but the word written in the relationship-to-inmate column was clear as day: *wife*. That's how I found out. I was friendly with all the guards by then, so when I asked if it was a mistake, they confirmed it wasn't and said she hadn't been to visit in a while."

I paused, remembering how I'd felt like I'd been kicked in the stomach that day. "Why did Max come to visit if you were already divorced...or annulled?"

Gray looked into my eyes. "My father had passed out at the office. The next day, they made the diagnosis of an inoperable brain aneurysm. One of his friends reached out to Max to try to get a message to me. He had no idea what had gone down between the two of us. She showed up. It was the first time I'd seen her since I'd told her I knew what she had done and was having our sham marriage annulled. I was curious to see what the hell would make her show her face. She walked into the visitor room. I told her not to bother sitting down and to say whatever she came to say. She smiled at me and said, 'Your asshole father has a brain aneurysm. He'll be dead before you get out.' Then she turned around and strutted back out the door she came in. Haven't seen her since."

I looked down at my feet. "So the day after the woman who stole three years from your life showed up and told you your father was dying, I told you to go fuck yourself and walked away."

When I looked up, a wisp of hair fell into my face. Gray reached out to push it away and stopped, pulling his hand back. "It's not your fault. I should have been upfront with you about Max from the beginning. Then you would have given me the chance to explain her visit that day."

I nodded, but his trying to take ownership didn't make me feel any better about what he must've gone through. "I'm sorry, Gray. I really am."

Etta came into the kitchen. I'd almost forgotten she was here. Gray took a step back.

"I'm sorry to interrupt, but if I don't turn the heat down on the gumbo, we'll be eating out." She walked over to the stovetop and took the large Dutch oven from the heat.

"What can I do to help, Etta?"

"You're a guest. You go take a seat, and Gray will set the table."

He didn't need to be told twice. He reached into the cabinet and pulled down the plates before taking out utensils. Clearly, he knew his way around the kitchen, and that warmed my heart a little. A grown man who still listened and quite obviously loved his childhood caretaker was a loyal one. And that meant more to me than all of the chemistry that still sparked between us.

I couldn't remember the last meal I'd enjoyed so much. Yes, the food was phenomenal, but the company was even better. During dinner, Etta continued to tell embarrassing childhood stories about Gray, and Gray seemed to relax more than I'd ever seen him. He smiled with his full face, flashing his dimples, and laughed from a place down deep that was reserved for true happiness. Our eyes met a few times, and I didn't tear mine away. Instead, I allowed the evening to just happen and had a better time than I cared to admit.

When Etta started to nod off in her chair while Gray and I shared cleaning up, I realized how long I'd stayed. "I should get going. I've been here eight hours, and Etta's tired."

Gray's face fell. "I'll walk you out."

Etta's eyes fluttered open when I went to get my purse. I leaned down and kissed her cheek. "Thank you for an amazing meal and wonderful company, Etta. I'll reach out to my friend at the traffic violations court to see if we can take care of your ticket without you having to appear."

"Thank you, sweetheart. I hope you'll come see me again soon."

"I'd love that."

———

Gray stopped me on the front porch. "Thank you for being so kind to Etta."

"It's my pleasure. She's really great."

"She is. Best thing I had in my life growing up. Even as an adult, I think she might've been the only one who never believed I'd done the shit I was accused of. Pretty sure my own father thought I'd done it. One of the worst parts of taking the deal was feeling like I let her down."

I shook my head. "There's no way you could ever let that woman down."

Gray nodded, but I could tell he didn't believe me.

We walked to the street where my car was parked. I unlocked the door, and Gray opened it for me, but I lingered before getting in. How was I supposed to say goodbye? A hug? A kiss on the cheek? A handshake felt awkward.

"Layla..." He stopped me before I'd sorted it out in my head.

"Yes?"

"Have lunch with me?"

"You mean like a date?"

"Or a non-date. Call it whatever you want. Just spend time with me."

I looked down.

I shouldn't. But that didn't mean I didn't want to.

Screw it.

No. Think with your head, Layla!

But it's just lunch.

There was no such thing as *just anything* with this man.

Yes.

No.

Yes. Why not? He deserves a second chance.

No. You'll only wind up hurt.

What about Oliver?

Gray's hand at my chin stopped my internal debate. I wasn't used to his touch, nor was I used to the way my body reacted to such a simple gesture from him. My breaths increased, and I became aware of my rapid heartbeat. He gently tilted my head up, forcing our eyes to meet.

"You want what we had to be over, that's fine. But give me a chance. Let's start something new."

I wanted to...I *really* wanted to.

"Just lunch...?"

"If that's what you want, just lunch."

I knew without a shadow of a doubt that the dumbest thing I could do was say yes. Which of course, didn't stop me. "Fine. Just lunch."

His face lit up like a kid seeing presents under the tree on Christmas morning. "I'll pick you up at eleven tomorrow."

"I'll meet you there."

He smirked. "You don't even know where we're going."

"Text me an address." I started to get into my car, but Gray grabbed my wrist, stopping me.

He looked into my eyes. "I promise you're not making a mistake."

I wasn't sure that was true, but I nodded anyway.

Getting into my car, I somehow managed to maneuver down the block without hitting anything. But once I was out of view of Gray Westbrook, I had to pull over to catch my breath. Putting my car into park, I leaned my head on the steering wheel. I'd just said yes thirty seconds ago, and already I had no idea what had possessed me to do it. Where had my common sense gone? Oh wait, I knew. It had been silenced by my blinding desire for the man, the same thing that had made me do stupid things a little more than a year ago, even under the watchful eyes of cameras.

Only this time...he was a free man, and there were no cameras...and nothing stopping us from doing all the things we had wanted to do to each other back then.

Chapter 14

Gray

I had stood before a judge and agreed to spend years locked up in a federal detention center, but I wasn't as nervous then as I was walking down the street to meet Layla. Maybe it was because then I'd known that when I finally walked out, I'd be a free man again, ready to start over with a clean slate.

With Layla, though, I wasn't so damn certain. If I blew it this time, there wouldn't be another chance. And I wasn't sure I'd ever feel free of her, even if she was done with me.

I arrived fifteen minutes early at the Starbucks around the corner from where I'd planned to take her and got both of us a coffee, another thing we'd never shared—a simple cup of fucking coffee—even though I knew exactly how she took it, because she'd written it in one of her letters.

She arrived right on time, and I stood next to the couch I'd made sure to grab because it was small and would mean we'd have to sit close.

"Hey."

She looked as nervous as I felt. I leaned down and kissed her cheek. The smell of her skin had more of an effect on me than when I was a horny teenager and got to second base.

I'd told her to dress casual because of where we were going, but seeing her dressed in a pair of jeans, fitted pale blue T-shirt, and some sort of high-heeled sandal with ribbon tied around the ankle confirmed that my idea of what to do this afternoon was right for more than one reason. Her dark, wavy hair framed her beautiful face, and instead of the usual red lipstick, her beautiful mouth was its normal color, only glossier. But none of that mattered when I saw her nose.

I had to swallow to keep my eyes from tearing up like a goddamn pussy.

"Your freckles are back."

She seemed flustered that I'd noticed and looked away. "I like to give my skin a break on the weekend. I'm going to grab some coffee. You want anything?"

I lifted the two tall cups from the table and extended one to her. "Blonde vanilla latte with extra vanilla syrup."

"*Oh*. Thanks."

My appointment wasn't for another half an hour, so I motioned for her to take a seat. "We have a little time before we have to go."

"Go? I thought we were where we were going. You said to meet you at Starbucks."

"That's right. *Meet me* at Starbucks. We have somewhere to go from here."

"Where?"

I grinned. "That's a secret."

She bit her lip, a rare sign of nervousness, and sipped her coffee. I couldn't help staring at her.

"You have to stop doing that?" she said.

"What?"

"Staring at me. It freaks me out."

"All right." I sat back into my chair and turned my head away from her. "So tell me what's been going on over the last year."

She elbowed me in the ribs playfully. "You know what I mean."

I turned back to face her. "Yeah, I do. You want me to me act like you're not all I think about, and that when I see you it doesn't take every ounce of strength I have to keep from grabbing your hair and making you remember what our lips felt like pressed against each other."

Layla took the slightest breath in, just shy of a gasp, but more than a regular inhale. She wanted to hide any effect I had on her. She looked away to break the moment before turning back, shaking her head.

"I made a list, you know."

I sipped my coffee, knowing exactly what she meant. Everything needed to be thoroughly analyzed. "Lay it on me."

"Pros," she started and grinned. "Let me think. That was a much shorter list."

"Easy now. I'm sure you're just missing a few. That's another reason we needed to spend some time together today. So I can help you balance that thing."

"Maybe I'll walk away with a whole bunch of new cons I hadn't thought of after this."

"You won't."

She rolled her eyes, yet smiled. "So cocky."

I winked. "My cock definitely goes on the pro side."

"That reminds me, I need to add *pervert* to the con side."

I leaned closer. "Give me a chance to make good on the dirty things I say. You'll move it to the pro side. I promise."

"Will we ever have a normal conversation again?"

I smirked. "Again? Did we ever have a normal conversation?"

She sighed. "You have a point."

"I'm just kidding. We *did* have good talks, Layla. You're beautiful, but I'm not celibate after more than three years because I can't meet a woman. We connected on a different level. I want you to give that a chance again."

She nodded but didn't look too convincing if she was saying yes.

"Would it make you feel better if I told you that you scare the shit out of me, too?"

Her lips parted, and she covered this time by bringing the coffee to her mouth.

I noticed a woman waiting for her coffee looking over at us and staring. Lifting my chin in her direction, I asked Layla. "Friend of yours?"

When she turned to look, her face and posture changed. It looked like she wanted to duck and hide under the seat. The woman waved, and Layla hesitantly waved back. "Shit."

"Someone you don't want to see?"

"It's my half-sister."

"From your father's other…"

"Family. Yes."

"She lives in New York?"

"She moved here a few months ago. And thinks we should be besties."

I glanced over at the woman now walking toward us with her coffee. "Well, don't look now, but your bestie is on her way over here."

The woman had an irritatingly high-pitched voice. "Layla! I can't believe I finally ran into you. I left you a few messages. I was starting to think you were avoiding me."

"No. Just busy." She pointed to me. "Even working weekends. I'm sort of in a client meeting."

"Oh!" She looked at me, her interest piqued. "Lucky you."

"But it was great seeing you." Layla laid it on thick.

"You, too. I'm having dinner with Dad next weekend. You should join. He'd love to see you."

Layla feigned disappointment like a champ. "Oh. Sorry. I'll be out of town."

The woman stuck out her bottom lip. "Okay. Well, I'll let you get back to work." She leaned down and went in for an awkward hug and air kiss. "I'll call you!"

"You do that," Layla said. "Take care."

When she turned back around, her shoulders slumped. "I hope wherever you're taking me, there's alcohol."

I looked at my watch. "It's even better. You'll love it. It will put a smile on your face and make you forget all about your crazy family. And you won't have a hangover tomorrow."

"I'm not sure I should trust you from the sound of that..."

I winked. "I like the way you're thinking. But you can trust me." I stood and held out my hand to help her up. "Ready to go?"

She looked at it for a few seconds, hesitating before placing her little hand in mine. Even though she let go after she stood—when I wanted to keep it—it felt like progress that she'd taken it at all.

Baby steps.

Progress.

We were quiet as we made our way out of the coffee shop and up the street. I was just about to let her in on where we were heading to cheer her up, when she surprised me by opening up on her own.

"She's really nice. I feel bad that I don't want anything to do with her. But I just can't bring myself to spend time with her."

"It's understandable," I said. "She's a constant reminder of something that's painful for you."

"But why doesn't it bother *her*? Shouldn't she see me the same way I see her? Just the fact that she *wants* to be friends makes me feel like something's wrong with me for not feeling the same way."

"Not everyone handles painful things the same way." I paused and thought about whether I should share the example I immediately thought of. Deciding maybe it would help my case, I did. "Look at what I did with Max. It could have been as simple as telling you I was married once and had it annulled when you asked. But I didn't even want to admit to it. I was embarrassed, and I hadn't done anything wrong. There's probably a little bit of you that feels the same about what your dad did."

She nodded. "Yeah. All these years and only Quinn knows the truth of my parents' odd relationship. And if I'm being honest, I had never even planned to tell her. His flight home on my sixteenth birthday got canceled, and I was upset that he was going to be with his other family on my day. Quinn and I got drunk, and I wound up telling her everything. I'd known what was going on for years by then, but I'd never said a word."

I looked over at her and nodded. "Forget the mistakes others make; just learn from them. That was one of Etta's mantras growing up. It's scary how appropriate it is for my life right now."

We arrived at the building that housed the animal shelter, and I stopped. "We're here."

"Where?" She looked around, and her eyes lit up as they rose to the sign high on the tall brick building: *New York City Animal Care*. "We're visiting dogs?"

"We can visit them all. But I'm here for one in particular. I adopted a dog, and today's my appointment to pick him up."

<hr />

"Oh my God." Layla landed flat on her ass and cracked up. Just like the first time I'd met Freckles, he'd acted shy and hesitant, sniffing her until he decided she was okay, and then he'd pounced and knocked her over to lick her face. This time I grabbed his collar, much like the volunteer had done when it was me.

"Relax, boy. Take it easy. I know she smells good, but you're embarrassing the both of us. Plus, I might be a little jealous."

Layla's smile was wide as she rolled her eyes and let me help her up. She stayed crouched down next to me, as Freckles finally turned his attention my way.

"There you go. It's about time you noticed I was here."

She looked on as I scratched behind his ears and gave him a good two-hand rub.

"And here I assumed you were referring to the attention I was giving the dog when you said you were jealous," Layla teased. "Now I'm not so sure. I think you might've been jealous of the dog giving me attention."

"You let me lick your face, and I won't even remember I have a dog."

She laughed.

The volunteer had said the center's Wi-Fi was down this morning, so they were a little behind in getting the adoption paperwork together. She'd suggested we hang out in the pet playroom while they worked on finalizing everything.

I would stay all day in this putrid-smelling room just to keep that smile on Layla's face. She looked so carefree in the moment.

Freckles ran over and got his shoe. I guess that thing was coming home with me if he still hadn't given it up. Layla took the shoe and pulled on one end while he happily pulled on the other.

"Is this what they're using for toys now? Whatever the fee is for adopting him, I think you need to double your donation."

God, that damn smile.

"It's his previous owner's. Sad story. He died…" I reached out and scratched the dog's back while the two of them played tug-of-war. "And this little guy got himself into trouble in the house for a few days before anyone found them. That's why he's shaved. When I saw him yesterday, he was covered in glue and mud. But that shoe is his owner's, and he seems to be attached to it."

"Awww. Poor baby." Layla released the shoe and scooped Freckles into her arms, snuggling him against her chest.

I could swear the dog looked back at me and grinned. Maybe I imagined it.

"I had a dog when I was little."

"I know. That was the start of your yeahway lists. You got a mutt that you named Muffin the Mutt."

She looked at me funny, her nose crinkling up. "You remember my dog's name?"

"Too creepy?"

Her lip twitched. "Maybe a little."

Ten minutes later, Carol, the volunteer who'd helped us when we came in, appeared in the doorway. "Looks like he's taken a liking to the Mrs."

I saw from my peripheral vision that Layla was about to correct her, so I beat her to the chase. "Can you blame him? Dog's got good taste."

I winked when my pretend wife gave me the evil eye.

"We're all ready with the paperwork. Sorry about the wait. We just need you to sign a few forms, and you'll be on your way."

I lifted the dog from Layla's arms and offered a hand to help her up.

"I'll be right next door when you're ready," Carol said. She began to walk away and then turned back and pointed to the beat-up loafer on the floor. "Don't forget Freckles' shoe."

Layla had been brushing the dog hair from her pants. Her head popped up. "What did she just say?"

"She said she'd be right next door when we're ready."

She narrowed her eyes. "After that."

"She didn't want us to forget his loafer."

"Yes, and what did she call the dog?"

"By his name, of course."

She playfully smacked my arm. "What's the dog's name, Westbrook?"

I grinned. "Freckles."

"That *was* his name already or that's what you named him?"

"I had nothing to do with it." I pointed to his nose. The little guy's freckles were front and center with his new shaved head. "But now I know why we bonded so easily. Me and Freckles. We're meant to be."

She shook her head, but the smile she wore hadn't disappeared. I extended my hand for her to walk through the doorway before me, but stopped her before she passed through to whisper, "I was referring to *both* Freckles, in case you were wondering."

Chapter 15

Gray

I wasn't ready to call it a day.

But after a trip to a nearby pet store to stock up on supplies, Freckles told me he was ready to go home. He actually laid down while I waited in the checkout line.

Layla placed the dog bowls in her hands on the conveyor belt while I added a twenty-pound bag of food, biscuits, some chew sticks, and a plastic shoe that I had a feeling would drive me nuts from squeaking.

She looked at Freckles as he yawned and made himself comfortable. "I think you have a lazy dog."

"Don't pick on your namesake." I paid the bill for my purchases and grabbed the dog food and one of the bags. Layla picked up the other two, and we walked back out to the street together.

"My little buddy's wiped out, and I could really use some help carrying all this junk to my place."

Layla gave me a face that said *you're full of shit*. "I could tie these bags to your belt loops and make you walk home like a pack mule while I go into the office for a few hours like I should've done today."

I grinned. "Or...you could come home with me and let me try to impress you with the view from my living room."

"If I help you, do you promise to be on good behavior?"

"I do." I looked down at my new dog. "But I can't speak for Freckles here. I'm not the only one that wants to lick you."

"Which way? Before I change my mind."

———

My palms started to sweat as I opened the front door to my apartment. I had no fucking idea why. I lived in a great building, the views were spectacular, and before my disastrous relationship with Max, I wasn't a stranger to entertaining. But with Layla, everything just felt important.

I couldn't have asked for a better reception if I'd ordered the sunset myself. The floor-to-ceiling windows in the living room revealed the most colorful, hazy sunset casting orange, yellow, and purple streaks across the sky. It wasn't quite fully dark, but it was dim enough that the lights of Manhattan bounced a glow all over the city.

"Holy shit." Layla made a beeline for the wall of glass. "I assumed you saying you had a great view was just a way to lure me up to your apartment."

I walked over and stood close behind her. God, what I wouldn't have given to pull her hair to the side and devour her beautiful neck. Together we looked out in comfortable silence until she broke it.

"You must've missed this."

I looked at her standing so close and began to salivate. "You can't even imagine."

If I didn't put a little space between us, I was about to fuck things up. I cleared my throat. "I need to give Freckles some water. Can I get you a glass of wine?"

"I'd love that."

Layla stayed at the windows as I filled Freckles' new bowl and opened a bottle of wine. It was getting dark fast, and by the time I joined her again, the light of the day was almost gone.

"When I was little and people asked me my favorite color, I would say rainbow because I loved the way all the colors looked together and couldn't pick just one," she said. "I think that's changed."

"Oh yeah?" I extended the glass of wine to her. "What's your new favorite color?"

She smiled. "Sunset. That's my new favorite color."

"Come on. Let me show you the view from my bedroom before it gets completely dark. It's different, but just as good."

"I don't even care if that's a line. I want to see the view."

"Seriously?" she said as she walked in. The two windows in my bedroom were smaller than the display in the living room, but they framed a view of the Hudson River, which currently reflected the last of the sunset and lights of the coming evening. "These are the best views I've ever seen in an apartment. I don't think I'd ever leave if I lived here."

"I'm sure that could be arranged."

Just as we'd done in the living room, we stood at the bedroom windows looking outside for a while. I'm not sure how long we were there, but when Layla turned around, it was totally dark.

Her big green eyes looked up at me. "What did you miss most?"

Before I could answer, she held up a finger, clarifying her question. "And you can't say me."

I thought for a moment. "I missed wanting time to slow down."

"What do you mean?"

"I wanted every day to pass quickly. I was basically wishing my life away. I missed the moments in life when I wanted time to stand still."

"I'm not sure I understand."

"How did you just feel watching the sunset in the living room? Like you were enjoying the moment, and maybe it would be nice to stretch it a few minutes longer...make time slow down?"

"Yeah. That's exactly how I felt."

"I missed *that* feeling. I missed having things that were so important to me, that I enjoyed so much, that I wanted them to last a little longer."

She looked into my eyes. "That's a really good answer. I guess it can encompass many different things—a sunset, a special moment with someone, hearing an old song, a rainbow."

I wanted to tell her that *this* was one of those moments in the worst way. But I held back for fear of scaring her. Instead, we both sipped our wine. Tension built inside of me. She had to have felt it, too. We were standing in my bedroom, in the dark, in silence. I looked over at the bed eight feet away, and my thoughts couldn't help but move to what it would be like to be inside her. I wanted to fuck her all over my apartment—a christening of sorts. Against the living room windows while she watched the sunset, in the bedroom on all fours while she watched the sun rise.

On the kitchen counter, in the shower, on the floor in front of the fireplace in the dining room, on top of my desk in the guest bedroom that I used as an office.

Layla's voice broke me out of my fuckfest fantasy.

"What are you thinking about right now? You seem so focused on something."

I sipped my wine. "I don't think I should say."

She tilted her head. Even though it was dark now, the green in her eyes sparkled. "Why not?"

"Because I promised myself I'd never do something stupid like lie to you again."

"Why would you have to lie to me?"

I pointed my eyes to the bed before meeting hers again.

"*Oh*," she said.

The tension we'd managed to keep on simmer suddenly intensified. The air grew thick as the seconds passed, neither of us making an attempt to move out of the dark bedroom. I heard her breathing turn heavier as she stared down at the floor, avoiding my gaze. When she looked up from under thick lashes and our eyes connected, I thought I might lose it.

So fucking beautiful.

So fucking sexy.

In my bedroom...

But I couldn't make the first move, even though I would have given anything to take that mouth, devour that neck, hear her moan the way I knew she did when I kissed her. It was a sound I'd never forgotten.

Her voice was so low, I almost thought I'd imagined it at first.

"Tell me what you were thinking."

"You won't hold it against me?"

She swallowed and shook her head.

"I was imagining waking up to a sunrise in my bed with you. I was imagining the sun coming up over the river and all the beautiful colors." My voice was gravelly, and I waited for her to stop me. She didn't. "You'd be on all fours in the center of my bed while I fucked you from behind, slowly, as you watched the sun rise."

Her lips parted. Yet she still didn't stop me, so I took that as a sign to continue.

"I want to fuck you up against the glass in the living room so the entire city knows you're mine."

Her breathing became more labored.

"I want to lift you up onto the kitchen counter, spread your legs wide, and eat you for breakfast."

"*Jesus*, Gray."

A jingling noise called our attention to the door, and we turned just as my new dog came busting into the bedroom. The big shoe he carried knocked against the doorjamb as he charged in. I'd honestly forgotten all about him. Freckles took a running leap and jumped right up onto my bed. He circled a few times before plopping down dead center in the middle.

It effectively broke the moment. *Maybe getting a dog wasn't such a great idea after all.*

Layla blinked a few times. I got the feeling she was relieved to have an interruption. She walked over to the bed and sat down. "Hey there, little buddy. How do you like your new home?"

I stayed at the window and watched their interaction.

Freckles got up and walked over to the edge where she sat. Layla extended her hand for him to smell, and he took full advantage, even adding in a few licks. Then, out of nowhere, just like he'd done to me the first time I met him and then to Layla earlier today, he jumped on her. Only this time, he didn't knock her on her ass. She fell back onto the bed and laughed while he hovered over her on all fours, licking her face.

Rather than stopping it right away, I enjoyed the moment. Layla's dark hair was sprawled all over my comforter, and she was laughing and smiling, so carefree. Eventually, I felt guilty for not calling my dog off, so I walked over to the bed and gave his collar a little tug.

"All right, buddy. Take it easy," I teased. "Save some of that for me."

Layla sat up with a genuine smile and wiped doggy drool from her face.

I still couldn't take my eyes off of her.

"What?" She patted her hair and righted her shirt, which had slipped from one shoulder. "Is my makeup all over my face or something?"

I shook my head. "Remember what you asked me before? What I missed most?"

"Yeah."

I looked between her eyes. "That was one of those moments. Just watching you enjoy the dog."

Warmth filled her eyes. "He's a sweet dog."

"How about his owner?"

She smirked. "He has his moments." Looking around the room, it must've dawned on her that it had turned dark. "We should go back to the living room. But thank you for sharing the view."

"My view is your view. Come for sunset, stay for sunrise."

She laughed, and I followed her to the kitchen, enjoying my own spectacular view of her ass. When she turned around at the bathroom in the hallway, she caught me, but didn't call me out on it.

"Okay if I use this bathroom?"

"Of course. There's one off the bedroom, also, if you want."

"Thanks. This is fine."

Freckles walked over to the front door and scratched at it. "Do you need to go out, buddy?"

He responded by chasing his tail in a circle at the front door. "I'm going to take that as a yes."

Layla came into the kitchen while I tried to attach the leash to Freckles' collar. "I think he needs to go for a walk."

"Wow. That's great that he just let you know. It took us months to train our family dog. Although he was a puppy, and I guess Freckles' previous owner had him trained. But still. Will be nice not to have to go through that."

"Why don't you relax? Stay here. Have another glass of wine while I take him out."

She walked to her purse. "Actually, I think I should be going anyway."

We'd spent the entire day together, and I still didn't want it to end. "You sure? There's a great little Italian place up the block. I was supposed to take you to lunch today, and we never made it. We can order in. Or go grab a bite, if you want."

"Thanks. But I think it's best. Plus, I have a ton of work to do."

Neither of us said a word the entire way down in the elevator. Once we were out on the street, Freckles pulled me over to a tree to relieve himself.

"Smart dog," Layla said.

"Yeah. I think I might've gotten lucky."

She looked down. "Thanks for taking me along today to pick him up. I had a really good time."

I couldn't let her go without pushing. Reaching out, I slipped two fingers under her chin and lifted so our eyes met. "Let me take you out to dinner. On a real date."

I watched as the wheels in her head spun. She bit her lip and looked away before giving me her eyes. "We take it slow."

"I can do slow." I responded way too fast. It was obvious that if she'd said *"Okay, but you have to eat a bag of shit first,"* I would have agreed.

She shook her head. "I hope I don't regret this."

My face lit up into what was probably the most obnoxious, over-the-top, cheesy smile. "That's a yes?"

"Fine. Yes." She held up a warning finger. "But it's dinner. *Slow*, Gray."

I wrapped one arm around her waist and pulled her to me. "I can do slow."

She narrowed her eyes. "I thought you said no lies."

"I did. That doesn't mean I *want* to do slow. But I *can*, and I *will*, if that's what it takes."

She rested a hand on my chest, applying a slight pressure that I suspected was telling me to keep the distance. "I need to take care of some things. Call me during the week?"

"Is wrapping you in my arms and hugging the shit out of you right now too fast?"

She giggled. "A hug is fine."

I pulled Layla into a tight embrace and buried my face in her hair. She smelled so fucking good. "You have no idea how happy you just made me."

"Ummm… If the thing poking me in the hip is any indication, I think I do know how happy you are."

We laughed, and while I hated to let her go, I tried to be good. I didn't even attempt to suck her face, though that was only the tip of the iceberg of what I wanted to suck. Although she *did* have to tug her hand from mine when it was time to walk away. I couldn't get myself to let go voluntarily.

Chapter 16

Layla

"Are we actually in the building on the same day?" Oliver walked into my office on Wednesday morning with his usual sunny smile.

On Monday he'd been in court all day, and on Tuesday I was out with a client in New Jersey until evening. We'd exchanged a few texts, and I'd told him I couldn't have dinner on Wednesday night, but suggested we have lunch instead. It was definitely easier to break things off over a quick lunch than a longer dinner, and I wasn't going to spend time with Gray until I ended things with Oliver. Even though Oliver and I had never talked about being exclusive, it just didn't sit right with me.

My phone buzzed on my desk, and I was glad it faced down. Gray had been texting me this morning, and I didn't want to show Oliver any disrespect. He was a great guy—a part of me wished I wanted to be with him instead of Gray—but the heart knows even if the brain hasn't caught up yet.

"I'm surprised I made it to work today." I closed the file cabinet I'd been digging in. "Mr. Kwan talked my ear off until eight o'clock last night."

Oliver and I had few crossover clients, and Kwan Enterprises used legal services from almost every department at our firm.

"Did he bring Jin Me or Song?" Oliver asked.

"Jin Me. Who's Song?"

He smirked. "His wife."

"Oh my God! He's married? I had no idea. I thought Jin Me was his daughter at first. She's, like, thirty, and he's probably in his late sixties. So it creeped me out when she put her hand on his thigh."

"Yep. Guy's a stud. He's been a client of mine almost as long as I've been practicing. There've been a dozen Jin Me."

"God, I never would've taken him for a cheater for some reason."

"It's always the ones you least expect." I knew Oliver wasn't referring to me, but I felt guilty nonetheless for having spent time with Gray.

"Umm… Yeah. I have to jump on a call. Lunch at one?"

"Greek?"

"Sure." I forced a smile. "That sounds great."

After Oliver disappeared, I sat and stared out my window for a while. I knew ending things with him was the right thing to do, whether things worked out with Gray or not. Because had my heart been with Oliver, it wouldn't have strayed so easily. But it was never easy to break up with a nice person.

My phone buzzed on my desk, calling my attention back from thinking about my upcoming lunch. Of course it was Gray. As was the earlier text that I hadn't looked at when Oliver walked in.

Gray: I'm flying to Chicago tonight for a meeting early tomorrow with a potential tech investment.

Gray: How about lunch today?

I texted back.

Layla: Sorry. Can't today. I have a lunch date.

After I wrote the text, I rethought my words and amended before hitting send.

Layla: Sorry. Can't today. I have plans for lunch.

Gray: Can you reschedule? I'll make it worth your while. Friend of mine is opening a French restaurant Uptown and hosting a critics' lunch—every entree in miniature size—a taste of the entire menu.

I debated what to tell him for a few minutes and decided to go with the truth.

Layla: I'm having lunch with Oliver today.

Archibald Pittman walked into my office and interrupted the rest of what I was about to text. His visits always made me nervous.

"Ms. Hutton. Just reviewed the billable hours. Nice job bringing our new client into the fold and pushing our other specialty work."

I had no idea what the hell he was talking about. "Uh. Thank you."

"Keep up the good work." He disappeared.

Still unsure of what he had been referring to, I texted Gray.

Layla: Did you happen to give any other legal work to the firm, outside of my department?

Gray: I don't share, Layla.

Hmmm. That was an odd answer.

Layla: I'm not sure I understand.

I waited for his text response, but instead the cell rang in my hand.

"I know you said we need to take it slow, but I can't fucking share, Freckles."

"What are you talking about?"

"Your lunch date."

"*Oh!*" I laughed. "Sorry, I was lost in our conversation. I mentioned my lunch with Oliver and then Pittman interrupted and mentioned something about a client giving the firm more business. I thought that might be you. It must've been someone else I work with."

"I did give the firm more business. They're handling the probate of my father's will and a real estate transaction I need done. I called Pittman and told him you'd sold me on bringing that work to your firm instead of leaving it with my father's attorney."

"Oh. Wow. You didn't have to do that. But thank you."

"You're welcome. Now can you do me a favor in return?"

"Sure. What?"

"Don't go to lunch with Pencil Dick. I can wait eleven months to see you. I can hold myself back from mauling you when you're in my apartment. I can go as slow as you want. But I can't fucking take the thought of you with another man."

As much as I hated to admit it, his possessiveness and jealousy were a turn-on in this situation—although I couldn't help but screw with him a bit.

"But I broke it off with Jared already."

"*Who?*"

I had to cover my mouth to stop my giggle. "Jared. And I was planning on letting go of Trent, too. Although I thought maybe I'd sleep with him at least one more time before breaking it off."

"You're fucking with me? Please tell me you're fucking with me."

I let him hear my laugh this time. "I'm having lunch with Oliver to end things. I was planning on telling you that, but then Pittman interrupted, and I forgot to mention that part."

Gray blew out a loud breath. "You think you're funny, don't you?"

"Yes. As a matter of fact, I am rather amused right now." I leaned back into my chair.

"I'm glad you're enjoying yourself. But that deserves a smack on the ass, and I'll enjoy the repay next time I see you."

"I might enjoy that, too."

Gray groaned. "Christ." Then I heard him cover the phone. "Can you circle the block once or twice, please?"

I heard the faint sounds of what must've been a driver saying, "*Sure thing, sir,*" before Gray returned to the line.

"I'm going to be late for my appointment at the bank because of you now."

"Me? What did I do?"

"You just told me you might enjoy me spanking you, and now I can't think of anything but the way your ass will look with my handprint on it. I can't walk in there with a swollen cock."

I shifted in my seat. "Oh."

"Have an early dinner with me? I can't wait to see you after you're officially mine."

"Don't get ahead of yourself. I said I was breaking things off with Oliver. I didn't say I was officially anyone's."

He ignored me. "Five o'clock dinner. I'll push my seven flight back to nine."

"I can't. I have a client at four, and need to prep for a case for tomorrow. When are you back from your trip?"

"Late tomorrow night. Friday then?"

"I have a kiddie birthday party Friday night. Saturday?"

"An event with my father's old partner. Sunday night?"

"I have an early deposition Monday that I'll need to prep for."

"Jesus Christ. And I fly out to the west coast on Monday morning. I can't wait two weeks to kiss you."

I smiled. "You could always come with me to the kiddie party. It's for my goddaughter."

"Will there be a quiet corner or a closet to push you in for a few minutes and kiss the shit out of you?"

I laughed. "I can't guarantee one. But there might."

"Fine. What time should I pick you up?"

"You're really going to come to a kiddie party with me?"

"Are you inviting me?"

"Sure, if you want. I'm sure Quinn would love to meet you. It's my best friend's daughter's party." I paused. "But full disclosure, I'm not sure she's your biggest fan. We sort of share everything, and she'll probably give you the evil eye and interrogate the crap out of you."

"Still worth it, just for the chance at getting you alone for a few minutes. Plus, I'm going to have to win over your friend sooner or later."

I loved that he was willing to work with anything I might give him. "I'll tell you what—we'll make it interesting. If you can get my goddaughter to give you a hug goodbye, and her mom to give you the thumbs up, I'll let you feel me up in the car on the way home."

Of course, he had no idea that my goddaughter pretty much hated men in general, and Quinn had considered visiting him in prison to chop his balls off at one point. But what fun would it be to fill him in on that?

"Sweetheart, you have no idea the lengths I would go to in order to win that bet."

"Six o'clock Friday."

"Can't wait."

The sound of my buzzer made me jump. I couldn't remember a time when I'd been this nervous for a date— if that was what you'd even call taking Gray with me to a kiddie birthday party at six o'clock on a Friday night. I pressed the intercom.

"You're a half hour early. Why do I think you did that on purpose so I wouldn't be ready, and I'd have to tell you to come up rather than coming down?"

"Because you're smart." His gruff voice and honesty made me laugh.

"Come on up."

I waited at the door for the elevator. I'd come home a little early to shower and get ready, but I still needed another fifteen minutes or so to do my makeup. Gray stepped off the elevator and strutted toward me. He walked with confidence and purpose—which was a turn-on for me. Something about the way a man stands and walks has always spoken volumes in my mind. It could be small—standing in the open-legged, feet-apart position that's a little wider than his shoulders, or the way he keeps his head up and looks straight head.

Gray ate up the distance to my door with his long, balanced strides. Even though it unnerved me, I stood my ground firm when he didn't look like he was going to stop.

He got right into my personal space and wrapped one hand around my waist. "I looked up the definition of slow on the way over here."

I perked one brow. "You did? What did you learn?"

"Moving or proceeding with less-than-usual speed or velocity."

"Very good. You've learned the definition of *slow*. How about *pulchritude*? I memorized that one for the SAT years ago."

Gray used the hand wrapped around my waist to press our bodies tighter. "*Wise ass*. I meant...*slow* doesn't mean stop. It means keep progressing forward, just at a slower pace."

"Yes, that's right."

I swear I saw a twinkle in his eye as a sly grin spread across his face. "Glad we're in agreement. Now give me that mouth so we can keep progressing forward."

I opened my mouth to respond, but his lips crashed down on mine before any words came out. I'd forgotten how soft his were, and how much they directly contradicted the hard need of his kiss. Gray wasted no time, his tongue dipping inside to taste me. I moaned into our joined mouths, and he responded with a growl that vibrated down to some interesting places.

Gray backed me against my apartment door, and then suddenly my legs were wrapping around his waist. I wasn't sure if he'd lifted me and guided my actions or if I'd done it all on my own. The crazy speed of my heart thumping made everything so much more fevered. My fingers threaded through his hair, yanking him closer. Gray ground his hips against me, and my eyes rolled into the back of my head. He was so hard, and my open legs left me exposed to the abrasive friction. *So decadently exposed.*

I moaned into our mouths again, and Gray pushed even harder. He fisted a handful of the flesh on my ass and squeezed to the point of pain. But that little bit of pain only served to turn me on even more. I was *absolutely screwed* when it came to going slow with this man. Because in that moment, if he'd unzipped and pushed my panties to the side, I'd have let him fuck me right against my apartment door for all the neighbors to see.

Luckily, although he was pretty damn good at reading me, he couldn't read my mind. So when he broke the kiss, I was breathless and panting, but at least I was still clothed.

I kept my eyes closed as I attempted to rein myself in, battling through my raging hormones to get back to some semblance of self-control. So I didn't expect the loud smack of Gray's hand connecting with my ass. My eyes flashed open.

"What the hell?"

"I owed you that for the other day on the phone—screwing with me about your lunch with Oliver and seeing other men." Gray rubbed the sting on my ass away with his hand.

There was no way in hell I was about to tell him my panties had just gotten a little wetter. Instead I took the moment to disengage from contact, because I didn't trust myself to honor my own request to go slow.

I swallowed and climbed down off of him. "I should leave you out in the hall while I finish getting ready after that."

"If that's what you need to do to keep control of yourself, by all means." He cupped the back of my neck and brushed his lips with mine. "But don't forget to change your wet panties."

I shook my head and *didn't* slam the door on him as I walked inside. "So full of yourself."

I heard him chuckle as I left him in the kitchen to go finish getting ready.

Gray didn't try to come into my bedroom during the twenty minutes it took me to do my makeup and get changed, which surprised me a little. But I got the feeling he would tow the line on *going slow*, yet he knew there were boundaries that would jeopardize things if he pushed.

When I was done, I found him in the living room, looking at the framed photos on my bookshelf. He had one in his hand. I walked over and stood next to him, looking at an old family photo of me with both of my parents.

"I don't even know why I keep that out. Maybe it's because I'm trained to keep up the charade of a normal family."

"You can love them both despite not approving of their lifestyle."

I took the frame from his hand and set it back on the shelf. Preferring a change of subject, I lifted one of me and Quinn in junior high. We wore matching clothes in the picture.

"This is Quinn. I have no idea why, but we used to call each other on Sunday nights and plan a matching outfit to wear on Mondays every week."

Gray smiled. "You were hot even in middle school."

"I'm sure you weren't so bad yourself."

The rest of the pictures on the shelf were of my goddaughter, Harper. Gray pointed to one. "I take it this is the guest of honor this evening."

"How could you guess?" I said sarcastically.

In the photo, Harper was lying down, watching TV from inside a long box. She'd been obsessed with boxes since she could walk, and her parents had made her various pieces of furniture out of them—including the bed in the photo. The ratty old box bed sat right next to the beautiful, empty canopy bed her parents had bought her.

Looking at my watch, I realized we needed to head out. "I just need to grab my phone and then we can get going."

"Give me the tour first?"

"Of my apartment? There's not very much to see. Unlike you, I don't have a view of the city. But if you look out my bedroom window around two in the morning, sometimes the guy in the building across the street is doing naked yoga."

"Great," Gray grumbled. He put his hand on my lower back and steered me toward my bedroom. "I'll take a tour of the room you can watch naked yoga from anyway."

I stopped short of actually going into my bedroom, mostly because it was all mattress. I had a queen-size bed in a room that should have had a double. But I was a restless sleeper and tended to roll around a lot. Pointing to the bed and dresser, I said, "This is it. Small bedroom, but it has a big walk-in closet."

Gray turned, crowding the doorway, and me. "How did it go breaking it off with Oliver?"

I tilted my head. "I show you my bedroom and you think of Oliver?"

Gray ran his thumb over my lips. "I think of how much I can't wait to fuck you on that big bed of yours, and I want to make sure nothing is standing in my way anymore."

God, I liked when he said he wanted to *fuck me*. I knew without a shadow of a doubt that our first time would be exactly that: *fucking*. Not making love or going all the way. There would be raw, primal fucking when the two of us finally got together.

I cleared my throat. "It went fine. We should get going."

Downstairs, I was surprised to find Gray's town car waiting. I'd assumed he meant he'd be driving to a kiddie party, not having a chauffeured car take us.

"A driver to a kiddie party?"

He waved off his driver who had started to get out when he saw us and walked ahead of me to open the back door. "I thought about it. But I need two hands to feel you up on the way home...after I win our bet."

Chapter 17

Layla

"You're really not going to tell me what this gigantic thing is?"

"I'll show you a gigantic thing..."

I rolled my eyes. "That thing in your pants better be outstanding *if* I eventually see it, for all the smack talk you've done about it. Now, tell me what's in this big box."

"I'll tell you for a kiss."

"I already kissed you."

"Is there a daily limit?" Gray pulled me from sitting next to him onto his lap in the backseat of the car.

I giggled and thought to myself, *I don't freaking giggle.*

"I've missed you, Freckles. Missed this—feeling like you were mine." He pulled my hair to the side and kissed up my neck. I sighed and closed my eyes. I'd missed it, too. Although, unlike Gray, I was taking baby steps and not diving into this relationship, so I kept the thought to myself.

"Can I ask you something?" I said.

"Anything." He inhaled deeply and kept his head buried in my neck. "God, I fucking love the way you smell."

"Do you think it's possible to love more than one person at a time?"

I felt him go rigid. "Is there something you want to tell me?"

I laughed. "No. I wasn't talking about me. But when I saw you looking at the picture of my parents, it got me thinking about how possessive you seem. Would you have been okay with me seeing you and Oliver at the same time?"

He pulled his head from my hair and looked into my eyes. "This is a hypothetical, right? You broke it off with Pencil Dick at lunch the other day?"

"Yes, crazy man. This isn't about us. I promise. I've just struggled my whole life to understand how my mother could accept my father having another woman—another family. And how my father could say he loved his families equally."

Gray looked relieved that I wasn't in love with another man. His posture changed, and he stared out the window, giving my question some thought. Returning his eyes to me, he said, "This is a tough question to answer. I don't want to hurt your feelings by telling you I don't think it's possible to love two people equally."

I sighed. "It's okay. Neither do I. But so few people know about my family life that I've never discussed it with a man. I thought maybe your perspective would be different than mine for some reason."

"I think there're different ways of loving people. But if you really love someone, like a man should love his woman, your heart doesn't have room to love anyone else the same way."

"So why wouldn't someone get divorced, then?"

Gray shook his head. "I have no idea. My gut wants to say because he looks at women like possessions."

"But you seem to be pretty possessive yourself."

"There's a difference between wanting to possess someone and being possessive."

"How so?"

"Possessiveness comes from a fear of losing something you care about. Wanting to possess something means you want to control it, take away its freedom."

I smiled. "You sound so wise, when normally you sound like a wise *ass*."

Gray's face turned serious. "Neither one of us had ideal role models for relationships growing up. But I like to think I at least learned what *not* to do. My father's loyalty was to his work, not to his wives. Mine won't be. Not anymore. I guess sometimes when your life is forced to stand still for a long period of time, it gives you the chance to look back. Things are clearer that way than when you're glancing over your shoulder and running forward."

For the first time, I initiated physical contact. I leaned in and brushed my lips over Gray's. When I pulled back, we stared at each other for a long time.

"Thank you," Gray whispered.

"For the kiss?"

"No. For the second chance."

Harper ran full speed at me when we walked in. She wrapped her little arms around my legs and jumped up and down, pointing to the enormous box in Gray's hands. I still didn't know its contents. "Is that for me? Is that for me?"

Gray bent down on one knee so he sat eye level with her. "Is your name Harper?" he asked.

She nodded her head fast.

"Is today your sixth birthday?"

More head nodding.

Gray looked at the box and shrugged. "Well, I guess it's for you, then."

"Can I open it?"

He glanced up at me for an answer.

"Oh no," I said. "You brought that massive thing here. You're not going to make me say she can't rip into it."

Luckily, Quinn walked over. She kissed me on the cheek and spoke directly to Gray with a stoic face and attitude. "Trying to buy my kid, huh? Hope you brought me something good. I'm expensive to buy off."

Gray leaned down and kissed Quinn on the cheek. He spoke with his sexy, gruff voice. "I brought you the best thing possible: Layla. It's a pleasure to meet you, Quinn."

She glared at him. "I'd say it was reciprocal, but the jury is still out on that."

Gray seemed to like that response. "You have every right to be skeptical. I'm glad Layla has protective friends."

Quinn hooked her arm with mine. "Why don't you take Aunt Layla's friend to the living room, and you can open your gift with Daddy in there, Harper." She turned to Gray. "I'm going to take Layla to the kitchen to open wine and talk about you. What can I bring you to drink?"

He threw her a dazzling smile. "A beer would be great."

The door to the kitchen was barely even closed when Quinn started. "Jesus Christ. You said he was good looking. Not *that*. That's Brad-Pitt-*before*-Angelina-level smoking hot."

I grabbed two wine glasses from the cabinet. "I really could fall for him, Q. It's sort of terrifying."

Quinn pulled a bottle of wine from a rack on the counter and the opener from the drawer in the center island. "You still don't trust him?"

"It's not that I don't. I'm afraid to. Honestly, why he lied makes a lot of sense. And technically, he wasn't even lying—his marriage had been annulled. He was at such a disadvantage, and our connection happened really, really fast. So part of me does understand why he didn't want to scare me away with his crazy history. And I believe his apology is sincere and that he cares about me."

A loud pop filled the air as Quinn pulled the cork from the bottle. "So what's the hesitation then?"

"He could devastate me."

Quinn held up the wine. "He could also lose his balls with the jagged end of a bottle."

"Oh my God." I handed Gray his beer and stood next to him as people crowded around Harper, who was tearing through her gift. "Don't tell me that big thing is a box of boxes."

My goddaughter had just opened the three-foot by three-foot square box that Gray brought, only to find another wrapped, slightly smaller box inside.

Gray grinned and sipped his beer. "You said she had a box obsession."

I *had* told him that, but *a year and a half ago*. "How the hell did you remember?"

"Told you, I remember every minute we spent talking together."

God, he really does. And him remembering this particularly random thing I'd told him about my goddaughter in passing so long ago really made me want to find that empty closet he'd threatened to push me in.

"That was so sweet of you. I only brought her a heart locket. She's going to be disappointed after this. Sadly."

He smiled proudly. "*And* the last box has an actual gift. It's a carved wooden box that's a puzzle to open."

I scowled at him. "This borders on bribery and might be considered cheating at our bet."

"My entire gift was under twenty bucks. How much did you spend?"

I brought the wine to my lips. "Bite me."

He looked around the room with a shit-eating grin on his face. "I'd love to. Is that closet around?"

I shook my head. "Come on, cheater, let me introduce you to everyone."

The party wasn't very big—mostly Quinn and her husband Brian's family and a few of the employees from the pub. Brian, being the suspicious New York City cop that he is, wore an inhospitable mask on his face as he shook Gray's hand. When Quinn had first told him I'd met a man *in prison*, he'd been vocal about suggesting I'd lost my mind. When he'd found out things ended the way they did, he didn't have to say I told you so.

Brian locked eyes with Gray during the shake. "Layla's like a little sister to me, and I carry a gun."

"Brian!" I scolded.

Gray put his hand up, motioning for me to let him handle it. He swallowed and nodded at Brian. "Understood."

It's funny, since I had decided to forgive Gray and move on, I actually felt bad for what he'd gone through and wanted everyone else to move on, too. People still saw him as an ex-con and a future suspect even when they knew the truth of his story. So while I partially understood Brian's suspiciousness, it also made me want to defend Gray.

"You know what, Brian—"

Gray slipped his hand around my waist and discreetly squeezed. My eyes flashed to his, and I knew he wanted me to let it go. So I did...for now.

Wagging a finger at Brian, I said, "We'll talk later."

We went out back, and I finished introducing Gray around. At least everyone else at the party was friendly. After I was done, we sat together on a lounge chair in the sun. It was a gorgeous late-spring day. I leaned my head on his shoulder.

"I'm sorry about Brian and Quinn."

"Don't be. If they weren't protective, they wouldn't be very good friends. I'm glad you have them."

"I know. But I want them to like you."

"I'm not planning on going anywhere, Freckles. Let them come around in their own time, and it will be genuine. You can't force someone's guard down." He kissed the top of my head. "I need to earn their trust just the same way I'm still earning yours."

A few hours later, as the party was coming to an end, I watched from a distance while Gray spoke to Brian. The guys were playing horseshoes under the lights, and Gray had joined in. I suspected he'd done it more to spend time with Brian than actually wanting to play.

Quinn walked over and sat in the Adirondack chair next to me. "I take it you dumped Mr. Twist?"

It took me a minute to realize she meant Oliver. "Yeah. He's a nice guy, but I realized when Gray walked back into my life that Oliver wasn't *it*. Even if Gray turns out to be not *it* either...what I feel reminded me what it should be like."

A loud yell brought my attention back to the game the guys were playing. Something good must've happened because Brian fistpumped into the air, and then I watched as he and Gray slapped a high five.

"The way to win my husband over is to be good at the silly games he likes."

I turned to her. "And what does Gray have to do to win his wife's approval?"

"Simple. Just make my girl happy and not sad."

Harper came running from inside with her cousin and jumped onto my lap. "Aunt Layla, wanna play with my boxes?"

"Sure, pipsqueak."

I wasn't quite sure how to play with boxes, but I let the little tyrant direct me on the back deck until the game ended and the guys walked back over. Brian lifted Harper from the box she sat in and tossed her into the air. She squealed like a little girl should when her daddy plays with her.

"It's late," he said. "What do you say I put you and your cousin to bed, but I let you keep on the light and bring some of these boxes with you?"

"Yay!!"

He set Harper down, and she yawned, right on cue.

"Say goodnight and thank you to everyone for coming."

Harper made the rounds, hugging all the women but keeping away from most of the men, as usual. I was rewarded with a giant, two-armed hug, and then she stopped and looked up at Gray, who stood next to me.

He crouched down to her eye level. "It was nice meeting you, Harper."

"Thank you for the boxes," she said.

She hesitated and then surprised the shit out of all of us when she jumped into Gray's arms for a hug.

Quinn and I were still shaking our heads when Brian carried her to her room.

Gray whispered into my ear, and goosebumps littered my arms. "One down, one to go."

He stood back up and began to unfold his shirtsleeves, which he must've rolled up while he was playing with the guys. Quinn elbowed me hard in the ribs.

"Oww." I turned to her, and she bulged her eyes in the direction of Gray's arms—his enormous, thick forearms.

God, I hope her analogy is true.

After the girls were in bed, Brian, Quinn, and I sat around in the yard with Gray, telling him stories about the three of us growing up. We laughed and had a few drinks. I thought it went a long way toward both of them warming up to my new... *What is Gray?* I suppose they'd warmed up to my new *boyfriend.* It was almost midnight by the time we decided to call it a night.

At the door, I hugged my best friend goodbye and promised I'd stop up to have dinner at her pub during the week. Brian and Gray shook hands, without the icy glare this time. When Gray embraced Quinn, she winked over his shoulder, right before giving me the thumbs up.

The thumbs up.

Of course Gray had to have turned his head at the exact same moment, but I couldn't be sure if he'd seen it— until he turned around. The gleam in his eyes confirmed he hadn't missed a damn thing.

The man had done the impossible in six hours—gotten a hug from the birthday girl and received the seal of approval from my best friend.

And I...

...I was about to get felt up in the car on the way home.

Chapter 18

Gray

A limousine waited at the curb.

"A stretch? Where's your town car?" Layla asked.

I waved off the driver and opened the back door for her, without answering. She looked at me, still waiting for a response, as I settled beside her in the back row and pulled the door shut. I spoke to the driver, giving him Layla's address, and ended with, "Take the long way. I'll make it worth your while."

I pushed a button on the overhead control panel, and the privacy glass began to raise. Once it hit the top, I tugged Layla from her seat next to me onto my lap.

"I believe I've won a bet, and I'm ready to collect my prize."

The smell of her perfume, or maybe it was her shampoo, made me insane. I felt like a teenager about to cop my first feel of the hot girl I'd fawned over all year. Only I was a thirty-one-year-old man about to embarrass myself by coming in my pants.

Her eyes grew wide when I reached for the bottom hem of her shirt, and it turned me on to no end to watch the heave of her chest grow. I'd waited to see her beautiful tits for so long. Now that the time had finally come, I wanted to memorize every change in her breath, every sound she made, so I'd know what she liked.

I lifted the fabric up to her navel and dipped my head to lick around her belly button before nibbling my way to one side of her waist and then the other.

Looking up so I could watch her face, I found her beautiful, green-blue eyes had turned a deep ocean blue. They darkened when she was angry or turned on, and I was fucking thrilled to finally be seeing this color for the right reason again. I lifted her shirt a little higher, to just under her breastbone.

Going in for a gentle kiss, I said, "I looked up the definition of *felt up.*"

Her voice carried a mix of amusement and sarcasm, with a side of raspy arousal. "I didn't realize *felt up* was in the dictionary."

"I had to use Urban Dictionary."

"Oh really? And what exactly did Urban Dictionary have to say?"

I ran my tongue along the skin at the bottom of her bra cup, tracing the shape of her breast. First one, then the other.

My lips vibrated on her skin as I spoke. "It said, *felt up* means to be touched on your private parts."

Pulling back to lock eyes with her again, I ever-so-slowly raised her shirt higher, exposing her bra. It was nearly impossible, but I didn't allow my eyes to drop down to take her in as I spoke. "Since it's ambiguous as to *what* should be touching your private parts, I'm going to go with tongue."

"And here I thought getting felt up meant a boy putting his hand under a girl's sweat..." Her voice trailed off when I nuzzled my mouth into her beautiful cleavage and licked a line from breasts to neck.

Layla shifted from the way I'd pulled her across my lap to straddle me. The skirt she wore parted, and I could feel the heat of her warm pussy through the material of my pants and her underwear. I groaned and used my thumbs to push down the cups of her bra before dipping my head to take in a pebbled nipple. She was right there with me when I bit down, keeping the pert bud between my teeth as I tugged before releasing and moving to the other side. She cupped my cheeks as I sucked, scraping her nails along the outline of my jaw. My hips rose to thrust into her, let her feel what she was doing to me.

When she moaned my name, I nearly lost my mind. I'd wanted nothing more than to hear that sound for so long. Moaning. *My name.* Her breathing was ragged as she ground against me. I hadn't planned on anything more than a make-out session and sucking on her gorgeous tits, but when she ground down against my rock-hard cock a second time, I realized she needed a release.

Yet I was afraid to push her too much, too fast. So I tested the waters, rubbing my thumb gently over the outside of her panties.

Fuck me.

They were soaked.

Shit started to snowball out of my control after that. I fisted a handful of her hair and pulled her mouth down to mine. Unlike the last time, I didn't have to encourage her to open for me. Layla's tongue slid inside my mouth with an eagerness that made me groan. Her shirt was still pulled up, and her tits were pressed against me so tightly that the hardness of her nipples against my chest—even through my shirt—felt like flint scraping against steel. Sparks were flying.

But it wasn't enough; I needed to set her on fire.

Lifting her up ever so gently, I cupped her pussy with the palm of my hand. Even though she ground right into it, I still wanted to hear her say it.

"Tell me you want me to make you come."

She started to respond, but her words were cut off by a gasp when my thumb pressed on her swollen clit through her slick panties. "Yes. Yes."

"Yes, what?"

"Make me come," she panted. "*Please*."

I gripped her hip with my left hand, lifted the slightest bit, and ripped the fucking panties from her skin with my right. The sounds of my desperation made her moan again.

I may come before her without her even touching my cock.

When I slipped two fingers inside of her, her back arched. I used my other hand to fist her hair, and yanked it back to expose her neck. Sucking hard on her delicate skin, I wanted to leave a mark to remind her what it felt like to have me finger-fuck her.

Her pussy was so snug. I slid my fingers out and then pushed them back in harder than she expected. She gasped, and my mouth dipped lower to find her nipple again.

"You're so wet for me. So beautifully tight. I love that I'll be your first in such a long time. And you for me." I increased the speed of my pumping fingers. They glided in and out smoothly now, her body relaxing a little and accepting the pleasure. Her hips began to rock.

"Are you on the pill, Layla?"

"Yes," she moaned.

"Good. I went to the doctor last week for a checkup. I'm clean. I'll bring you the papers to show you, if you'd like." I added a third finger at the exact moment I gave her hair another good, hard tug, and her moan sounded like a song.

"We've had barriers between us for years. I want nothing between us when you're ready. I want you bare so I can fill you with my cum."

I stretched my thumb to press on her clit, which I'd purposely been ignoring, and when she started to chant *yes, yes, yes*, I wasn't sure if she liked what I was doing or couldn't wait for me to come inside her, too. I liked to think it was both.

I felt her pussy clench around my fingers and pulled my head back to watch the magical moment of her explosion. The sight was more captivating than anything I'd ever seen. Her muscles throbbed as she cried out my name, and then her face went tense before a glow of relaxation hit. Her eyes closed, and she rode a wave of euphoria.

Beautiful.

Just fucking beautiful.

Eventually, I let go of my tight grip on her hair, and she collapsed forward onto me. Face pressed to my shoulder, her breathing stayed ragged for a while. When it leveled out, she turned her head to face me, and I caught the best lazy smile on her lips.

I smiled back from ear to ear. She'd been the one to orgasm, but that happy face was the best gift she could have given me. Wrapping my arms around her, I kissed the top of her head. *This*...this was another of those moments when I wanted time to stand still.

"God, I think I really needed that." Layla's voice had already turned groggy.

"I think you did, too."

"Damn. The boys in high school really had no clue what they were doing if this is feeling me up."

I chuckled. "Is it crazy that I have an urge to beat the crap out of a bunch of faceless high school jocks who got to feel your tits before me?"

She laughed. "Crazy? Yes. But also really sweet."

I felt the car slow and looked out the window. We were already through the tunnel and back in Manhattan. I had no sense of time when it came to this woman. From the first day I'd met her, the hours seemed to fly by.

"We're almost to your place," I whispered and kissed her forehead.

She perked up and looked outside. "Wow. That was really fast."

I looked at my watch. "We left Quinn's place almost a full hour ago."

She smoothed her hair and grinned. "Damn. I guess time flies when you're having fun."

A few minutes later, just as we'd both gotten ourselves situated again, we pulled up outside her apartment. My hard-on wasn't about to go away on its own, but it had at least gone down enough to be able to walk.

"I'll walk you up."

Layla bit down on her lip, her eyes skirting from mine as she deliberated over something. "I didn't take care of you. Do you want to come in for a little while?"

It was an invitation I'd have given my left arm for a few weeks ago. Yet when I looked in her eyes and saw hesitancy, I knew she wasn't ready for that.

"As much as I want to say yes..." I slipped two fingers under her chin and lifted so our eyes met. "As much as I *really* want to say yes, I should go."

She looked both relieved and disappointed, but nodded.

I decided it was safer to say goodbye at the door. After she unlocked her apartment, I held onto the doorjamb with both hands. "Come with me to a party tomorrow night. It's my father's partner's sixtieth birthday, so it won't be as much fun as a six-year-old's, but I'd love to take you and show you off. Grant is also my godfather."

Layla's face softened. "I'd love that."

"Will you still feel that way if I tell you it's black tie?"

She smiled. "I'm sure I can dig something fancy out of my packed closet."

I nodded. "Seven o'clock."

"Okay."

Leaning down, I brushed my lips with hers, even though I really wanted to devour that mouth again. "Thank you for tonight, Freckles."

She blushed. "Pretty sure I'm the one who should be thanking you after the car ride home."

"It was my pleasure. I can't wait to do it again very soon...only next time...with my tongue."

Chapter 19

Layla

*I*t's big.

And hard.

It's been a really, really long time.

I chewed on my pen cap and stared down at my notebook.

Really, really hard, I added. So much so that apparently it deserved two spaces in the *pro* column. And I underlined the *really. Both* of them.

I'd gotten ready early, so all I needed to do was slip into my dress. Since Gray wasn't due for another half hour, I'd started a pro and con analysis of sleeping with him. After twenty minutes, my pro list was pretty long, yet my con list had only one item. But if I'd dropped my collection of pros and the single con onto a scale, I was pretty sure the weight of that one negative might still tip the scale to its side.

Could break my heart again.

That was really my only reservation anymore. I'd forgiven him. I'd accepted everything he'd told me as the truth. I'd even admitted to myself that we were unfinished business I couldn't move on from, no matter how hard I'd tried.

Yet I was still terrified. Deep down, part of me worried that I wasn't any different than my mother—that I wasn't capable of seeing a situation for what it really was and would accept a man who was something other than what I ultimately wanted.

I thought back to the day I'd realized my mother was in denial. I was fifteen, and my dad had left the day before for his usual four days on the west coast—with his *real* family. My mom was sitting at the kitchen table, drinking a cup of tea while looking through travel brochures for Hawaii. I'd gotten excited and asked if we were going on a vacation.

She'd smiled and said yes. "Your father was going to surprise us, but I found them in his suitcase when I was unpacking him from his business trip."

Business trip. That's what she always called the time he spent with his wife and other daughter.

My smile had faded. *Sure.* He was going to surprise us with a trip. They weren't brochures his wife had stuck in there for him to pick a nice place for his *real family*. I'd shaken my head and said, "Mom...there is no trip."

"Of course there is," she'd said.

I'd searched her face, thinking she couldn't possibly believe it. But she had.

It made me sad.

We never went to Hawaii that summer. But Dad did happen to have a two-week absence, and when he'd called to talk to us, the area code for his *business trip* was 808. *Maui.*

How could she not have seen it? I was just a kid, and I saw it clear as day. The only logical explanation was that she justified everything in her head because she wanted to be with him. And admitting that the man she loved was a liar would have meant it was wrong for her to be with him. Love is supposed to be blind, but it's not supposed to make you deaf, dumb, and stupid, too.

Putting away my notebook, I decided to get dressed. If I truly planned on giving this relationship a chance, I couldn't spend my pre-date time reminiscing about my parents' poor example of a relationship and all of my trust issues.

I'd decided to wear a gown, rather than a cocktail dress. Black tie could go either way, and I was in the mood to dress up. I'd spent an inordinate amount of money on the thing and had only worn it once—to a charity event I'd attended for a client along with a few others at my firm. It was the most beautiful, deep shade of midnight blue. It had a simple, sleek silhouette with a neckline that cut low, but still managed to cover up everything and pull off elegant. Delicate beading cinched my waist in a belt-like pattern and made my curves seem even curvier. When I'd worn it to the previous event, I'd gotten a ton of compliments— from men and women.

My buzzer rang right on time, and I told Gray to come up while I lined my lips in an extra bright shade of red. He stepped off the elevator just as I unlocked the front door, and I let out a little sigh. God, he looked gorgeous.

His usually messy hair was slicked back and to the side, and his tuxedo fit him perfectly. He looked like an old-fashioned movie star, a gentleman. Although when he prowled to the door and wrapped his arm around my waist, his mouth was anything but gentlemanly.

"You look good enough to eat."

I rested my hands on his chest and teased, "Maybe I need to lose another bet at the party tonight."

Gray growled and took my mouth in a kiss. I loved that his hands always found my face when he kissed me. He cupped my cheeks and tilted my head to the side while he sucked on my tongue. I imagined how it might feel if his head was between my legs and he sucked there with the same intensity. Before he broke the kiss, his tongue retreated and then came back to flutter against mine.

Oh my God.

I hadn't imagined what his tongue would feel like on me; *he was showing me.*

"You don't have to win or lose a bet, sweetheart. Just say the word. I'm salivating at the chance to burrow my tongue in that tight little pussy of yours."

I shivered. God, I loved that dirty mouth of his. "I think you better stay out here while I get my purse."

When I turned to walk inside, Gray stayed firmly planted in the doorway.

"I was teasing, you know. Come in."

He shook his head slowly as his eyes raked up and down. "Trust me. I need to stay out here."

"I should've brought business cards. Slipped them into my dress."

We'd just finished talking to the third couple Gray had basically told they should move their legal business to my firm. It hadn't even dawned on me that the majority of the people I'd be meeting tonight were prospective securities clients—even though it made perfect sense since it had been Gray's father's business, and we were at a party for his partner.

He looked down at the neckline of my dress. "Pretty sure you have nowhere to hide anything under there."

Gray walked us to the dance floor and pulled me into his arms. I wasn't surprised to find that he danced like he kissed—aggressively, holding me pressed against him. He had grace and rhythm and led with a strong hand.

"Where did you learn to dance?" I asked.

"Not from the ballroom dancing lessons one of my stepmothers enrolled me in when I was eleven."

I furrowed my brow. "You didn't go, yet you learned how to dance?"

"Etta taught me. It was part of the deal I made with her. I wanted to take karate lessons, not ballroom dancing. My stepmother insisted dancing was a skill necessary for a man who would grow up going to social engagements. Etta used the money for the dancing lessons to pay for the karate lessons no one knew I took, but I had to let her teach me how to dance."

The most adorable vision of an eleven-year-old Gray dancing with Etta made me smile. "I love that. And she did a good job teaching you. You also have a certain assertive way about you that makes you naturally a good partner."

Gray nuzzled into my hair and used his hand at my back to tug me closer. "I can't wait to dance with you horizontally."

He smelled so good, danced wonderfully, kissed me like it might be his last, and I knew from feeling him straddled beneath me in the limousine last night that he was also well endowed. It was debatable which one of us couldn't wait more than the other.

After the song was over, we sat down at our assigned table. We'd been seated with Grant's children, two women about my age, or a little older maybe. They were both very friendly when Gray had introduced us earlier in the evening.

"So what do you do, Layla?" the one named Chelsea asked.

"I'm an attorney with Latham & Pittman."

"What's your specialty?"

"I do mostly SEC and transactional work."

"Oh. So you're familiar with the lingo all of these people use, then?"

"I'm afraid so." I smiled.

"I'm an art appraiser." She poured wine from one of the bottles set up on the table. "Which means all I hear when most of these people talk is *blah blah blah*."

I laughed. "People in the industry tend to use a lot of acronyms and like to talk shop."

"How did you and Gray meet?"

"Umm..."

I was totally unprepared for that question and had no idea how to make *we met in prison* sound anything but a little nutty.

Maybe because it *was* a little nutty.

Gray must've overheard and seen my face as I tried to figure out an appropriate answer.

"She taught a class I took," he said with a wink. "I was hot for the teacher."

We sat around talking for a while. At times, Gray would be in one conversation and I'd be in another with someone else, yet his hand was always across the back of my chair or his thigh pushed up against mine. I loved that he seemed to need to stay connected to me in some way, because I felt the same.

Eventually, a gentleman came over and asked to steal Gray for a few minutes to talk shop. While he was gone, I took the opportunity to find the ladies' room and freshen up. I fixed my hair, blotted on fresh lipstick, and right before I was about to leave, I decided to actually go to the bathroom before rejoining the party.

I closed myself into the stall and gathered all of the material of my dress to one side before hovering over the toilet in my high heels. I'd heard heels clacking on the tile floor and voices, but didn't pay any attention as I put myself back together, smoothing my dress back into place. Just as I went to open the lock on the stall, I heard a woman say Gray's name. I stilled to listen.

"And the woman he brought? She's an SEC attorney. How convenient. I guess he figures next time he gets caught bilking a client, he'll have free representation at least." I recognized the voice as Chelsea—Grant's daughter, and the same woman who'd been so nice to his face.

The other woman cackled. "Wish I was an attorney. He might be a criminal, but he's still hot as hell. I'd let him drill me in exchange for some free legal services."

"My father believes he's innocent. Can you believe that? Then again, he was also partners with Gray's father. Maybe he just likes assholes."

The two of them stuck around for a few more jabs at someone else and then slithered back to the party. I stayed frozen in place, still locked in the stall. That woman had smiled and acted friendly to both our faces. I'd been so consumed with my own thoughts on Gray, I'd never stopped to consider that he'd lost more than just three years of his life.

That time in prison would follow him around forever. People would pretend to move past it, but there'd always be a shadow of suspicion. I'd seen it happen to criminal clients—an innocent man wrongly accused of rape. Even after his name was cleared, people still looked at him funny. There was always a morsel of doubt. Maybe, just maybe, he'd done it and gotten away with it. Only in Gray's case, not only had he not done it, he hadn't gotten away with it either, and he'd lost his freedom for years.

I wasn't quite sure how to handle what I'd just heard. Should I tell him? Could he possibly already know? My instinct told me he had no idea these people were fake and talking about him behind his back. I stayed in the bathroom for a few more minutes to collect my thoughts, and then headed back out to the party.

Gray was coming down the hall to the bathroom as I exited.

"There you are. I was about to send out a search party for you."

I forced a smile. "Sorry. Women take forever in the bathroom."

He studied my face. "Is everything okay?"

"Yes. Sure," I lied.

"Dance with me again." He put his arm around my waist and guided me to walk with him. "It's the only way I can get my hands on you in public without making a scene."

179

Once we were on the floor, I broached the subject of Grant's daughters to see if he realized they were two-faced assholes. "Grant's family seems nice."

"Yeah. Grant was one of the few people who never doubted me when I said I was innocent. And his daughters are great, too."

My heart ached. God, I hated that he'd done something so admirable to save a woman he'd cared about, and people would forever have doubts. I guess I wasn't very good at hiding my face.

"You sure everything is okay?"

"Yes, fine."

There was no point in telling him what I'd overheard at this moment. I'm sure it would just hurt. But realizing people would hesitate about him for a long time made me realize I needed to stop my own hesitation. Either I was in or I was out. It wasn't fair to him to be like those women.

In that moment, I decided to take a chance—really take a chance. Jump in with both feet.

"How long do we need to stay?" I asked as we swayed on the dance floor.

Gray looked disappointed. "Do you need to get home early?"

"Yes."

"Work on a Sunday?"

"Well, maybe, but no."

"Are you not enjoying the party?"

"I'm not really in the mood for a party anymore."

He pulled his head back. "Would you like to go somewhere else?"

I caught Gray's eyes and looked into them deeply before gently brushing my lips to his. "Your place."

Gray froze. He searched my eyes, and I got the feeling he was afraid to believe what I was telling him.

"My place?"

I leaned in and whispered. "What was it you said you wanted to do to me while the sun came up?"

One minute we were on the dance floor, and the next we were heading toward the door. I laughed as I worked to keep up in my heels. Gray was practically running for the exit.

Outside, he rushed to the curb and raised his hand with an ear-splitting whistle, flagging down a passing taxi and whipping the door open for me.

I couldn't stop laughing. "But we came in your town car."

"No time to wait for him. Get in."

Chapter 20

Gray

I didn't want to fucking disappoint her.

Halfway to my apartment, I started to realize I needed to grab a quick shower for a few minutes of privacy when I got home. My cock was straining for release just sitting in the back of the cab and holding her hand. There was no fucking way I was going to be able to satisfy her like this. My performance would rival a teenage boy's shitty first time. I'd be lucky if I didn't come in my own hand trying to get my dick out of my pants.

I kept my distance, not wanting things to heat up only to be forced to extricate myself to cool down. In the elevator, I put my hands in my pockets to keep from touching her. She stood so close, smelling like fucking heaven, and the thought of pressing her up against the glass in the tiny car was unbearable. I wanted her to look in the mirror and watch her reflection when I rammed into her from behind.

But once we were inside my apartment, avoiding her became a challenge. Freckles met us at the door and ignored me in favor of licking Layla. *Smart dog.*

I thought the distraction might be the perfect excuse to slip away for a few minutes. "I'm going to grab a quick shower."

Layla stood and grabbed the lapels of my jacket. "You want some company?"

Fuck.

Maybe if I got my dick good and sudsy, she wouldn't notice that I shot my load before she even touched me.

I dragged my fingers through my hair. "On second thought, how about some wine?"

"Umm. Sure. Wine sounds good." Layla walked to the open windows in the adjoining living room to look at the view. It was a clear night, and the city was lit up through the darkness.

I took my time opening a bottle of her favorite and pouring two glasses. Passing one to her as I joined her at the windows, another bright idea hit me. If I could knock back a few drinks, it might slow my libido a bit.

I swallowed half a glass and untied my bow tie, leaving it hanging loose around my neck. I tried to avoid looking at the gorgeous woman standing next to me, but couldn't help myself.

God, why does her collarbone have to look like that? That neck... I wanted to bite it in the worst fucking way.

Without even realizing, I finished off the other half of my wine. But Layla realized. She glanced at the empty glass in my hand, still holding the one she hadn't sipped yet.

"Is something wrong, Gray?"

She turned to face me, and the glow from the moon cast light across her face. She looked like an angel—one I wanted to do evil things to. I shoved my hands into my pockets again for safekeeping, and almost forgot she'd even asked a question.

"No. Everything's good."

She squinted.

Goddamn it. "Fine." I shook my head and let out a loud rush of air. "I haven't been with a woman in a very long time."

She grinned. "Are you concerned that you forgot how do to it?"

"Wise ass."

"It's like riding a bicycle. I'm sure you'll do fine."

Riding. Did she have to use that word? I couldn't fucking wait until she rode me. I abruptly opted for another glass of wine. When I returned to the windows, Layla turned her back to me. She pulled her hair to one side. "Could you help me with the zipper? I want to get out of this gown."

I looked up and silently spoke to God. *Haven't I had my share of shame? Just give me this. A solid ten minutes without embarrassing myself. Is that too much to ask? I just donated three damn years.*

The room was so still that every tooth separating from the zipper echoed. Goosebumps broke out on Layla's neck, and I heard the hitch in her breathing as my hand reached the end of the zipper near her very fine ass.

She turned around, locking eyes with me before slowly slipping the dress from her body. It pooled into a giant sea of blue at her feet. I closed my eyes and counted to ten before looking up. But nothing could have reined me in when I caught the sight standing before me. *God, she is gorgeous.* Layla wore nothing but black lace panties, a matching half-cup bra that her full tits were just about spilling out of, and a sexy pair of stilettos. Her waist was so tiny, I could cover it by wrapping both my hands from front to back. And *her legs*—a mile of silky smoothness that my tongue couldn't wait to lick from toe to thigh.

"*Fuck.*" I shook my head and took a step back, unable to take my eyes off of her. "Layla...you're going to have to promise that you'll give me multiple chances to make up for my poor performance the first time I'm inside of you. I'm about thirty seconds from finishing, and we haven't even started yet. You're beautiful."

"I think I can help you out there." She suddenly dropped to her knees.

And if I'd thought she was beautiful before—*this*... nothing could hold a candle to this sight. *So. Fucking. Beautiful.* I was definitely going to embarrass myself, but at least I might have a fighting chance if I'd already let one go.

Layla reached for my belt, and thank God her fingers still worked, because I was completely incapable of doing anything other than staring down at her. Unlike with her dress, when she slid the zipper to my pants down, I couldn't hear the teeth separating because the only sound I heard was the rush of blood pumping through my ears. My heartbeat was out of fucking control.

"Jesus," she whispered as my cock sprang free. "Now I think I'm the one who's a little nervous."

Layla licked her painted red lips and looked up from under thick lashes. "Don't stop. I'll swallow for you."

Jesus.

Fucking.

Christ.

She leaned forward, licked the glistening precum off my crown, and flashed the most devious smile before opening wide and sucking me into her mouth. I felt all the self-control I'd been holding on to slipping from my grip.

My fingers threaded into her thick hair, and something about feeling the bob of her head in my hands made me snap. I groaned and tightened my grip on her hair with a little tug. She let me set the rhythm with my hands, and somehow I miraculously held back from turning what was the best feeling I'd ever had in my life into face-fucking her until her throat was raw.

The sight of her head bobbing faster and faster, each time taking me a little deeper, was the sexiest thing I'd ever seen. When I felt her hand start to massage my balls, I realized this moment was totally worth waiting three years for. Hell, I might've donated another three if this was waiting for me when I got out.

I'm so close.

So damn close.

Forget shame. Forget dignity.

I groaned and Layla responded with a sound that was almost a hum and then suddenly she swallowed, and I hit the back of her throat.

"*Fuck.*"

"*Yes.*"

"Fuck. *Take it all in...*"

Within seconds, I felt my balls draw up, and I knew I was about to explode. Even though she'd told me not to stop, I still felt compelled to warn her. I might want to fuck her face, ass, tits, pussy, and anywhere else she'd let me stick my cock, but I wasn't an animal, after all.

"Baby..." I managed to groan. "I'm gonna come..."

She responded by digging her nails into my ass, and I quickly lost my battle. Spurts of cum let loose while my entire body shuddered. I wasn't even sure how I remained standing with the intensity of my orgasm.

After taking a minute to gather a little strength, I lifted Layla from her knees and into my arms. She nuzzled into my chest, which was still clothed.

"Jesus, that was..." I was truly at a loss for words. "That was..."

Layla wrapped her hands around my neck. "Just the beginning. That's what that was."

Chapter 21

Layla

The bedroom was pitch dark.

Gray hadn't touched me since we walked in, but I could feel him behind me. His hot breath tickled my neck while he spoke.

"I want to watch your face while I'm inside you, but depriving you of sight will heighten your other senses, so it will have to wait." He grazed his fingers along one of my arms, and every hair on my body rose. God, he wasn't kidding—my other senses were intensified.

The raw, sexual chemistry that had been sparking between us since the first time we laid eyes on each other grew like wildfire. My body was so on edge that when Gray grabbed my hip, I jumped a little. His other hand swept my hair to the side and then his mouth came to suck along the pulse in my throat.

"Put your hands up. Lock them together behind my neck."

I lifted my arms and did as instructed. Gray's hands caressed their way up my body. When he reached my breasts, he squeezed hard, and I let out a little moan.

"I've been dreaming of this for years," he whispered. "So many fantasies. I can't wait to play them all out with you." He pushed down the cups to my bra and pinched both nipples.

"Tell me about them." My voice sounded sultry. It almost didn't sound like me. Then again, I'd never been this aroused in my life.

Gray's mouth stayed at my ear while his hands massaged the nipples he'd just awakened with a delicious ache. "I want you to stand in front of a mirror and play with your tits while I suck on your neck, with my fingers inside your pussy and my cock buried deep in your ass."

I gasped. "What else?"

His hands traveled painstakingly slowly down my body and slipped inside my panties. "I want you to sit on my face and ride it. I want my nose buried in your pussy while I suck on your clit."

He slipped one finger inside of me, then a second.

"Oh God."

"You're so wet for me."

I leaned my head back against his chest.

"When I see you in your office, behind that big desk of yours, you're so in control and powerful. I want to take that away from you, make you drop to your knees and suck my cock."

I let out a nervous laugh. But he wasn't kidding.

Gray used one hand to pull me against him while his fingers kept gliding in and out. His erection was fully hard again and pushed all the way up to my lower back. I could feel the smooth, hot skin of his crown against me.

"I want to fill every part of your body." He slipped another finger inside me. "With my tongue, my fingers, my cock...I want to own your cunt, your ass, your tits, your mouth."

"God, Gray."

He withdrew his fingers and spun me around. I felt lightheaded, and my knees were weak. He slipped my panties down and took off my bra before walking us forward a few steps. My eyes still hadn't adjusted to the total darkness enough to see in front of me.

"The bed's in front of you. Bend forward at the waist and rest your head on it. Spread your legs nice and wide for me."

Gray dropped to his knees and then his mouth came up directly between my parted legs. He didn't start slow. He buried his face in my wetness, lapping like he couldn't get enough and then sucked hard on my clit. My orgasm began to build, and I worried I might fall on top of him.

"So sweet..."

He slipped a finger back inside me.

"So tight..."

He groaned and flicked my clit with his tongue.

"So fucking wet for me..."

The wave that had been threatening in the distance suddenly crashed down on me without warning. I moaned as my body began to pulse on its own.

Just as I started to come down, Gray scooped me up and placed me on the bed. His body came over mine, then his lips. He devoured my mouth in a kiss filled with more passion than I'd ever experienced. His touch was strong and dominating, with perfect control just shy of forceful. Composed, yet needy, our lips meshed, tongues entwined, and bodies wrapped around each other. We separated only briefly, just enough so Gray could take off the shirt he still wore.

He shifted slightly, lining his thick head with my opening. But then he stopped.

"Can I take you bare?"

We'd already had this discussion, but I loved that he asked anyway.

I wrapped my legs around his waist, encouraging him. "Yes, please."

This close, I could see the bright whites of his eyes and watched as they closed for a minute while he pushed inside.

With his girth, he must've been aware that he needed to go slow. Never breaking our gaze, he took his time, easing in and pulling back out, then pushing in a little farther with each new stroke. Once he was almost fully seated, he stilled and muttered against my mouth. "*Fuck. You feel so fucking good.*"

After my body started to relax and loosen, Gray reclaimed my mouth and began to go harder. Faster. Deeper. Strokes became gyrating thrusts, and he sank deeper and deeper each time until the base of his cock was grinding against my clit. Nothing had ever felt this good—certainly not the first time. And this was only the beginning.

My orgasm began to build again, muscles pulsating around him. "Gray..."

He sped up his pace. "Fuuuck. Right there with you, babe."

The sound of our wet bodies slapping against each other echoed in the room. The scent of sex permeated the air, and my body hummed from his touch. I felt utterly and completely consumed by this man. That feeling pushed me over the edge, and my orgasm throbbed to life. Gray kept up the perfect pace as I rode a long, blissful wave. He whispered in my ear while I moaned, telling me how good it felt inside of me, how my body belonged to him, and how hard he was going to come. After I finally started to go limp, Gray sped up his pace before sinking deep and filling me with his own release.

He kissed me for a long time after that. Slow, beautiful, romantic, sensual kisses that a young girl dreamed about. Kisses you felt in your heart.

If I hadn't been so enraptured by the moment, I might've worried that what I felt in my heart was a lot more than a kiss.

Gray joined me in his shower the next afternoon. He walked in wearing nothing but what I was beginning to think was an endless erection and a face that told me he planned to make good use of it.

His hair, which had been slicked back for the party, was now disheveled in the way only a man could look sexy after a marathon night *and morning* of sex. He didn't ask to join me, and oddly that turned me on immensely.

I'd been facing the water spray and didn't move as he opened the glass door and stepped inside. Gray wrapped his arms around me from behind, one hand squeezing my breast and the other palming my stomach as he pressed his dick to the crack of my ass. "Morning," he groaned. His head dipped down to nibble on my shoulder.

"I think technically it's afternoon."

"Whatever it is, it's a good day when I wake up to find you already undressed and wet."

I laughed. "You say that like I'm a different kind of wet than washing in the shower."

His hand snaked down between my legs, and he pushed two fingers inside me. "Isn't it?"

I had to put both my hands against the tile. "I think you might be a sex addict."

"I think I'm addicted to *you*." He moved his mouth to my ear, and his voice turned raspy. "Are you sore?"

I was a little sore. But his fingers glided in and out of me, and it didn't hurt too much. "Maybe a little."

Gray stopped and pulled out. "Sorry."

"It's fine." I turned around and hooked my arms around his neck. "Totally worth it."

He smiled and leaned his forehead against mine. "Oh yeah?"

I nodded. "It's a good kind of sore. The kind that makes me smile when I feel it instead of wince—because I remember what last night felt like."

"Thank you. It's a gift to hear that, Freckles. It really is." He gently kissed my lips. "Turn back around. Let me wash you instead."

I sighed with true contentment and handed him the soap before turning back to face the warm stream of water.

He lathered up and started to wash my back. Quite quickly, his hands were concentrating on my lower half, fingers breaching into my butt crack.

"You know, if you're sore..." His voice was sultry—pure sex—as his fingers traced down farther, stopping at my rear entrance to rub a circle and apply a bit of pressure. "...there are other ways I could bring you pleasure."

"*Fiend*. I think today we'll just stick to you washing my back. I need to get home and work. You've been a distraction the entire weekend. A *good* distraction, but I need to catch up before I get to the office tomorrow."

Gray's soapy hands rose to my shoulders, and he rubbed. "Can we do that together?"

"What? Work?"

"I have to go to the west coast tomorrow afternoon, and I'm not ready to give you up yet."

"Sure. But you might get sick of me. We've been together all weekend."

"Sweetheart, I plan on us being together a hell of a lot longer than a weekend."

Chapter 22

Layla

Gray: I think you're turning me soft.

I tossed my glasses on my desk and sat back in my chair with a schoolgirl smile. The text was a welcome break after the Monday I'd had. I'd spent the morning in a tough deposition and early afternoon reading a boring case in my office. What should have taken me a half hour had already taken me almost two. I really needed to finish up because I had a new client coming in soon.

Layla: I hope it isn't a part I like hard...

Gray: Shit. Don't say *hard*. I just landed in L.A., and I'm in a cab on the way to meet a potential business partner. Now I'm going to have to make a stop at my hotel first.

Layla: LOL. What part of you is turning soft, *fiend*?

Gray: The inside. Is it possible to be pussy-whipped after only being inside said pussy for two days? I just heard a damn Taylor Swift song while walking through LAX and thought of you.

I sighed.

Layla: What song was it?

Gray: Fuck if I know. I said I was pussy-whipped, not a pussy.

Layla: I think you need counseling. What time are your meetings today and tomorrow?

Gray: Tonight at five and the other at eight, L.A. time. It'll be late your time after my dinner meeting ends, so I'll call you tomorrow. I moved up tomorrow's meeting from the afternoon to the morning so I can take an earlier flight home. I want to make it back to take you out to dinner tomorrow night.

Layla: Okay. Any special reason?

He typed back.

Gray: Yes. I miss you.

The man could seriously make me swoon. Just as I went to type back, my secretary buzzed. "Your three o'clock appointment is here."

I hit the intercom button on my desk phone. "Okay. Thanks. Give her the standard retainer agreement to read over while she waits. I need about ten minutes to clear my desk and run to the ladies' room."

"You got it."

I allowed myself another minute to read back through my text exchange with Gray, treating the messages as fuel to get through the dragging day. For a woman who'd been terrified of a relationship with him not too long ago, it certainly seemed like I'd gotten over it. We'd spent Friday and Saturday evenings together at different parties, then spent Saturday night through Sunday afternoon having sex as many times as humanly possible. Sunday evening we'd both caught up on work while sitting across from each other in my living room. We'd passed takeout containers back and forth and shared silent smiles until we finished at eleven o'clock and turned in together. It felt like the best of both worlds—the excitement of something new, yet the comfort of something familiar. I even kept his dog when he left town this morning, rather than force the sweet little guy into a doggy hotel.

I really needed to get my ass in gear and not keep my appointment waiting too long. My fingers hovered over the keys, debating my response to his text for a few heartbeats. *Screw it. In for a penny, in for a pound.*

Layla: I miss you, too.

———

Mackenzie Cartwright, my afternoon consultation, entered my office with one of those fancy strollers and a sleeping little girl. Can't say that had ever happened before. Aside from the fact that eighty percent of my clients were men, the women I occasionally provided services to kept their business and personal lives very separate. I didn't have a clue whether most of them even had a family.

I extended my hand. "Layla Hutton. It's nice to meet you, Miss Cartwright."

She corrected me. "It's *Ms.*"

"Oh. Yes. Of course." I waved to the three guest chairs on the other side of my desk. Please, have a seat. Can I get you anything to drink?"

"No, thank you. But if we could please keep our voices down so my daughter doesn't wake up, that would be great."

"Sure," I said, realizing I hadn't actually lowered my voice at all. "Sorry." I whispered. "Of course."

I walked around my desk and waited for Ms. Cartwright to settle in. She wore a light jacket—even though it was probably seventy-five degrees out today—and dark sunglasses. But she took her seat without removing either.

Okay. Whatever.

"So...the paralegal who did your intake and set up the appointment said you have a partnership disagreement you want advice on?"

She seemed to be staring at me. I waited in awkward silence for her to finally answer.

"That's right."

"Why don't you start from the beginning?" I looked down at the client intake form the paralegals complete during a phone interview before we bring on a new client. "It says here that you suspect your partner is misappropriating funds?"

She stared at me some more. This was the oddest initial client meeting ever. Again, I waited for her response through a long, awkward silence.

It gave me the chance to take a good look at her. She was attractive, but a little too thin. Her high cheekbones, which could have looked modelesque with another fifteen or twenty pounds, instead jutted from her pale, grayish skin. Upon closer inspection, I thought her thick dark hair, which covered a good portion of her tiny face with heavy bangs, might actually be a wig. I tried to see her eyes, but they were hidden behind the dark tint of her oversized glasses.

At some point, the waiting and checking each other out just became weird, and I felt the need to prompt her response again. "Have you spoken to your partner about the issue yet?"

"Yes."

Okey-dokey, then. I was only going to get one-word answers, apparently. Normally these were the types of responses I got from the client of opposing counsel during a deposition, not from my own. Clients seeking help usually couldn't wait to tell me their stories.

"And what is your partner's position on the misappropriation? Does she admit to having taken the funds?"

"He."

"Oh. Okay. Does *he* admit to having taken the funds?"

"No."

"Is he still a signatory on the partnership bank accounts?"

"Yes."

"Okay. Well, the first thing we can do is go to court and ask for an injunction that restrains him from being able to withdraw any money or cash any checks without *both* your signatures. That way, you're still able to utilize the partnership funds for legitimate business purposes you can agree on, but neither of you will be able to make a unilateral decision to withdraw for personal use."

"Fine."

"Do you have an accounting of the funds that you believe were misappropriated?"

"No."

"How about a rough idea?"

She stared at me some more.

Frustrated, I motioned with my hands for her to speak. "Is it...one thousand, ten thousand, a hundred thousand? It doesn't have to be exact. We'll call it estimated at approximately..."

"Six million."

I raised my brows. "Six million?"

"Yes."

I felt like I was being punked. Who comes into a law office to discuss their partner stealing from their business, yet doesn't want to actually provide any information, and when the estimated theft is dragged out of them...it turns out to be *six million dollars*?

I put down my pen and stopped taking notes. Something was definitely off. "And these funds...these were taken from business profits?"

She shook her head. "They were funds we both contributed from a prior business venture we were part of. Transfers from our old firm."

"Start-up investment capital, then?"

"Yes."

"You each contributed an equal amount of the start-up funds?"

"I'm not sure."

I squinted. "Okay. So eventually, if we went to a trial on something like this, we'd have to prove who put in what and where it came from. Would that be a problem?"

A sweet little voice stole both our attention. "Mama."

With a giant stretch, the sleeping beauty in the stroller came to life. The little girl was gorgeous. A massive head full of dark curls, pert little nose, and pale green eyes. I smiled at her, and she shot me a toothy grin before covering her face with the blanket, playing shy.

Apparently, her mother's bizarre, curt speech only extended to me. The woman leaned over to her daughter with an ear-to-ear luminous smile and pulled down the blanket a tiny bit to expose the girl's eyes.

"I see you," she said in a sing-songy voice.

The little girl shrieked and pushed the blanket down, revealing the same big smile as her mother. I watched the two of them, fascinated by the sudden change in the woman. Her cold had turned off as if her daughter were the sun that warmed her. They played for a minute, and then the woman unlatched the safety belt from the stroller and lifted the little girl out and onto her lap.

Her beautiful pale eyes were framed with the thickest dark black lashes. "Your daughter's eyes are stunning." I said.

"She gets them from her father."

I couldn't stop looking at the little girl. With pale eyes like Gray and dark hair like me, she looked like a child the two of us could have together someday.

I shook my head at that thought. The fact that my brain had even just gone there unnerved me a little.

"Say hi, Ella." My strange client had become a different person. It was as if she'd forgotten how to be friendly until she had her daughter's smile as a reminder.

"Hi!" She waved.

"Hi, Ella," I said. "How was your nap?"

The little girl smiled and lifted a hand to her chin, almost as if she blew me a kiss.

Her mother pushed one of her unruly curls behind the little girl's ear, and I noticed she wore a hearing aid. *Ah.* Sign language. She hadn't blown me a kiss.

"Well, I should probably be going," the woman said. "What do you need to get started?"

"The names and addresses of the parties, and the name of the bank and account number where the funds were stolen. That should be enough to at least get us a temporary injunction for the bank."

She rattled off two bank accounts almost faster than I could jot down the numbers. The one-word woman certainly could machine-gun off information now.

"Great. And your partner's name and address?" I asked.

She abruptly stood and started to strap the little girl back into her stroller. Once she finished, she adjusted the sunglasses on her face and looked at me. "Aiden Warren."

Aiden Warren... Why did that name sound so familiar to me?

I tilted my head. "The name is familiar. Would you happen to know if he was ever a client here? I'll need to check for a potential conflict of interest, if he was."

"I don't think so. But I believe we might have a mutual business associate."

All of a sudden, a memory popped into my head. It was a conversation I'd had with Gray.

> *"When did you realize it was Max who*
> *had set you up?"* I'd asked.
> *"About a month after I started my*
> *sentence, a buddy of mine came to visit.*
> *He'd been on the subway and happened*

to see Max, only she didn't see him. She was too busy sucking face with Aiden Warren.*"*

"So you got suspicious because she was cheating?"

"Aiden Warren was the guy who we thought set us up."

I blinked a few times. "You're..."

Her face remained expressionless. "Mackenzie Cartwright *Westbrook*. My friends call me Max. And, yes, she is *his* daughter."

Chapter 23

Gray

Where the hell are you?

I'd turned on my phone as soon as we touched down, but still had no response from Layla. After my delayed flight, it was already almost eight o'clock here on the east coast. I'd assumed when she hadn't responded earlier in the day that she'd been busy with work. But my messages were showing as read, and she must've had *two minutes* to shoot me a quick response by now.

Stepping off the plane with my carry-on luggage, a bad feeling came over me as I headed to the airport exit. I dialed Layla's number. It rang once and went straight to voicemail—which meant she'd pressed ignore.

I wanted to think the best of the worst—I'd pissed her off somehow, and she was letting me know it. But the protective part of me couldn't help but worry. What if she'd been walking to lunch and some asshole driver was texting and blew the red light while she was in the crosswalk? Or she got sick in the middle of the day and was sitting in an ER somewhere. My strides ate up the walk out of the airport. Al was picking me up. He'd be idling somewhere nearby since you couldn't sit outside of JFK waiting for

204

a passenger, so I texted him to pull around to the arrival terminal.

"Layla's apartment." I spoke before even slamming the door shut.

"You got it, boss."

Al looked in the rearview mirror before pulling away, but also checked on me. "Good trip?"

I settled back into the seat. "Yeah. Just a long day."

Traffic was light, so when we arrived at Layla's, it was just about nine o'clock.

"Give me about ten minutes, and I'll let you know what I'm doing."

"You got it," Al said.

I looked up at Layla's window when I got out of the car. It was dark and showed no sign of anyone being home.

Her building had a vestibule with a locked door. A tenant had to buzz you in to unlock it. I pressed the bell and waited for her voice to come over the intercom.

But it never came. Three buzzes and one last-ditch attempt to get her on the phone were all fruitless. I ran my fingers through my hair, the knot in my stomach pulling tighter.

"1275 Broadway, Al." I slammed the car door shut. "Layla's office."

Al glanced back again. "Everything okay?"

"I hope so."

━━━━━

Archibald Pittman walked out the front door with another man just as my car pulled to the curb. The smart thing to do would have been wait until he was gone, but the ride from Layla's apartment had elevated my anxiety to a whole new level. There was no fucking way I was wasting thirty seconds just to avoid her boss.

Striding to the door, I looked down at my phone to avoid making eye contact. It didn't stop Pittman from noticing me.

"Grayson?" He stopped his conversation and called to me while I tried to pass.

I looked up. "Archie. Good to see you."

"Are you heading upstairs at this late hour?"

I pulled an excuse out of my ass. "Time-sensitive contract, has to be sent back to the west coast tonight."

"Glad to see my staff is looking after your needs."

"Yes." I offered a curt nod, anxious to get inside the building. "Well...time's ticking. You have a good night."

I was already four steps closer to the building before he could finish reciprocating his goodbye.

The elevator opened to Layla's floor, and I was relieved to find the double glass doors still open. Of course, the reception desk was empty at 10PM, so I weaved my way into the inner offices. The hallways were lit, but most of the office doors were closed. I made the final turn, a left, and saw that the fourth door down—Layla's office—was still open, although the lights were off.

I didn't expect to see anyone, and since it was dark, I almost missed her when I first entered her office. But the lights suddenly flickered on. They must've been on a motion sensor that I'd activated by stepping inside. I found Layla sitting at her desk looking right at me.

My brows drew down. "Were you sleeping?"

"No."

"What's the matter?" Papers were scattered all over her desk, which was normally neat and organized. A few were even on the floor.

I took a few steps closer and got a better look at her face. The skin around her eyes was puffy and red. She'd been crying.

"Layla, answer me. Did someone hurt you?" My blood started to pump at what might've happened. All the worst thoughts started to run through my mind. She was alone in the office at night sitting in the dark...her desk was a disheveled mess...she'd been crying... Did someone attack her?

She stared, saying nothing. I walked behind her desk and turned her chair to face me. Crouching down, I tried to remain calm and keep my voice steady. "Layla. Talk to me. What happened, sweetheart?"

A page on the edge of her desk caught my eye, and I turned my head, sure I was seeing things. But I wasn't.

I picked up the paper. The picture was a few years old, but there was no doubt it was Max. I remembered the article well. Kiplinger's had done a story on the rise of women traders, and Max had been featured, along with a few other industry up-and-comers. The piece had come out a few months before we opened our firm.

My eyes traveled over the rest of her desk.

What the fuck?

I picked up another paper—an article about our partnership.

Another paper—the UCC filing on our partnership.

Another—copies of my criminal court sentencing documents.

The entire desk was covered in papers about me, Max, or our now-defunct firm.

Layla was looking at me when I turned my attention back to her.

"What happened. Why are you researching Max?"

She looked away, staring out her office window into the darkness outside for a minute before turning back. "I met her today."

I searched her eyes, trying to hold back firing off a million questions because I saw there was more she needed to say.

She closed her eyes for a while, taking a deep breath before reopening them and then looked directly into my eyes. "She came to my office...*with your daughter*."

"Start from the beginning, Layla."

I'd had to take a seat after I made her repeat what she'd said three times and told her I had no idea Max had a child, much less one who could be mine.

"I had an appointment on the calendar with a new client named Mackenzie. I had no idea Max was short for Mackenzie, so I didn't think anything of it." Layla's voice was eerily calm. "The woman showed up and acted really strange. She had a little girl sleeping in the stroller. She said her partner stole six million dollars from her. Then her daughter woke up and—she was beautiful.... She had your exact same green eyes. Only I didn't realize they were yours at first. When I complimented them, she said the little girl had her father's eyes."

"And she said it was my child?"

"You really had no idea?" She looked back and forth between my eyes.

"Of course not!" I stood and began to pace. "This is fucking nuts. I can't have a child with her."

"Why not?"

"Why would she have kept it from me?"

"Why would she steal from you and set you up when you both had more money than you knew what to do with already?"

I sat back down. With elbows on my knees, I held my head in my hands while I rubbed my temples. "I can't answer that. Because none of it ever made sense to me."

Layla was quiet for a moment. Her voice sounded so vulnerable and scared when she spoke. "You really didn't know?"

It was at least the third time she'd asked me that question. *Jesus Christ.* I was so busy getting over the shock of what she'd told me, I hadn't even begun to think about what this meant to the two of us if it were true. Looking up, I saw so much pain in her eyes. Suddenly everything I'd waited to have for more than two years felt like it was slipping through my fingers.

I got up and walked back around behind her desk, where she still sat in her chair. Crouching down again, I took her face in my hands. "I haven't seen Max in more than a year. Last I'd heard, she'd moved to Florida. I didn't even know she was in New York, and certainly not that she was coming to see you and playing some sort of sick game. I had no idea she had a child, and I wouldn't put it past her for this entire thing to be made up, Layla. You have to believe me." I moved my face closer so all we could see was into each other's eyes. "I had absolutely no idea about any of this. *No idea.*"

She searched my face and nodded.

I let out a sigh of relief, even though I knew it was only temporary.

The sound of keys jingling forced my attention from Layla to the hall, just as a uniformed security guard stopped in the doorway. "Building closing in fifteen, Layla."

She nodded. "Oh. Okay, Frank. Thanks."

The guard looked at her face and me crouched down beside her. "Everything okay?"

"Yeah. Everything's fine. We'll clear out in a few minutes."

He nodded. "Have a good night."

When he walked away, I pushed hair from her cheek. "You look exhausted. Come home with me."

She shook her head and started to sweep all the papers strewn over her desk into a pile with her hands. "I have Freckles at my house, remember? Plus, I'm exhausted. I really want to sleep in my own bed tonight."

She was already slipping away from me mentally. I couldn't let physical distance add to that. "Can I come home with you, then?"

I saw the hesitancy in her face.

"I'll sleep on the couch if you need some space. Just don't push me out the door and close it, Layla. Please."

Reluctantly, she nodded.

That night, she let me sleep in her bed. I wrapped my arms around her and pulled her tight, holding on for my life. Because I knew. *I knew.* The shit was about to hit the fan tomorrow.

Chapter 24
Layla

The bed was empty next to me in the morning. Cold, too.

Daylight wasn't yet shining through the blinds from outside, but I had no idea if it was the middle of the night or early in the morning. Reaching for my phone to check the time, I spotted the kitchen light on from underneath my closed bedroom door.

Five AM. I wasn't a late riser, but it had taken me a long time to fall asleep, even after I'd rolled over and pretended to have conked out. So this morning, I was dragging. Part of me wanted to roll back over and forget everything, but I knew sleep wouldn't come. I needed to get up and take a shower, think about everything that had transpired with the clear head of a new day. But I also needed to know if Gray was still here. I sensed he was, so I got out of bed and padded from the bedroom.

I found him with a coffee cup in his hand, staring at the screen of his laptop in the living room. The overhead light was off, but the glow of the screen illuminated his face. Gray was always handsome. It would be impossible to not see that through any emotions he wore; his chiseled bone structure didn't allow the beauty to disappear like it did with some men, depending on their mood. But this morning he looked tired. His green eyes reflected the dark circles under them and looked strained from lack of sleep.

"How long have you been up?" I walked to the kitchen and took a coffee mug from the cabinet.

Gray set the laptop down on the coffee table and shifted in his seat to face the kitchen. "An hour or two?"

I fixed my coffee and leaned against the counter to sip. "Did you sleep at all?"

"I think it was more like a short nap. You?"

"A little longer than that." I eyed his laptop. "What are you working on? You didn't look that excited to be reading whatever it was."

"Some revisions to the offer on that tech firm you reviewed the contract for. My partners want to make an offer today. They think another venture capitalist is interested, and if we extend an offer with a short window of acceptance, they won't have time to finish their due diligence or make a competing offer."

I nodded. "Let me know if you need me to do anything."

Neither of us said anything for a few awkward minutes after that. I hated the feeling of an elephant being in the room and preferred to get things off my chest.

"Are you going to contact her today?"

He patted the couch next to him. "Come sit."

This was going to be a push and pull. I could already see it. I'd try to put some space between us—physical or mental—and Gray would fight me on it.

"I prefer to stand while I drink my coffee."

He frowned, then proceeded to get up and walk to the

kitchen to stand across from me. My U-shaped kitchen was small, so the distance between us was only a few feet.

Push.

Pull.

He looked down at his feet. "I searched the Internet for her contact information this morning and got an email address and office number that look current. I don't even have a telephone number for her."

"What do you mean? How can you not have her number?"

"I tried to call her once after I figured out what she'd done. But she'd changed her cell phone number, and my email came back undeliverable."

"Oh." I hesitated for a moment. "I have it. I mean, she gave all her contact information when my paralegal set up the appointment. If you need it…"

Gray's eyes locked with mine. "She's already dragged you into whatever game she's playing enough. But thank you."

"What are you going to say when you contact her?"

Gray shook his head. "I have no fucking idea. But I guess I should start with '*Do I have a daughter?*'"

At two in the afternoon, I'd had the most unproductive day of my entire career. I read a contract four times and sat in a staff meeting where the attorney next to me literally had to kick me under the table when someone had posed a direct question to me, and I hadn't even heard them speak. I tried to order lunch with my assistant, but couldn't decide what to eat, so I'd lied and said I remembered I'd brought in some leftovers.

A knock on my door interrupted my lengthy staring-at-the-window session.

Oliver smiled and stayed in the doorway. "Hey. How are things going?"

Even though we worked for the same firm, in the same building, I hadn't seen him since we had lunch and I'd broken things off.

"Good. Busy."

He nodded. "Not sure if you heard, but Elizabeth Waring is leaving."

"Oh? No. I hadn't heard. Is she going someplace good?" Elizabeth was a good friend of Oliver's, an attorney in the intellectual property division who he worked with often. We'd had lunch all together a few times.

"She's retiring."

"Retiring? She's what...thirty-five?"

He smiled. "That's what we call people who leave private practice and go work for the government. She took a job at the U.S. Copyright Office."

"Oh. Good for her. She'd said she wanted to have kids. That will make her life easier—working a regular nine-to-five and not having to worry about billable hours."

"Yeah. She's happy. Not going to get that here at any age. Do you know the difference between Pittman and a leech?"

"No. What?"

"After you die, a leech stops sucking your blood."

I laughed. "That's very true."

"Anyway. Just wanted to say hi and let you know we're taking her out for her last day if you'd like to join. Next Friday night at The Rodeo Bar around the corner."

My brow arched. "The place with the mechanical bull?"

"That's the one."

"And I thought the family law department had the wild ones."

He smiled. "You should come. It'll be fun."

"Thanks for the invite. I'll try."

After Oliver left, I sat back in my chair—because I hadn't slacked off enough for the day. *Such a nice guy.* And I'd bet he didn't have any secret children he didn't know about. And considering the bar had let him in, I was pretty sure he wasn't a convicted felon, either. But of course, I couldn't fall for him. That would've been too easy. Apparently, complicated was more my thing.

My phone buzzed on my desk. *Speak of the devil.*

Gray: Dinner tonight?

Just seeing his name light up my phone gave me a jolt. Of course I wanted to see Gray. That was part of my problem. I didn't know when it was time to walk away from the man. Or rather, *I knew*, I just couldn't do it when I was near him. It made me wonder if this was how my mother had felt—letting her heart control her head when it came to my father and his secret family. I needed to be stronger than she was, so I decided to tell a little white lie.

Layla: Sorry. Have plans tonight.

Push.

Pull.

I pictured Gray sitting at his desk, the muscle in his jaw flexing as he read my decline of his invitation. I knew the next text to arrive wouldn't be a simple okay. I needed a little space right now, and he wanted to crowd a small room and lock us both in it.

Gray: Work?

If I answered just *no*, it would seem dodgy and vague now. But I didn't like lying. So instead, I decided to make my lie into a truth. Rather than texting Gray back right away, I sent a text to Quinn.

Layla: My day is in need of homemade hooch. Know of a place?

She texted back.

Quinn: You're in luck. I just made a fresh batch. I added in some acetylsalicylic acid this time.

I laughed.

Layla: Isn't that what aspirin is made of?

Quinn: Damn straight. Too birds, one stone. What time you coming?

Layla: Soon.

Quinn: Soon? The clock behind the bar says it's not even three. Do I need to replace the batteries? Or do we have some serious shit to discuss that you're leaving that office before seven at night?

She knew me well.

Layla: Don't waste the batteries. I might need them for my vibrator soon. XO

Now, I'm not lying.

Switching chat strings, I opened the one with Gray.

Layla: No. Plans with Quinn.

Gray: Okay. Be safe.

I wanted to leave our conversation at that, but I was curious about whether he'd reached Max and wanted to talk about it over dinner. It would be just like Gray to make sure to deliver that type of news in person.

Layla: Did you reach Max?

Gray: Not yet. Left two messages. Receptionist said she's out of town today.

I took a deep breath in and out and tossed my phone on my desk. *Screw it*. What was I waiting for? The whistle to blow at five o'clock?

I opened my desk drawer and pulled out my purse. Not even bothering to put away the file I'd been working on, I decided my day was over.

It's five o'clock somewhere.

Quinn's jaw hung open. And that was saying something. My best friend had an Irish dad and owned a bar. There wasn't much that shocked her.

"So she had his baby while he was in prison for the crime she committed, and as soon as he starts to get his life back in order, she shows up to drop a bomb?"

"It appears that way." I sucked back a third shot of homemade whiskey and winced at the burn that traveled down my throat.

An older gentleman who must've been a regular—he looked familiar even to me—held up his empty beer mug from the other end of the bar. "Hey, Q. How about a refill sometime today?"

Quinn waved him away and responded without even turning her head in his direction. "Go around and fill your mug yourself, Frank. It's on me, but it's self-serve this afternoon."

The old guy practically hopped from his seat to help himself.

Quinn leaned her elbows on the bar and settled her head into her hands. "So, let's fast forward and play this out. For whatever reason, she didn't tell him he has a kid. But it turns out it really is his. What does that mean to you and Gray?"

"I have no idea."

Quinn tilted her head. "Having a kid isn't the end of the world. Of course, it's the end of your sex life, money, nice figure, and youthful skin, but it's not the end of the world."

I laughed. And hiccupped. Sort of a hiccup-laugh combo, which sent Quinn into a fit of laughter, too. It wasn't even really that funny, but I think we both just needed the laugh.

Quinn wiped tears from her eyes. "You know, come to think of it, having a relationship with a guy who has a kid isn't that bad. They generally only have the monsters every other weekend and get to be the good guy in the parent duo. They don't have to wake them up for school or squeeze their little necks to get them to brush their teeth at night. It's like the best of both worlds. You get to have kids without the full-time responsibility."

"You have to squeeze their necks to get them to brush their teeth at night?"

"Just a little in the back. But it's more for me than for Harper."

Some actual customers started to come into the bar—
ones Quinn couldn't offer self-service to. So I was left
to ponder and drown my sorrows in alcohol alone for a
while. And ponder I did.

What would I do if that little girl was Gray's daughter?

I'd dated a guy who was divorced once. He had a four-
year-old. I hadn't ruled him out because he had a child, so
why would Gray be any different?

Because the guy I dated was just that—some guy I
dated.

Not the man I'm in love with.

The man

I'm

In love

With.

That bore repeating in my head.

Slowly.

I guess it didn't really come as a shock. I'd fallen in love
with Gray two-and-a-half years ago. It was just the first
time I'd actually admitted it to myself. Which meant...I
guzzled the rest of my drink.

After five hours of sitting at the bar and wallowing in
self-pity, I finally headed home. Quinn made sure I made
it safely into the back of the cab and took down the driver's
ID number—letting him know she had it—to ensure he
took me straight home.

Once there, I went directly to my bed, without even
taking my shoes off, and plopped down face first. I'd just
started to doze off when my phone chimed, indicating a
new message.

I felt around for the end table without lifting my head and had to squint to make out the words. It was a text from Gray.

Gray: I came by your place a little while ago but managed to talk myself out of ringing the buzzer. I don't even know if you were home, but it felt good to be in the same place you might be. I'm giving you the space you want, but that doesn't mean I don't want to be with you. Please know that, Freckles.

I loved him even more after reading that text. Yet I couldn't let him push. We'd only just worked things out, and I didn't think our relationship was ready to add a child. Ignoring his words, I texted back.

Layla: Did you talk to Max?

Gray: Her office called me back and told me to meet her there tomorrow at 9AM.

Jealousy shot an arrow through my heart at the thought of them together in one room. It was ridiculous. I knew that. The man loathed her. But I felt what I felt. Love was possessive. It didn't matter who the intruder was; it only mattered that someone was circling what I considered mine.

I swallowed the lump of wariness in my throat and responded with all the enthusiasm I could muster.

Layla: Good luck tomorrow.

Chapter 25

Gray

I drummed my fingers on the arm of the chair, growing more restless by the minute.

Max's secretary had showed me into a conference room—one with a long table and more than a dozen chairs. But more importantly, one that had glass panels, which allowed everyone who walked down the hall to see in. At first I thought perhaps it was standard operating procedure—the secretary didn't know who I was or have any reason to think my business with Max today required any sort of privacy. But as the minutes ticked by, I realized Max left nothing to chance. She'd have instructed her staff to put me exactly where she wanted me, so the fact that I was sitting in a fishbowl was definitely not an accident.

Max was nervous about my reaction. Considering I felt like a ticking time bomb, her assessment was probably on point. Any minute I thought I might explode. And whoever was in my way? God help us both.

At ten after nine, the door to the conference room opened and Max walked in. If she was nervous, it didn't immediately show. She marched to the opposite side of the table, set down a large file wrapped with a rubber band

and her cell phone, and took a seat across from me. She folded her hands on top of the folder and looked at me without a word.

It had been more than a year since I'd laid eyes on her, and that time had not been kind. Max was always tall and thin. In the mornings, she went for long runs—sometimes the distance of a marathon runner prepping for a race—when she was stressed. During the time we were being investigated, she lost a lot of weight, running two and three hours a day, but she'd still looked healthy, even if on the thin side.

But the woman sitting across from me looked like she'd been stressing a fuck of a lot. Her cheeks were hollowed, her shoulders seemed half the size they used to be, and the V-neck of her shirt displayed collarbones that jutted out in a way that was more skeletal than sexy. If I wasn't so fucking furious, the way she looked might've been alarming.

"Good to see you, Gray. You look well," she finally said.

I slammed my hand against the table, causing everything to bounce, and she jumped.

"What kind of sick game are you playing now?" Venom dripped from my voice.

She quickly composed herself, straightening her spine. "I know you're a good man, but I needed to see who our daughter was going to be around before I decided to tell you."

"*Our* daughter? If she's my daughter, why *the fuck* would you wait more than three years to tell me?"

A man opened the conference room door and looked at Max. "Everything okay in here?"

Max's hand went to her ear. She'd always had a habit of playing with her earring when she was nervous. *Good. You should be fucking nervous.*

"Everything is fine, Jack. Thank you for checking."

The man gave me a second glance, and probably seeing daggers in my eyes, he hesitated and looked at Max again.

She had to reassure him. "Really. We're fine. Gray and I go way back. We were just having a heated discussion over the futures market."

The guy nodded, even though he looked like he didn't believe a word she'd said, and slowly shut the door.

Max cleared her throat. "If I'd told you I was pregnant three years ago, you might've fought harder for your freedom, and then I wouldn't have had my immunity."

I stared at her. She'd basically just admitted everything I'd figured out was true. Not that I had any doubt about it, but I'd never expected her to come clean.

"Why are you suddenly telling me all of this? I've been out for almost two months, and you go to my girlfriend's place of employment pretending to be a client so you can introduce her to a child you claim is mine?"

Max slid the folder in front of her across the table. I didn't move to pick it up.

"I had no plans to tell you ever. I'd gotten what I wanted and moved on to start my life in Key West."

"And what changed?"

She moved her eyes to the folder. "It's all in there."

My voice was eerily calm. "No more games. What's in the folder, Max?"

She pushed back from the table and walked to the window. My patience wore thin during the long minutes she stared outside, but somehow I managed to wait until she spoke.

She kept looking out the window as she started. "I have stage four metastatic breast cancer. It's spread to my lungs, liver, bones, and brain. My MRI, PET scan, and medical papers are all in that folder—along with a DNA test proving that Aiden is not the father and one proving that you are. I submitted your toothbrush and razor so they could collect a sample."

She walked back to the table, held the top of the chair she'd been sitting in, and looked me straight in the eye. "There's also a letter I wrote to you included in that folder."

Of all the shit I'd imagined she might say today, that wasn't it. I stared into her eyes. This was a woman who'd fed me lies for years, and I'd fallen for them all. I'd lost three years of my life because of her expertise in lying…. And yet…I could swear she was telling me the truth.

I slid the thick folder to my side of the table and removed the rubber band. With a deep breath, I opened it and began to sift through the pile of papers. Most of it was medical gibberish I didn't understand. Words jumped out from the page as if they were highlighted and flashing, even though they weren't.

Palliative treatment

Histopathology

Neutropenia

One particular section on the bottom of a Memorial Sloan Kettering PET CT study seemed to read in plain English more than the others. It confirmed everything she'd said, citing large tumors in her head, lungs, liver— *the site of a double mastectomy even.*

I looked again. My original assessment of her weight loss suddenly became clear. No body fat, thin face...I started to notice things I hadn't before. Her skin was a sallow grayish yellow, her thin face had aged twenty years, and her hair was a different color and much thicker than it had been—she was wearing a wig. Once voluptuous, with curves even when she'd run herself too thin, she now had no breasts.

I closed my eyes for a moment and swallowed. It did nothing to clear my jumbled mind. Opening them, I looked up at the woman who'd stolen years of my life, along with my reputation and dignity. I didn't want to see her as human. I wanted to see her as the monster I'd spent three years cultivating my hatred for—but I couldn't. All I saw was a frail person. A woman. A mother. Someone's child who was thirty years old and dying.

The inside of my chest felt hollow. My voice softened. "How long do you have?"

"Six months...maybe."

I dropped my head into my hands. It felt like the room had started to spin. "I'm sorry."

She took the seat across from me again. "So am I, Gray. So am I. I know it's not enough. And I'm not expecting your forgiveness. Sometimes it takes staring death in the face to make you look back at your life and realize you didn't live it in a way you're proud of. I'm not proud of much that I've done at all. I lived for money and power, disregarding anyone who fell in my wake. But I am proud of Ella. She's innocent and sweet, and full of love and life." She paused. "I guess I'm lucky she took after her father and not me."

I looked up at her. "Are you sure she's mine? How do I know these tests aren't manipulated?"

Max smiled sadly and reached into her blazer pocket. She slid a photo across the table.

Lifting it knocked the breath right out of me. The little girl was all me. Big green eyes, dark lashes, creviced dimples punctuating her crooked smile. A fucked-up thought popped into my head. *She looks just like my father*.

I swallowed and tasted salt in my throat. "I need some time to digest all this."

"Of course."

I stared down at the photo of the beautiful little girl. "Can I keep this?"

"Of course."

Standing, I felt numb. I took the folder and nodded at Max before turning to walk out. With my hand on the glass door, I asked, "Anything else you want to confess before I go?" It was my idea of a sad joke.

But Max looked down.

I shook my head. "Fuck—what now?"

"Aiden stole all the money from me that we stole from you. I really would like your friend to try to get it back. It's Ella's inheritance."

Unbelievable. I opened the door and spoke without looking back. "You're a real piece of work."

Chapter 26

Gray

Rattling the ice cubes in my empty glass, I stared at the mess of my life strewn all over the living room couch and floor. The folder Max had given me contained everything—her medical papers, her will appointing me as Ella's sole guardian, a seven-page letter that detailed all of the whys, hows, and whens of her illness and pregnancy, and my daughter's birth certificate and medical files. She'd even admitted in writing to the details of the con job she'd pulled on me. It was a shitload of information. But it was the photo of my daughter sitting on top of the papers that I kept coming back to.

My daughter.

I wasn't sure I'd ever get used to even thinking the words, much less saying them aloud. Ella Kent Cartwright had been born on Valentine's Day almost three years ago. Max had listed the father's name as unknown on the birth certificate but gave Ella my mother's maiden name as her middle name—*Kent*.

I picked up Ella's picture to study it for the thousandth time. I had no idea how to take care of a child—a daughter, no less. But my heart swelled every time I looked at her adorable little face. I felt like my life had once again been sucked into a tornado, and where it would spit me out was anyone's guess. But I knew one thing for sure: I needed to meet Ella as soon as possible.

Stumbling to the kitchen, I refilled my glass, cursing at the empty bottle while I poured the last drops.

I needed to talk to Layla. She'd texted me an hour ago, and I still couldn't bring myself to respond. What the fuck did I write back?

Yes, I have a daughter.

And...pretty soon I'll be a single dad to a nearly three-year-old I've never met.

What I wanted to do was lie—tell her Max hadn't shown up for our meeting and just spend one more night in denial. But...*no lies.* That's how I'd lost her in the first place.

The discussion certainly wasn't one that should unfold via text. It was almost eight so I figured Layla would be home by now.

Gray: Is it okay if I stop by so we can talk?

Her response came quick.

Layla: No.

My heart started to pound, and I fumbled my phone, dropping it on the floor when I started to text back. I heard another phone ringing in the background while I swiped my cell from the floor. I was so laser focused on finding the reason she didn't want me to stop by that I didn't realize it was my own home phone.

Gray: Are you still at work? I could come pick you up and we could ride to your place together.

Layla: I'm not at work anymore.

Shit. She just didn't want me to come over.

Gray: Too tired?

My phone rang again. This time I heard it loud and clear, but chose to ignore it. Whoever was calling wasn't as important as Layla.

Layla: Actually, I'm not.

Fuck.

I started to text back and then thought better of it. Instead, I hit *Call*. She answered on the first ring.

"We need to talk, sweetheart," I said.

"I agree. So why don't you answer your home phone already?"

I was thoroughly confused for a few heartbeats. "How do you know my…"

"Because I'm standing downstairs, waiting for you to tell your nice doorman to allow me to come up."

I picked up my house phone and held it to the other ear. "Norman?"

"Yes, sir, Mr. Westbrook."

"Can you please send Ms. Hutton up?"

"Will do."

"And for future reference, Ms. Hutton is welcome any time she wants."

"You got it."

I hung up the cordless and returned to my cell. "Get your ass up here, wise ass."

I waited in front of the elevator doors. Freckles, on the other hand, took his trusty shoe and charged right inside when the door opened.

Layla bent to pick him up. "Are you glad to see me or trying to escape in the elevator?"

I wanted to keep that smile on her face forever. Suddenly, a sobering thought hit me. I hadn't wanted to have a serious conversation over text. The same might've been true for her. She could be here to dump my ass in person.

I attempted to push the thought out of my head and remain positive. "This is a pleasant surprise."

She finished scratching Freckles and set him down. "I figured you'd been avoiding me all day because you had news you didn't want to share and wouldn't lie when I asked you."

I forced a smile. "You know me well."

On the inside, I was a fucking wreck, unable to think straight, but that didn't stop me from soaking her in. She wore a red business suit—a skirt and jacket, with a white, silky camisole underneath. Holding Freckles, the thin fabric clung against her bra, and I could make out the pattern of lace underneath. Her long, toned legs were shapely and smooth, and she wore black high heels that I'd have opted to have stitches in my back just to feel them puncture my skin. But it was her nose that did me in. She hadn't covered her freckles. Somehow that gave me a beacon of hope to cling to.

While I was busy ogling her, apparently she'd done the same to me. Except what she found wasn't as pleasant.

"You look terrible," she said.

"Then it's a good thing you look so beautiful and can pick up the slack."

"Are you...going to invite me in so we can talk? Or are we just going to stand in front of the elevator and stare at each other?"

"How would you feel about staying right here?"

She forced a smile. "Come on. Give me a drink. From the looks of you, I have a lot of catching up to do."

After I poured her a glass of wine and grabbed myself a bottle of water—I'd had enough—we went to the living room. I'd forgotten the mess all over the place. Sweeping papers from the couch, I made room for her to sit.

Layla's eyes landed on the photo I hadn't been able to take mine from today. She picked it up and stared at it while sipping her wine.

"She's beautiful. The photo doesn't even do her justice," she said softly.

"I've done nothing but stare at that for hours."

Her eyes flickered to meet mine. "She's yours?"

I blew out a deep breath. "Max gave me DNA results to show that Aiden isn't the father and testing she claims was done with a sample from my toothbrush and razor, which is positive for paternity."

"Do you believe her?"

I looked at the photo still in her hands. "I think I would've believed her with that photo alone."

Layla smiled sadly. We stared at each other in utter silence for a long time. I didn't know what to say, and I thought it best to let her digest it and not force it down her throat.

Eventually she looked away. "Why did she keep it from you?"

"She said she found out she was pregnant right before I took the deal, and she thought I might not take it if I knew I had a child on the way. I might've fought for my freedom, and that would've put her immunity deal at risk."

"God," she gasped. "That's ruthless."

I shook my head and looked down at my feet. "I didn't think anything else could shock me."

"Does she want you back? Is that why she told you the way she did—through me? Showing up at my office like that?"

"No. She said she wanted to see who her daughter was going to be spending time with."

"There are obviously more normal ways to go about doing that. Like perhaps letting the father know he *has* a child before stalking his girlfriend?"

"There's nothing normal about Max. I learned that the hard way."

We were again quiet for a few minutes. I needed to tell her the rest, but wasn't sure how to tell her the life I'd just gotten back was about to be turned upside down. Her next question, though, opened the door.

"So what happens now? Is she going to let you see her? Will she fight you for visitation and your legal rights?"

I waited until Layla drank her wine and lifted her eyes to meet mine again. "Max is dying. Stage four breast cancer that has spread to...everywhere."

Her jaw dropped, and her hand clutched at her chest. "Oh my God, Gray."

"She decided to tell me because she's running out of time and wants to help make the transition easier."

"The transition?"

"To me having custody."

"Wow." Layla rubbed at one temple. "I…I don't even know what to say."

I took the wine from her and set it on the coffee table so I could take both her hands in mine.

Looking into her eyes, I said, "Say you'll date a single father who doesn't have a fucking clue what to do with a kid. Say this isn't going to scare you away again."

She looked down. "Gray…this is a lot."

"I know. And I'm not asking you to take it all in right now. Fuck, I haven't even let it all sink in."

She looked up at me. Her mind seemed to be jumping all over the place like mine had done all day, clicking the puzzle pieces into place. "That's why she's so thin. The wig. The big sunglasses."

I nodded. "She doesn't look good."

"Did you get to meet Ella today?"

I frowned. "No. I left Max's office with my head unscrewed and came home to read a seven-page letter she'd given me in a file with a bunch of legal documents. The letter had her cell phone on it and said to text when I was ready to see Ella. I sent her a text earlier, but haven't heard back yet."

"Ella wears a hearing aid. I noticed it when Max moved her hair the other day. It completely slipped my mind."

I nodded. "She had medical records in the file for Ella, too. She has Connexin 26. It's a genetic condition that can cause mild to total hearing loss. Her case is mild, but it can become progressively worse over time, so Max is teaching her sign language as a precaution. My father had it, too. He didn't wear a hearing aid, but he should have. He just made everyone repeat themselves all the time."

"Jesus, Gray. I don't know what to say. You've missed almost three years of your child's life."

"I'll have to make up for it."

She stared into my eyes, and I watched hers fill with tears. I thought she was sad about this latest wrench in things. A lone tear slipped down her cheek, and I wiped it away with my thumb.

"I'm sorry I have all this baggage. If I were a better man, I'd walk away from you and not leave all this at your feet. But when it comes to you, I'm completely selfish. I can't help myself. I'm sorry I'm upsetting you. But I can't let you go again. I had no choice last time when you walked away."

More tears started to fall. I blew out a deep breath and wiped her cheeks again. "I'm sorry. Please don't get upset. I'll figure this out. We'll figure this out. It kills me to see you crying because I let you down again."

"I'm not crying because you let me down." She sniffled. "I'm crying because you lost years with a child you haven't even met yet."

I pulled her to me and wrapped her in my arms. It felt like I could finally breathe again. I stroked her hair.

"It's a lot, I know. And I don't expect you to say anything at all today. You need some time. But there's one more thing I need to say."

Pulling back, a sad smile threatened at her lips. "I'm not sure I can take much more."

I took her hand in mine and brought it to my lips for a kiss. "This doesn't have anything to do with Max. But it's important that you know."

"What is it?"

"Tomorrow or whenever you reflect back on everything—when you think of all this bad stuff I just unloaded on you—I need you to also remember one other thing." I paused and waited until she was really looking into my eyes before continuing. "I'm in love with you, Layla Hutton—so fucking in love with you it hurts to think about losing you."

She smiled. "Gray..."

I pressed my lips to hers to stop her from speaking. "Shhh. We've talked about enough heavy shit for one night. How about I pour you another wine and we take a hot bath together?"

"I don't know, Gray. I should go..."

"If you go, I'm going with you. You're not getting rid of me that easily. We can go to your place if you want, but I'm not leaving you alone...not tonight after I just sprang all that shit on you."

She seemed conflicted, but after a few minutes she finally nodded.

Layla accepted my offer of wine, but turned down my suggestion of a bath together. When we climbed into bed that night, I held her in my arms as tightly as I could without hurting her. But even through my iron grip, I felt her slipping away.

Chapter 27

Layla

I woke up to the sight of a sleeping Gray. He looked so peaceful. My heart ached for everything he'd lost: three years of his life, his business, his reputation, experiencing the birth of his daughter—her first few steps, her first haircut, first words, first...*everything*. So I wanted to be here for him, to stick it out. But the thought of building a new life that now included a three-year-old and her mother who was about to die scared the living shit out of me.

The self-protection mechanism in my heart wanted me to run the other way as fast as I could. But the part that beat wildly every time Gray walked into the room kept me here watching him sleep.

Last night I couldn't stop thinking about something my mother had always said. After I'd realized we weren't my father's only family—that she was actually *the other woman* and I was her bastard child—I'd asked my mom on more than one occasion how she could put up with something like that. Her answer was always the same: *"When you love someone, sometimes you need to put their needs first."*

I'd always thought that was a cop out, that her accepting that my father *needed* to have two families was bullshit. Yet I always kept my tongue in check, never wanting to upset her or speak badly about my father, who was so good to me...when he was around.

But inside, every time she said love meant having to put his needs before her own, all I could think was *Yeah, and you just taught him that your needs always come second*. Growing up, I'd vowed to put my own needs first if I ever fell in love.

Gray's eyes fluttered open on that thought.

"Hey." He reached out and ran a thumb along my cheek. "You're still here."

"Did you think I'd be gone?"

He gave me a soft smile. "I was afraid to fall asleep and have my grip on you loosen for fear you'd slip away."

"Well, I do have to get my ass up and go to work. I need to go to my apartment to shower and get clothes, too. So I better get moving."

He reached around to my back and hauled me flush against him. "Shower with me."

"That isn't exactly conducive to getting to work on time."

Gray buried his head in my hair. "We can be fast."

The way his hot breath on my neck made me instantly aroused, I knew that was a crock of shit. "How about, I'll take a shower here, and you can make us some breakfast?"

"Let's negotiate," he grumbled against my skin before trailing a line of kisses up my neck. "We shower together, and I'll eat you for breakfast while you wash. Multitasking."

I bent my head back to allow him better access and smiled. "Nice try. But I have a ten o'clock deposition that will go most of the day, so I need something to fill my belly."

"I'll give you something to fill your belly."

Laughing, I pushed him away so I could get up. "I'll have to take a rain check."

After a quick shower, I wrapped my hair in a towel and put on the shirt Gray had worn yesterday. It hung to my knees like a dress as I followed the smell of bacon to the kitchen. Gray stood in front of the oven shirtless, wearing a pair of black sweatpants. His back muscles were ripped without him even flexing, and they tapered down to a slim waist. No matter how confused my head happened to be at the moment, my libido knew exactly what it wanted.

I walked behind him and scratched my nails down his back, not so lightly.

Gray groaned. "You have no idea the willpower it took to stay out here, knowing you were naked in the other room. Scratch me again, and I'm going to say fuck the self-control, and you're going to be up on the kitchen counter with your legs spread and late for work."

He plated the bacon, grabbed some toast as it popped from the toaster, and turned around to face me. His eyes looked down to a noticeable bulge in his pants.

I covered my mouth and giggled. "That just happened now?"

"I woke up in bed next to you. It had started to go down a minute before you dug those nails into my back. Now you've made it rear its needy head again."

I took the plate from his hands and tried to ignore my own needy head—although mine was north of my waist. "Bacon and toast?"

"I'm out of eggs. It was that, peanut butter, or a steak."

"Good choice."

"Sit. The coffee just finished brewing. I'll fix us both some."

Although Gray had plated a second serving of bacon, he left it on the stovetop and sat across from me with only his coffee.

"Aren't you going to eat your bacon and toast?"

"After I get back from a run. I can't eat before I hit the pavement."

I sipped my coffee. He hadn't asked how I took it, yet made it perfectly. My heart warmed. "What's on your agenda for today?"

His easygoing smile fell. "I checked my phone while you were in the shower. Max wrote back late last night. She said I could meet Ella this afternoon. I suggested the park across the street. There's a kid's play area and a dog run. I'm going to rearrange my schedule to work from home today. I told her to text me a time, that I'd make myself available as soon as she can get there."

"Wow. Okay. Are you nervous?"

He ran a hand through his hair. "I'm terrified. A man's not supposed to show fear, but I'm afraid this little girl will take one look at me and start crying."

"Oh my God." His vulnerability touched a weak spot inside of me. I got up and knelt down next him. Taking his hand, I said, "She's going to love you, Gray. Children have a sixth sense when it comes to knowing who's a good person. And I watched you with Quinn's daughter. I told you Harper isn't a fan of men *at all*, yet she took to you."

"I bribed her with a gift I knew she'd love."

"Maybe. But trust me, you wouldn't have gotten that hug from her if she didn't have the sense that you were a good person. And whether you know it or not, you were good with her. You're a natural. When you spoke to her, you didn't look down at her. I watched you. You bent down and spoke to her at eye level. You treated her as a person, not a little kid, and you actually listened when she talked. That's pretty much all you need to start. The rest will come to you."

"I've never changed a diaper in my life. I watched muted YouTube videos on it last night after you fell asleep."

I smiled. "You'll be fine. We'll figure it out. Besides, most kids are out of diapers by the time they're three. So that's one less thing to worry about."

He'd been looking down at our joined hands, but his eyes jumped to mine. His gaze was intense.

"What?" I said.

"You said *We'll*."

My forehead wrinkled.

"We'll. You said, '*We'll* figure it out.'"

I hadn't even realized it, but he was right. "I guess I did."

Gray pushed his chair back and lifted me into his lap. He cupped both my cheeks in his big hands.

"Of anything you could say to try to make me feel like I wasn't going to screw this up, that gives me more hope than anything. Because with you next to me, I can do anything."

———

"I called Al." Gray finished tying his running shoes and stood just as I emerged from the bathroom, dressed and brushing my wet hair. "He'll be downstairs in five minutes. He'll take you home to get dressed and then drop you off at work."

"Oh. You didn't need to do that. I could've taken the train."

"It's my pleasure."

My eyes did a quick sweep of the clothes Gray had thrown on to go running. A second skin, black Under Armor shirt and a pair of running shorts.

"I like your outfit."

"Oh yeah?" He stalked over to me and wrapped his hands behind my back. "I'll wear it every day, then."

"I think it might start to smell after a while."

"I'll buy multiples."

One hand slipped under the back of my shirt and began to caress my skin. It froze where my bra should've been, and then felt around, as if he was verifying his initial conclusion.

"You're not wearing a bra."

"I shoved it in my purse. I wore it yesterday."

His hand traveled from my back to my front and cupped a bare breast. "I like this. Easy access. But I don't like the thought of you traveling like this on the train."

"I'm not taking the train. You just said Al was picking me up."

"Yes, but you didn't know that when you got dressed."

"Well, then it worked out nicely, didn't it?"

Gray squinted at me and pinched my nipple. "Wise ass."

I reached up on my tiptoes and leaned in to whisper in his ear. "If you don't like the thought of me riding the train with no bra, you probably would've hated that I have no underwear on either."

Gray mumbled something about self-control right before his lips crashed down on mine. He kissed me passionately, and it was the first time since Max had walked into my office that things felt normal again between us. I sighed into his mouth, and he backed me toward the bed. I barely registered my back hitting the soft mattress, but I definitely felt the erection prodding at my hip. As much as I hated to, I forced myself to cut things off before we went any farther.

Placing two palms on his chest, I gave a gentle nudge. "I have to get to work."

"I'll call Pittman and tell him I had an emergency you needed to attend to this morning."

"Then I'd have to bill you for the hours."

"Bill me for a month. I don't give a fuck as long as I don't have to let go of you."

I laughed and shoved him a little harder. "No, really. I have to go."

"Fine." He pouted, but got up.

In the elevator, the playfulness continued. My panties had been sticking out of my unzipped purse, and Gray and I had a fight over them. He pulled. I yanked. I wanted to stay in this little box, our own little world where we'd briefly forgotten anything else existed.

But too soon, the doors slid open in the lobby. An older couple was waiting to get in, and Gray thought he could use that to his advantage. His eyes glinted in victory, assuming I'd let go, embarrassed that we were fighting over a black lace thong.

Instead, I cleared my throat and took a step forward, still refusing to give up the panties. I looked at the woman. "Sorry. My brother is a cross-dresser, and sometimes I catch him stealing my panties."

The woman's eyes bulged while Gray released the underwear. I flashed him a wicked smile of victory over my shoulder as I exited the elevator.

"Cute. Very cute," he called after me as the doors closed behind him. "That's Mrs. Elsworth. She's the president of the co-op. I'm sure my cross-dressing will be on the agenda at next month's board meeting."

I laughed through the lobby and all the way to the front door. But my laughter abruptly ended as I stepped onto the street.

Stopping short, I caused Gray to crash into me. He steadied both of us and kept me from nearly toppling over. Thinking I was still playing around, he squeezed me and lifted me off my feet, swinging me around until he came full circle and got a look at the two people standing in front of his building.

Max and Ella.

Chapter 28

Layla

Neither one of us knew what to say or do. Gray held on to my shoulder so tightly, I was certain I'd have a bruise later.

"What are you doing here?" he snipped to Max, who straightened her spine at his tone.

"I texted you twenty minutes ago. Ella's sitter called in sick, so I decided to bring her to the office with me. Your place is on the way, so I thought..." Max looked back and forth between us. "If this isn't a good time, we can come back."

Gray didn't respond. I turned to see him staring down at Ella. The beautiful little girl stared back up at him with his same stunning green eyes. Seeing his daughter in person for the very first time seemed to have sent him into some sort of shock. When he continued to just stare and say nothing, I tried to nonchalantly take hold of his bicep and squeeze in an effort to snap him out of it before he scared Ella and his worst fear came true—she started to cry.

"Gray..."

He blinked a few times and looked at Max. His face was a mix of lost and terrified. It reminded me of a little boy who wouldn't get off his bed, for fear there was a monster under it, so he didn't know how to get out of his room.

Max knelt down to Ella and began to speak, while also signing with her hands. "Sweetheart, this is Mommy's friend, Gray. Say hello."

Ella extended her fingers and crossed her thumb in front of her palm, then made a saluting gesture from her forehead while she said, "Hello." The motion appeared as though it might be sign language and not really a salute.

Gray looked at me, at a complete loss of what to do, how to respond. I nodded my head back toward the little girl and pointed my eyes down to her. Thankfully, he followed my muted directions.

Kneeling down to her eye level, he cleared his throat. "Hi, Ella."

She signed something without adding the words this time.

Max prompted her, "Ella, add the words, sweetheart."

Ella did the same sign and then said, "Park."

Max looked at Gray. "I told her we were going to meet my friend and then the three of us would go to the park."

Gray nodded. And then the awkwardness that had started to wane came back—at least for me anyway. Max turned in my direction. Her hard stare silently communicated that a fourth wasn't welcome on their family outing.

She flashed me a Botox smile. "You remember, Ms. Hutton, right, Ella? She's Mommy's attorney."

I heard her loud and clear.

Luckily, Gray's driver pulled to the curb at that moment. I couldn't wait to flee.

"There's my ride. I should get going to work." I smiled down at the little girl. "Bye, Ella." Squeezing Gray's arm, I forced half a smile. "I'll talk to you later."

Then I scurried to the car before anyone had a chance to say anything else.

Slamming the door shut, I let out a few panting breaths as I watched the three of them out on the street. I'd never been so glad for tinted windows before.

Ella reached her hands up toward her mother, and Max leaned down to unlatch the little girl and help her out of the stroller. I couldn't take my eyes off the three of them, even as Al started to pull away from the curb. My neck craned to watch out the back window. We only made it a few car lengths before hitting a line of traffic, so I had plenty of time to study their interaction.

Max finished folding up the stroller, and Ella took one of her hands. Then she spoke to her daughter, who extended her other hand toward Gray. My heart broke watching him struggle with how to react. Holding your daughter's hand should be the most natural thing in the world. Yet he looked stiff and terrified. After a few heartbeats, he took hold of her little hand. Gray couldn't stop staring down at his daughter—which I understood completely. After a minute or two, the three of them finally started to walk in the direction of the park.

My car inched forward at a snail's pace, with a long line of cabs in front of us waiting to make a left turn. Eventually, I no longer had to crane my neck, and the three of them passed us. Gray seemed oblivious that he'd even walked by his own town car.

I stared at their backs as they walked. With tiny little Ella in the middle holding their hands, they looked like any other family walking in New York City. The longer I watched, the more my eyes started to lose focus.

God...a family.

I'm not ready for that.

We're not ready for that. We'd barely gotten over our own problems and started to move forward. Couples were supposed to go through stages to prepare them for being ready for a family. Even if I'd gotten pregnant, we would have had nine months to warm to the idea.

My eyes began to come into focus as they walked farther up the street, but my vision also started to play tricks on me. While Ella and Gray were crisp in my line of sight, Max began to fade away. A little at a time, I watched the woman turn into a shadow and then completely disappear. Erased from the picture, she vanished. When she came back into focus a few seconds later, I swallowed my breath. I no longer saw Max...she'd been replaced by...me. Staring, the vision seemed so real—Gray and me walking hand in hand with Ella between us.

That's how it would be, wouldn't it?

Fade out Max.

Fade in Layla.

I shut my eyes to get rid of the vision, only to realize it wouldn't go away. I still saw it.

Fade out Max.

Fade in Layla.

I shut off my phone during the deposition. It had been difficult to focus the entire morning, and ten minutes into questioning the defendant, I realized I kept staring at my cell, waiting for something to come in from Gray. My client deserved better representation than that, and I *needed* to throw myself into my work to maintain my sanity today.

It was nearly five o'clock by the time I turned it back on. Messages started to flood in, the majority of them from Gray. Most had been sent within a minute of each other, capturing his stream of thoughts.

Gray: She's incredible. So smart.

Gray: She didn't cry.

Gray: I might've when I got home.

I smiled sadly at my phone, reading that one.

Gray: You were right. She's already potty trained.

Gray: No more YouTube diaper videos. Thank God. It felt fucking weird to watch a naked baby.

Gray: She hugged me goodbye.

Gray: I didn't want to let go.

The time on his texts had a long lapse, then...

Gray: I can't wait for you to get to know her, too.

I'd never been a big drinker, but in that moment, I wished I kept a bottle of something in my desk. I could use a giant swig to calm my nerves.

Gray's last text had come in about an hour ago.

Gray: Hope your day was good. Dinner tonight?

I avoided responding to that and instead scanned through my other missed texts. There was one from Quinn, one from a client, and one from Kristen...my half sister. For some odd reason, I chose to open that one, which usually I'd avoid like the plague.

Kristen: Just passed a great little Korean restaurant. Dad's favorite. We should have dinner there all together. Talk soon!

I heard her chipper voice, even in a text.

My desk had a stack of missed call memos, so I focused on those for a little while. But by six, my phone had started buzzing again, and I really didn't have to look at the name to know who it would be.

Gray: You read my texts an hour ago. What's going on in that head of yours, Freckles?

I smiled.

Layla: Sorry. Deposition was all day, and then I had to return some business calls before it got too late. I'm glad everything worked out with Ella.

I watched my text turn to delivered, then read. The dots started to jump around as he responded, then stopped. A moment later, my cell rang in my hand.

Gray responded to my hello in a sexy, throaty tone. "I needed to hear your voice."

"It sounds like you just woke up."

"Nope. Just came back from a run."

I'd forgotten that his run had been interrupted this morning. "Oh."

"So were you really busy or just avoiding me?"

I answered on reflex. "I was busy."

"Layla..."

I rolled my eyes. "Fine. I was avoiding you. But *I am* busy, too."

I heard the gloat and smile in his voice. "Haven't you figured out by now that you can't avoid me? If you hadn't responded soon, I'd be at your office checking on you. I'm not giving up on us that easily, sweetheart. I understand it's a lot at once, and I'll give you time to take it in if you need it. But I want to know you're not pushing me away, and it's just time you need."

In the midst of his life being turned upside down, he was the levelheaded one. It felt like I should be there for him to lean on me. But I was scared. Each time I made the decision to move forward—take a chance to be all in—something else pushed back. The least I could do was be honest.

"I watched the three of you walking to the park this morning. It just hit me...you have a family now."

"Max isn't my family."

"I know. I just meant...the three of you looked like a family. And I realized that being with you, meant..."

"I don't expect you to replace Max in Ella's life, if that's what you're thinking."

I sort of was. I sighed. "It's just hard. I'm...I'm...scared, Gray."

"Me too, babe. Me too. But I'm more scared of losing you again than of all the other shit coming my way. We'll figure it out."

God, he was so sweet. "Okay."

"Dinner tonight?"

I just wasn't up for it. The last few days had taken a mental toll. My first instinct was to lie and say I had plans. But I went with honesty because he deserved at least that much. "I need a night at home, by myself, Gray."

He took a minute before answering. "I understand."

I hated the hurt in his voice. "Are you seeing Ella again soon?"

"The day after tomorrow. Tomorrow I have to fly up to Chicago for the day to meet with my partners and the CEO of a company we're investing in. I won't be back until late. But Max and I had a civil conversation while Ella was playing at the park. I'm going to spend as much time as I can with the two of them, so she can get to know me. Once Ella's more comfortable, Max will drop out of the picture for my visits. I want you to get to know her, too, if you can handle that."

"Let's take things one step at a time. Focus on you and Ella. You don't need to worry about me right now."

"I can do that better if you tell me you're not kicking my ass to the curb."

I smiled. "I'm still with you."

"I might make you repeat that every day, Freckles. Like a mantra."

Chapter 29

Gray

Google had become my best friend.
How to sign "how are you?"
What do three-year-olds eat?
Toys to buy a three-year-old child.
Girl toys to buy a three-year-old.
Things to talk about with a three-year-old girl.
Stage four breast cancer.
What the hell is Yo Gabba Gabba?

Today I was going to Max's apartment to spend time with her and Ella at home. When she'd suggested I come to her place, I automatically wanted to say no way. *No fucking way I want to be stuck inside the same four walls as you—even if the place is the size of a palace.* But after I gave it some thought, I realized I needed to be more flexible and do what was best for Ella. I needed to do whatever would help her open up to me, and that would probably happen best on her own home turf, rather than in a stranger's apartment. So I didn't fight it. My feelings for Max, my instinct to fight everything she wanted, had to take a backseat to my little girl.

My little girl.

It was truly surreal.

Max had said that Ella's favorite thing to do was take long walks. She loved to look around the busy city from inside her stroller. So when I stopped off at the toy store up on 82nd Street—the one I passed by all the time, but never went inside—I knew what to get her the moment my eyes landed on it.

The Radio Flyer 4-in-1 Stroll 'N Trike, in pink. It was like a stroller and tricycle all in one. She could learn how to pedal if she wanted, but it had a footrest for when she got too tired. I found myself tugging on the three-point harness and asking a teenage store clerk safety questions that made his face wrinkle like I'd just sprung a pop Physics quiz on him.

I arrived at the address Max had given me and was surprised to find it was a brownstone in Brooklyn rather than a swanky penthouse on the Upper East Side. I personally liked the quiet streets of this area, but Max had always been about the hustle and bustle of Manhattan.

I rang the bell, and Max opened the door. She was dressed in a white tank top, and it really hit me then how much weight she'd lost. When I'd seen her the other day, she'd had on a sweater. Of course I'd seen it in her thinned face, but that wasn't the half of it. The full visual was pretty damn alarming. Her collarbones and shoulder blades jutted out—all the meat was gone. She was little more than a skeleton with skin, and that skin was sallow.

She stepped aside for me to enter. Apparently I hadn't done such a good job of hiding my thoughts.

"It's from the chemotherapy. That's why I stopped it. Refractory vomiting. The anti-nausea and vomiting medicine stopped working. I couldn't do it any more. I want to enjoy what time I have left with my daughter, not spend it with my head hanging in the toilet bowl."

I nodded and walked in.

Max looked at her watch as we stood in the foyer. "Ella's late getting up from her nap. She usually sleeps for an hour, but she's a little over. I don't wake her if she goes long. I feel like her body knows when it's time to get up. But I can wake her if you want?"

Yes. I can't stand here with just you.

"No. It's fine. Let her wake up on her own."

Note to self, nap length is determined by the child, not the adult. One less thing to Google. I felt like I should have a notepad and pen.

"I was just going to make some tea. I drag by the early afternoon. That's why I only work mornings now. The caffeine helps me keep alert enough to watch Ella play. What can I make you?"

"Tea is fine."

I didn't really want to be inside Max's place, and definitely not making small talk. But what the hell was I supposed to do?

On the way to the kitchen, I glanced around a bit. The brownstone she lived in was pretty damn nice—custom millwork, high ceilings, wide-plank, white oak flooring, glazed windows with stained glass, a shit ton of light.

"Nice place," I said.

Max filled a cast iron kettle with water from the tap. "Thank you. It will be yours soon. I left it to you in my will."

"What?"

She set the kettle on the stovetop and turned on the flame. "I bought it with the money I stole from you. It's the least I could do. Don't take under two million for it when you sell it. There's no mortgage."

She'd shocked me twice in the span of two minutes. "I don't know how to respond to that. Thanks, I guess?"

Max leaned against the kitchen sink, while I stayed on the other side of the spacious center island. Distance from her was welcomed.

"There's also ninety thousand in my savings and a term life insurance policy. I left the policy benefits to Ella, but you're the trustee, so you can manage it for her."

It was fucked up to be having this conversation. But when do you have this type of talk when you only have a few months to live? You never know what day will wind up being your last. No point in waiting.

"Okay. Any other legal things I should know?"

She looked me straight in the eyes. It was the first time I'd let that happen since I'd found out what she'd done. Even when she'd come to the prison to tell me my father died, I wouldn't look at her. I couldn't do it the other day at the park, either. But I did today for some reason. Maybe seeing her physically wasting away had given me an ounce of compassion.

"When I went to see Layla, I was curious about her—jealous, even. But I also wasn't lying. Aiden stole all the money that we stole from you. You should get it back."

I shook my head with a sardonic laugh. "You were really two peas in a pod, huh?"

"I'm sorry for what I did to you, Gray. I know there's no apology big enough for losing years of your life. God knows I see that now. But I truly am."

I stared at her. The woman had suckered me into a marriage, stolen millions of dollars, had me imprisoned for a crime she'd committed, and hidden the fact that I had a daughter for years. And yet...a part of me believed her.

What the fuck is wrong with me?

"Why'd you do it?" I asked.

That had been the number one thing I'd pondered over and over during the first months of my sentence—until I decided it didn't matter, and that I wouldn't ever move on by focusing on shit I couldn't change.

Max looked down for a few minutes. When she looked up, there were tears in her eyes. "You didn't really love me."

"What the hell are you talking about?"

"I loved you."

"You have a really fucking funny way of showing it."

"For years I wanted you, and you didn't see me. You saw me as your partner, not one of the women you took out and slept with."

"I fucking married you!"

"And you *still* didn't love me the way I loved you."

"So you decided to screw one of our employees, steal money, and set me up? To what? Punish me?"

"I thought Aiden really loved me."

"You can't be that fucking desperate for a man to love you."

"I'm sorry. I know it doesn't make sense. But I was angry that after all those years of loving you, you still didn't love me like you should have. Once we got married, I thought about backing out of what Aiden and I had planned. Deep down, I still loved you and thought maybe you would finally love me back. But you didn't see me as the love of your life."

I stared at her, completely dumbfounded—and too damn angry to continue this conversation. When her tears started to fall, it made me even more pissed off at myself. I shouldn't have felt bad for her. Yet I did.

What the fuck is wrong with me?

"I need to take a walk. I'll be back in a little while."

I walked for a good hour along the nearby promenade. Actually, at some point, I started to jog, then run, then sprint as fast as I possibly could. It wasn't until I was bent over, with my hands on my knees gasping for air, that I realized what I'd done. I'd needed my breath to catch up to the speed of the shit flying through my head.

What the fuck was wrong with Max? I hadn't loved her enough? We were fucking friends, business partners. I'd never had a damn clue that she had feelings for me. It wasn't like she'd told me, or even made any advances in that way. I'd thought we'd gotten married on a whim, while drunk on an island vacation celebration. It was a joke at first, until she'd suggested we give it an actual try. After a bit, I'd started to settle into the arrangement. It had seemed convenient for both of us. So maybe I didn't love her the way a man should love a wife, but that's a reason to ruin my life?

All this time, when I'd reflected back, I'd assumed she was just pure evil. I'd had no idea that she was batshit crazy *and* evil. We're talking Glenn Close, *Fatal Attraction,* bunny-boiling crazy here.

After I'd calmed down, I realized I needed to put this shit out of my head for the sake of my daughter. Ella had to be my priority now. I couldn't let Max steal any more time from me. So I walked back to her house, took a deep breath, and rang the doorbell.

The little face that yelled my name when the door opened gave me strength to go back inside.

"Today is Wednesday," Ella signed as she spoke. I really needed to learn a shit ton more sign language. I'd learned a few words and sentences on various YouTube videos, but Ella seemed like she had an entire language down.

"Yep. Today is Wednesday. Can you teach me how to sign that?"

Max had left us alone once Ella seemed comfortable with me. I was grateful to concentrate on her and not have another pow wow with her mother.

Ella nodded and went through the motions of signing the words again.

"Like this?"

I signed them, and she cracked up.

"No. Like this, silly."

She did it again, and I'll be damned if I saw any difference. But I gave it another shot anyway.

She laughed again. Apparently I'd still done it wrong. Ella folded my thumb and pinky down, bringing them to touch together, and then stopped and showed me the same position of her hand. "W."

"Ah. I get it now. The three fingers form the letter W."

I had no idea when kids started to spell, but I was pretty damn sure it wasn't before the age of three. Yet my daughter knew Wednesday began with W. My chest expanded a little bit.

Ella held my hand, guiding it to draw a circle with my three fingers. "Wednesday," she said as we looped the circle closed.

I tapped her nose with my finger. "How'd you get so smart?"

"From my daddy."

I froze. What the—had Max told her? I thought we'd agreed it was best to wait a while, let her get to know me before we told her who I was. Or...maybe she referred to Aiden as her father. That thought made me feel sick.

"Your daddy?"

She nodded fast. "Mommy says I'm smart like my daddy."

When she didn't add any more, I thought it best to change the subject.

"So...it's Wednesday." I signed it, and apparently third time's the charm because my performance earned me a big, toothy smile. "Do you do something special on Wednesday?"

She laughed at me again. "White. We wear white." Ella twirled, showing off her outfit. She wore a white shirt with gold, sparkly letters that read *Mermaid Life*, coupled with a pair of white shorts. Her sandals were white, too.

"Oh." I looked down at my clothes. I had on a pair of khakis and a navy polo. "I must've gotten my days mixed up."

She scrunched up her button nose and began to tick off the days of the week with her little fingers. Her pointer was first. "Monday Magenta." Middle finger. "Tuesday Turquoise." Ring finger. "Wednesday White."

I interrupted her by signing the word Wednesday and then winked. Her smile grew.

She kept going, ticking off through one hand and starting on the next. "Thursday Teal. Friday Fuchsia." (Which she adorably pronounced *foo-sha*.) "Saturday Sage. Sunday Sapphire!" She slapped her hands down to her sides when she finished.

"You always dress a color to match the day?"

She nodded.

I really needed that fucking notebook.

"Which one is your favorite?"

"Sapphire! Blue, blue, blue!"

"Blue is my favorite color, too." At least it was now after seeing how happy it made her. A thought popped into my head. "Do you remember Layla?"

She nodded.

"Her favorite color is rainbow."

Ella cracked up. "Rainbow's not a color!"

"Maybe not. But when you like a lot of them, why pick just one? Special girls can have any favorites they want."

Max popped her head into the room. "Everything okay here?"

"Mommy, Mommy!" Ella jumped up and down. "My favorite color is rainbow!"

Max looked to me and smiled back down at her daughter. "It is, is it?"

"It's Layla's, too! We're special so we can have more than one color as our favorite!"

Max's smile wilted. "That's nice, honey. Do you want your snack now?"

"Yes!" She jumped up and down, delivering her answer. Her energy glowed.

"I'll make two plates."

A few minutes later, Max returned with two small plates, one for each of us. *Wednesday. White. Apple slices and peanut butter.* Maybe I should've taken those notes in my phone.

We sat together on the floor in the living room, with our plates on the coffee table. While we were eating our apples, I noticed Ella was using her left hand to eat. "Which hand do you hold a crayon with, sweetheart?"

She raised her left hand.

"I write with my left, too. Most of the world writes with the other hand."

"Mommy writes with a different hand."

That's because you take after your daddy.

When we were done with snack time, Ella asked if we could go for a walk. I had forgotten all about the stroller-trike I'd bought her. I'd left it in the vestibule when I came in. I collected our plates, and Ella and I went to look for her mother.

We found her in the kitchen, drinking a protein shake.

"Ella wants to go for a walk."

"Oh, okay. You two have fun."

Ella ran to her mom and tugged at her shirt. "You come, too, Mommy."

Max's eyes flashed to me. *Ella first*, I reminded myself. I gave her a silent nod.

"Okay. Let me get a sweater."

While Max got her sweater, I showed Ella her new stroller-trike. She literally squealed. Then she took off running back to the living room. I watched from the hallway as she pulled open the end table drawer, picked something out of a box, and crammed it into an envelope. She sped back to me just as Max came back with her sweater.

Holding the envelope up to me, Ella said, "Thank you!"

Curious as to what the hell was going on, I slipped the card out of the envelope. It was a small note card with a silver *Thank You* printed on the front, and the inside was empty.

Max started to laugh. "Ella, honey, we're supposed to fill those out before we give them to people."

Ella frowned.

Max explained. "I don't let her use the toys she gets as gifts until we write a thank you note."

The kid was damn smart. And I didn't need anything written. I knelt down to her. "My thank you card is perfect the way it is. You're very welcome, Ella."

"Can I try it?"

I glanced at Max, who nodded.

"Absolutely. How about if I push you around the block once, and then I hop on and you push me around?"

Ella let out a loud belly laugh. I couldn't imagine ever having a bad day if I could wake up to the sound of that.

"You're too big!"

I patted my waist. "I did gain a pound or two."

Max locked up the house while I strapped Ella into her new ride. I guided her feet to the pedals and showed her where to put them if she got tired.

The minute we started walking, I could have let go of the handle that pushed the thing. Ella pedaled her own weight almost immediately. The stroller-trike had a canopy top to shield her from the sun, and Ella was in her own little world, pedaling away. She wouldn't hear us talking, but I spoke low anyway.

"Does she have any allergies?"

The peanut butter snack had made me think about how many kids seem to have nut allergies these days.

"Feathers. I had her allergy tested because she got a rash from a pillow. The only thing she tested positive to was feathers."

"Any medications?"

"No. Just a children's vitamin every day."

"What is she afraid of?"

Max glanced at me and looked down with a big sigh. "Me going away."

"Going away?"

"I've read a dozen books on how to prepare a child for the death of a parent. Children her age don't really understand the concept of death. They see it as temporary or reversible. I guess it makes sense, since they watch cartoons where characters are flattened by a car and then blow up to their normal size and walk around again. I tried to explain death to her by saying that sometimes mommies and daddies have to go away, even when they don't want to. I thought she'd understand that, but a few days later, I had to go upstate for the afternoon to a business meeting, and when I told her I was going away, she started to sob. So I think I screwed that lesson up pretty good."

I smiled sadly. "She told me her daddy is smart. I assume she thinks Aiden is her father?"

"What?" Max scrunched up her face. "No. I never introduced Aiden as her father. We broke up when she was less than a year old. I doubt she even remembers him."

"So who was she talking about then?"

"You. I talk about her father in the general sense once in a while. She thinks her daddy is away on a long business trip. She has no concept of time and hasn't really ever questioned it."

I raked my fingers through my hair. "Jesus."

After a twenty-minute walk, Ella had tuckered herself out from pedaling so much. Max looked like she had exerted all of her energy, too. I walked them into the house, and the two of them went to the bathroom. While I waited, I took out my cell phone. I was shocked to find out it was almost five thirty. It seemed like I'd just gotten here.

"Would you like to stay for dinner?" Max asked when she returned.

The truth was, I wasn't ready to leave Ella yet. There was so much to learn, so much to catch up on. Yet I also didn't want to take over Ella's routine and throw her off. Google had said the introduction of a partner should be done gradually—not that I was any kind of a partner to Max. But I figured the concept was the same.

"I should probably get going. I don't want to push my luck and outstay my welcome with Ella. She's probably pretty accustomed to having one-on-one time with you."

"Oh. Okay."

"When can I see her again?"

"Friday is my last day of work. I have half days until then. So my schedule is pretty flexible."

"You're taking time off?"

"I'm leaving. I love working—the highs and lows of the market were an important part of who I am. But since my diagnosis, I've known I'd eventually leave to spend the last of my time with my daughter. I can feel the changes in me coming faster now. My strength is going, and simple things are getting more difficult."

The last of her time.

I felt a heaviness in my chest. My daughter would soon have no mother. Not to mention, as horrible as she was to me, Max was only thirty years old.

I nodded. "Okay."

"How about the day after tomorrow? Ella has a checkup at one, but we could get together afterward?"

"Can I come to the checkup?"

"Umm... Sure. Of course. Ella's going to have to get used to that anyway."

Ella ran out from the bathroom, and I suddenly pictured her bigger—maybe eight or nine years old. She wouldn't want a man at her checkups by then.

"Ella, Gray is going to leave. But we're going to see him again really soon."

"What day?"

The corners of my lips twitched. Even if she wasn't mine, I'd think this kid was pretty damn awesome.

I knelt to talk to her. "Friday. Can I guess what you'll be wearing?"

She grinned. "Fuchsia! Pink!".

I cupped her cheek with one hand, stroking her baby soft skin with my thumb. I'd done it without thinking, but it didn't scare her away. My daughter seemed comfortable with my touch. I wondered if that was a physiological thing. I'd be Googling that later for sure.

"I'll see you soon, sweetheart."

Without warning, she jumped into my arms and wrapped hers around my neck. I got choked up as she allowed me to engulf her in a tight embrace. When she was done, she hopped away, as carefree as before she'd given me the hug—blissfully unaware that she'd just rocked my entire fucking world.

Max smiled warmly. "I think this was a great visit."

I stood. "Me too. Take care of yourself, Max."

Chapter 30

Layla

I hadn't noticed the appointment on my calendar until after lunch.

"Hey, Peggy." I buzzed through the telephone intercom to my assistant. "Did you just add the appointment at four o'clock today?"

"I added it this morning. Mr. Westbrook called and asked if you could squeeze him in as the last appointment of the day. You were on the phone, so I didn't clear it with you. But nothing was on your calendar. Do you need me to change it?"

"No. It's fine. I just thought maybe I'd missed it there. Thank you."

Gray and I hadn't seen each other in a few days. He'd been spending time with his daughter, and I'd kept myself busy with what I did best—working fifteen hours a day. I missed him, but things were a lot more complicated than just having a boyfriend now.

A part of me had thought I could step back from where we were in our relationship, but the more we were apart, the more I realized there was no going back to casual and taking things slow—not that Gray and I had ever really done casual. We'd had that special connection from the very first time we'd met.

When we'd talked on the phone last night, he hadn't mentioned he needed to speak to me about work, so I took out my phone to text him and see if everything was okay. But as I did that, my office phone rang, and I was summoned to one of the partner's offices to discuss a new case. It was typical for associates to have to drop what they were doing and spend a few hours in a partner's office when they felt like it. They didn't exactly feel the need to schedule time when it might be convenient for everyone. Hence, the reason I'm on a first-name basis with the security guards who lock up the building. Whatever a partner needed just piled on top of whatever *I* needed to get done.

I didn't get back to my desk until just before four o'clock. I'd been fighting a futile attempt to not check the time every few minutes during my meeting. Peggy buzzed before I could even finish putting on a fresh coat of lipstick.

"Your four o'clock is here."

"You can send him in."

I stuffed my purse into my desk drawer and folded my hands on my lap, waiting for Gray. My heart sped up hearing his footsteps come down the hall. He definitely had a distinct stride—and he was walking at a fast, no-bullshit pace.

He came through my door with a cocky, devious smile. Stopping to look at me as he stepped into my office, he said not a word. I stayed quiet as well, but damn if my body didn't say a lot. My nipples pebbled, the hair on my arms stood up, and my pulse started to race. I shifted in my seat, and the light in Gray's eyes flared.

He closed the door behind him and very slowly clicked the lock shut.

When he turned back around, I raised a brow. "Is our business so sensitive that my door needs to be locked?"

Gray wore a dark, three-piece suit, the kind that fit him in all the right places and made his already confident persona shoot up tenfold. His tie was a beautiful blue color that would have normally reflected the color of his eyes, only they were darkening right in front of me.

"If it were up to me, I'd leave the door open while I make you come. In fact, I'd prefer if the office heard it. But I thought you'd rather have privacy."

God, he was so arrogant. And I loved it. I so, so loved it.

I folded my arms over my chest. "Pretty sure of yourself, aren't you?"

"That I can make you come? Absolutely."

"I wasn't referring to that. I was referring to the fact that you think I'd let you try, in the middle of the day, in my office."

He smirked. *That smirk.*

I braced as he walked toward me. Grabbing one arm of my high-back chair, he swung it around and then surprised me by lifting my ass out of it and up onto my desk. He raised a knee and used it to spread my legs, then pushed his hips between them as he pressed a kiss to my jaw. "I missed you."

His voice alone could make me wet. In fact, it might have. "Did you come to..." I trailed off as his mouth moved to my throat. "Did you come to see me about business?"

He kissed his way up to my ear. "I came to make you come."

One of his hands slipped between us and under my skirt—easy access. I felt my face heat as I let him rub up and down the silk of my panties. I should *not* be doing this. Yet I did nothing to stop it from happening.

"We shouldn't." A feeble attempt, at best.

Fingers slipped under the silk of my underwear. "Are you sure?" He found my clit and started to massage it. "You're already wet. I can make it quick."

Before I found words to respond, one finger slid inside of me.

My eyes shut, and I swallowed whatever answer I'd been about to give. I couldn't even remember what that was. He gently pumped in and out a few times, then pulled out and thrust back in with two fingers. I moaned, and he silenced me with a kiss.

"Shhh. I wanted to lick you first, but I don't want you to get in trouble. So we'll have to do it this way before I taste you so you're more relaxed."

His hand went to work. Curling his fingers inside me just right to rub that sensitive spot, he relentlessly pushed in and out. The man had magnificent fingers. Not three minutes ago, I'd been steadfast that we were playing a cat-and-mouse game, and I was never going to fool around with him in my office in the middle of the day. Now I was propped up on my desk, stretching the material of my skirt as I tried to open my legs wider, and shamelessly moaning into his mouth.

"That's it. Come for me, baby. I can't wait to lick you clean."

At that moment, I honestly didn't give a shit how reckless I was, the climb had begun, and all I could do was hang on and wait until I was on the other side. Gray's hand—the one that wasn't busy working miracles— threaded into my hair and tugged my head back so we were nose to nose. "I want to watch you come. Show me, beautiful. Show me."

His thumb pressed firmly onto my clit, and everything inside of me coiled. It felt like I might explode if I didn't release. Sensing my desperation, Gray thrust in and out harder and faster, pushing me over the edge. I gripped my desk for dear life and hung on as I rode the pulsating waves of pleasure. Gray's intense eyes watching me came in and out of focus as it crested. Our gazes locked; I couldn't have looked away if I'd wanted to.

On my way down, he tugged at the hem of my skirt and lifted my ass so he could push the fabric up to my waist. Still in a complete fog, I had no idea what he was doing—only that the exposed cheeks of my ass were now sitting on the cool top of my wooden desk. Gray dropped to his knees and began sucking on my swollen bud. My body roared back to life. I had been ready to snuggle and nap, but one lash of his tongue had me realizing the party was just getting started.

Giving in completely, I lay back on my desk and reveled in the feel of his tongue flicking and sucking, penetrating and promising. When my orgasm hit, I wasn't sure if it was a second one or if the first had just ebbed until it had enough strength to form the next big wave.

Gray didn't stop until I was boneless. Spent, I looked up at the ceiling, catching my breath as he slipped off my panties and righted my skirt. Then he scooped me up into his arms, took a seat in my chair, and plopped me onto his lap. My head was spinning.

Gray kissed my forehead. "This has been a productive meeting. You're very efficient. I'm glad I stopped by."

"I'd say something witty, but I don't think my brain is functioning yet."

He chuckled. "That's good. Because I figured it's been working overtime and needed the break."

I leaned my head against his chest. "I have been working a lot."

"I was referring to your brain overthinking everything when it came to us."

"Oh."

A few minutes later, Gray said, "I hate to eat and run, but I actually do have an appointment with an attorney across town in a half hour—the attorney for the company we're investing in. Apparently he's an old friend of my father's."

"I'm glad you said *old* and *he*...considering how you just treated this attorney when you waltzed into her office."

Gray lifted me from his lap and settled my ass back on my chair. His kissed my lips. "I'm seeing Ella tomorrow afternoon. Picking her up at noon and taking her out for the first time alone. I'd love you to come with me?"

"I don't know, Gray. Maybe you should do that on your own if it's the first time."

He searched my eyes. "I want you to get to know her."

"I'm...I will. I'm just...not yet."

He nodded and forced a smile, but I knew I'd hurt him. "Okay. Dinner tomorrow night, then?"

"Sounds good."

Guilt had kept me tossing and turning all night. Saturday morning I'd gotten up extra early to work from home, but I couldn't concentrate. The memory of Gray's smile when he'd asked me to spend the afternoon with his daughter—and the way I'd made it fall when I told him I wasn't ready for that—was haunting me.

I tossed the pen on the dining room table and sat back in my chair. It's an afternoon with a little girl? I spent time with Quinn's daughter, Harper, all the time. Why was I making such a big deal out of it?

Because I never wondered if Quinn was going to be in my life forever, that's why. Growing up the way I did, I'd learned that kids need consistency. Popping in and out of their lives sends a message that you can't undo with words—*you aren't my priority*. So I hesitated to take that step now.

But what if I took a child out of the picture? I was crazy about Gray in a way that I'd never experienced with a man. Something inside of me just knew what we had was something special—and that scared the living crap out of me. So, was it Gray who was moving too fast? Was it getting to know Ella and both of us growing attached? Or was I just avoiding jumping in with both feet, even though I had no doubts about the way I felt, because I was afraid to get hurt again?

Damn it.

I'm such an idiot.

I picked up my phone to call Gray and realized it was already eleven thirty.

While it rang, I ran into my bedroom and stole a glance in the mirror.

Pretty scary.

He answered as I pulled the tie from my hair with my cell cradled between my shoulder and ear.

"Hey, beautiful." He sounded genuinely happy to hear my voice. It confirmed I'd finally made the right decision.

"Are you on your way to Ella's?"

"I am."

"If the invitation is still open, I'd like to come."

"Are you sure?"

"I'm sure."

"Well, I'd love that. We just crossed the bridge to Brooklyn, but I can turn around."

"No, that's okay." I hopped on one foot while taking off my sweatpants. "I'll meet you there. It'll be quicker. I'll just grab a cab. I don't want you to be late."

"We can turn around and get you. It won't make me that late."

"No, Ella is expecting you. Text me the address. I'll meet you there as quick as I can."

He laughed. "Okay, crazy girl. Whatever you say."

***

My cab pulled up in front of Max's house at eight minutes after twelve. Gray exited his usual town car as I jumped out. I must've looked frantic.

"I'm sorry I'm late."

"Don't be." He cupped my cheeks. "I'm just glad you decided to come."

I exhaled and held his wrists. "Me too."

He leaned in and placed a soft kiss on my lips. "It means a lot to me."

I knew it did. "We're late."

"Max kept me waiting around for three full years. I think she can handle a few minutes delay."

I smiled. "That's true."

Gray held out his hand to me, and I put mine in his to walk to the door. "This is a really nice neighborhood. I love old brownstones."

"She bought it with the money she stole from me."

"Shit. That sucks. Sorry."

Gray rang the bell, and a minute later, Max opened the door. Her smile faded as soon as she saw he wasn't alone. I wasn't sure what she had against me, but clearly she wasn't happy I'd come along.

"I didn't realize you'd be bringing someone for your visit with Ella."

"Not someone," he said with a stern tone. "*Layla*. I'm sure you remember her from when you sandbagged her in her office."

Max forced a smile and pulled her cardigan sweater closed. "Come on in. Ella is washing up."

Luckily, we didn't have to stand around and make nice. Ella came flying down the hall wearing an enormous smile. "Gray!"

She stopped in front of him and signed something.

Her excitement must've been contagious—I found myself smiling as wide as she was, even though I had no idea what the heck was going on.

Gray shocked me by signing something back. His performance earned a clap and squeal from Ella. "You 'membered!"

Her mother corrected her. "It's *re*membered, Ella."

Gray turned to me. "It's Saturday." He pulled on the material of his pale green polo and then began to sign. "Saturday. Sage."

It hit me that the two of them were wearing the same shade of sage green. Ella had on a light green T-shirt.

I wrinkled my brow with a curious smile. "I didn't realize the days of the week were color-coded."

Ella tugged at Gray's shirt and asked him to help her get her new stroller from the closet, which left me standing alone with Max.

She didn't even pretend to smile. Instead, she started right in. "It'll be a lot to handle soon, stepping into the shoes of a dead woman whose child is devastated."

My mouth opened and stayed that way. I'd been expecting her to be a bitch, but *Jesus*...really? What the hell did I say to that? I stayed quiet because she'd rendered me speechless, not out of respect to her.

She figured she'd continue since I was, apparently, all ears. "She needs to bond with her father. Don't interrupt that to play house. If you're not going to be a mother to her, let them be. A loss from a breakup is no less than a loss from a death to a child. You'll devastate her when you decide to walk away."

Gray and Ella walked back, smiling. He took one look at me, and his smile faded. "Everything okay?"

Max answered. "We were just discussing my prognosis."

276

Gray's face turned solemn, and he nodded like he understood. "Oh." He rubbed my arm. "You ready to go, babe?"

I nodded.

Outside, I stood back and watched as Gray strapped Ella into a car seat in the back of the car and loaded the pink stroller into the trunk. When the three of us were alone in the backseat, Ella said something I didn't hear, and Gray threw his head back in laughter. The two of them had definitely connected on some level already. Suddenly I felt like a third wheel and thought maybe it hadn't been such a great idea to come.

I'd been lost in thought and heard Gray's voice, yet the words he'd said were out of reach.

He squeezed my hand. "You okay? You seem like you're somewhere else."

I looked out the window and noticed we were already going back over the bridge to Manhattan. The first ten minutes of the drive were gone. "Yeah. I'm fine. Sorry. Where are we going, anyway?"

"I thought we'd get out at 72nd Street and walk over to Conservatory Water."

"That's the place where they race the model—"

Gray shushed me and winked. "It's a surprise for her."

I smiled. "I guess I need to get used to spelling things."

Ella had been swinging her legs and looking out the window as we crossed the bridge. But she heard the word *spell*.

"I can spell my name!" She signed as she called out the letters. "E-L-L-A."

Gray beamed. "I'm not sure learning Hindu to converse in private would matter. She'd pick it up faster than we could. Smart as a whip."

Ella pointed to her head. "Daddy gave me my brain."

My eyes grew wide. Gray lowered his voice and whispered to me. "It's not what you think. I'll explain later."

Traffic was light, so we breezed over to the park. Again I watched the interaction between Gray and Ella, fascinated by how at ease he seemed to be with his little girl already. Once he unloaded the pink stroller with pedals from the car and strapped Ella in, he told Al to meet us back at this spot in two hours.

Ella watched everything going on around us as we walked toward the water, which gave Gray and me a chance to talk.

"She's obsessed with the E.B White *Stuart Little* book and movie," he said. "Her mother mentioned some of her favorite things in the letter she wrote me. So I watched it the other night to have something to talk to her about, and I realized that a big part of the movie takes place in this park at the Conservatory Water—the place where everyone sails the remote-control sailboats. Max said she's never been here, so I thought she might recognize it from the story."

I smiled. "That's really sweet. I bet she's going to love it."

No sooner than the words left my mouth, Ella validated my thought. She shrieked and pointed toward the lake filled with boats as it came into view when we turned the corner.

"Stuart, Stuart!" she yelled.

It reminded me of the kind of thing my dad would have done when I was growing up—on days he was my dad and not someone else's.

For the next hour, Ella stayed glued to her seat, watching the hundreds of motorized sailboats floating around. Even though Gray had been clear that Stuart Little wasn't really on any of them, I was pretty sure she was checking for herself. At one point, she climbed onto Gray's lap and made herself comfortable. The look on his face was priceless. Happiness radiated from him.

After we had lunch, Gray suggested we get some ice cream, so we all walked over to a stand and then sat on the park bench.

Ella licked her cone and turned to speak to me. "Did you know my mom has cancer?"

I coughed my ice cream down the wrong pipe.

Gray made sure I was okay and then took over the conversation.

"Yes. We know about that."

Ella licked her ice cream and pondered for a while. "She's going to die."

This time it was Gray who choked. I walked to the ice cream cart and grabbed us three bottles of water. Gray chugged half a bottle, and his voice still croaked when he spoke. "That happens sometimes when people are sick, sweetheart. Unfortunately."

"Are you going to die?"

God, this is the most bizarre conversation. And I was glad as hell that Gray had jumped in to tackle it.

"Not for a very long time, I hope." Gray pulled her ponytail. "I haven't even gotten all of my colors for each day of the week down yet. So I hope I have a long time to go."

She laughed and went back to her ice cream. To Ella, the conversation could have been about the weather. Yet Gray looked like he needed a drink, and I thought I needed more than one.

The sun had started to set as we pulled onto the side streets that led to Ella's house. She'd fallen asleep in the car, and I'd rested my head on Gray's shoulder and closed my own eyes. The entire day had been pretty surreal. As terrified as I'd been before coming today, watching Gray with his daughter—getting to spend time with the two of them—had actually alleviated some of my concerns.

In my mind, I could see the three of us together. While that still terrified me, I could visualize moving past it as time went on. That was all I needed—to get on a path that could get me there.

"You look tired." Gray brushed hair from my face as we pulled to the curb in front of Max and Ella's brownstone.

"What gave you that idea? The fact that my arms are limp by my sides, and I drooled on your shoulder on the way here?"

Gray side-glanced at Ella, who was still sound asleep. "Why don't you stay in the car and relax while I carry her in." He leaned closer so our lips were touching, and I could feel them move while he spoke. "You're going to need your energy for when I get you home."

Chapter 31

Gray

I took my time walking to the door.

Ella's sweet little breaths blew on my cheek with each exhale as her head rested on my shoulder. A few weeks ago, I never would've thought this would be my life. If anyone had told me I'd be stalling before I rang the bell to return my daughter to her dying mother, I'd have told them they were fucking nuts.

And the nuts part wouldn't have been that I had a daughter; it would have been that I could fall so hard and so fast for a child I hadn't even known existed not too long ago.

But Ella was special. Smart, funny, with a zest for life that I'd forgotten existed, not to mention—I looked over at her sleeping face—adorable, even when she was drooling on my shirt. I was still terrified, and a part of me couldn't yet fully comprehend the enormity of what would be happening sometime in the near future, but I wanted it. I wanted to take care of this little girl, protect her from all the evils in the world, and be a father who was there for her. They say children learn from watching their parents, not by what parents say in words. Well, the same holds true for children who didn't have the best role models. I'd learned from my father what *not* to do.

I'm a firm believer that everything happens for a reason. If I'd found out I was having a child three years ago, when my work was the most important thing in my life, I might've followed in dear old Dad's footsteps, letting everyone else raise my kid and focusing on money and power. But the years of nothing to do but think had given me direction. Ella's needs would come first...no matter what. So would Layla's.

I rang the bell and waited to return my sleeping beauty. After a few minutes, I rang it a second time. Still no response, so I began to dig into my pocket for my phone when the door finally opened. Max looked like shit compared to this morning. And this morning she'd looked pretty damn awful.

"What's going on? You okay?"

She had a blanket wrapped around her. "Yeah. I'm just cold. I fell asleep on the couch."

I squinted. "It's eighty-something degrees out. Do you have the air on too high?"

"No. It's a side effect from some of my medicines. Cold and sleepy."

I reached out and felt her head. She wasn't warm.

Max attempted a smile, but it looked like she didn't have the energy. She stepped aside for me to come in. "How long has she been sleeping?"

"Maybe a half hour. She conked out on the drive home."

"Would you mind putting her in her room?"

"Sure."

I walked my princess to her room and laid her down on the bed. She stirred, but rolled on her side and never opened her eyes. Tucking her in, I kissed her forehead before backing out of her room, trying not to make a sound.

Giving a shit about Max's well being caused me to have mixed emotions. I wanted to walk right past where she sat in the living room—giving the same fucks she'd given about me as I'd rotted in prison for three years. But I was human. Not to mention, she took care of my daughter. So I needed to make sure she was capable of doing that.

"You going to be okay?" I stood in the archway between the hall and living room.

Before she could answer, a teakettle whistled.

"I don't want that to wake up Ella." She stood and walked into the kitchen.

I followed. "Do you have anyone who helps you? Checks in on you?"

She took the kettle from the heat and moved it to a different burner. "I don't have many bridges that I haven't burned. I have Paula, who works for me. She takes care of Ella while I work."

I knew Max was an only child like me; she and her mother weren't close. As far as I remembered, she had an aunt in Connecticut she got along with pretty well. What was her name? Betty, Betsy... Her last name was Potter, and I remembered it was close to those children's books about rabbits. *Beatrix.* That's it. "What about Beatrice?"

"She died last year. Stroke." Max opened a cabinet and reached up for a mug. "Would you like some tea?"

"I'm sorry to hear that. No tea. Thanks."

She poured a mug full of hot water and dipped a tea bag in. Turning around she said, "I'll be fine. I can handle her still, if that's what you're worried about."

"I can take her for the night if it's too much."

"No." She shook her head and looked down. "I'll know when it's too much. I won't put her at risk, even though I do want to spend as much time as I can with her."

I nodded.

Max let out a big sigh. "I need to say something you might not like."

What exactly did she think had come out of her mouth in recent years that I *did* like? The lies, the manipulation? I bit my tongue.

"What's on your mind, Max?"

"I'm concerned about Layla."

"What about her?" I snapped.

"Ella is going to lose her mother. That's going to devastate her. But there's nothing either one of us can do about that."

"Understood. But what's that got to do with Layla?"

"Ella will grow attached to her. She'll seek out another woman. It's natural. She will want a mother figure."

I clenched my jaw. "And?"

"And when Layla walks away, it will be no different than a death in Ella's mind—another loss when she's already so vulnerable."

"You sound pretty fucking sure she's walking away."

"You're a hard man to walk away from, Gray. But she's not ready for a family yet."

"You spent, what, a half hour in her office a few weeks ago? Pretending to be a client when you really just wanted to stick your fucking nose into my business? And you know all this about her?"

"We spent a few minutes together today talking. I watched her with you and Ella."

I shook my head. "You're fucking unbelievable."

"You see what you want to see in women, Gray. Always have. I guess it has something to do with your kind mother and losing her at such a tender age."

"What are you, Sigmund Fucking Freud? You have no idea what you're talking about."

And what the hell was I still doing standing here? I turned around and started to walk toward the door, never looking back as I spoke. "I'll be here Sunday at noon to pick up Ella."

Layla had been quiet the entire ride back to Manhattan. I hadn't noticed for three quarters of it because I was still steaming from my little conversation with Max. That woman had balls to try to tell me about my love life. I'd decided to keep her thoughts to myself, rather than unload them on Layla. There was no point in making the strain between her and Max worse.

"You're quiet." I laced my fingers with hers as we exited the bridge. "Everything okay?"

She smiled, but it didn't reach her beautiful eyes. "Yeah. Just tired."

"Are you still up for going out to dinner?"

"I'd actually rather stay in, if you don't mind."

I lifted her hand to my mouth and kissed it. "Whatever you prefer. While I love the idea of showing you off in a sexy dress, I'm a big proponent of naked Chinese, too."

I wasn't even sure if she'd heard me. Layla seemed off in another place. She looked out the window and then turned to me. "Ella is amazing."

I smiled wide enough for both of us. "Am I a conceited bastard if I say I agree?"

She genuinely smiled this time. "Not at all."

We pulled up outside of her apartment building, and I jogged around to her side of the car to open the door. Then I told my driver to take the rest of the night off.

Helping Layla from the car, I explained. "I don't plan on leaving tonight, unless you kick me out. And if that happens, I can take a cab."

Once we were upstairs, Layla disappeared into the bathroom, and I opened a bottle of wine and poured two glasses. Something about the way she was acting still seemed off to me, but I thought perhaps I was over-examining everything at this point because of the shit Max had planted in my head. That woman was pure fucking evil.

I handed Layla a glass of wine when she came back to the kitchen. "Are you hungry? You didn't eat much of anything this afternoon except that ice cream. Why don't I order us something?"

She sipped. "Sure. That sounds good."

"What are you in the mood for?"

"Whatever. You can pick."

I took her wine glass from her hand and set it down on the kitchen counter, along with mine. Wrapping my arms around her waist, I pulled her against me. "If you're allowing me to pick whatever I'm in the mood for, you might go hungry."

I brushed her hair back from her face and waited until our eyes met. "Thank you for today. It meant a lot to me to get to spend time with my two girls together. But I'll admit, as much as I enjoyed it and wouldn't trade it for the world, I'm glad I have you all to myself right now."

"It won't be that way when...I mean, it won't be that way when Ella is living with you."

"I'll have to soundproof the bedroom walls." When she didn't smile, I pulled back in order to examine her expressions better. "Talk to me. What's bothering you?"

"Nothing." She shook her head. "I don't know. I just got my period, so I'm feeling a little moody, I guess. Plus, I'm tired. My iron is probably a little low."

I wanted to believe it was nothing, so I didn't push. After our wine, Layla took a shower and left me to pick out something to order for dinner. She'd directed me to the menu stack in her desk drawer and told me to be careful because the drawer was sometimes wobbly.

Wobbly was an understatement. I pulled out the drawer, and the entire thing derailed from the track. The wooden bottom popped out, and the contents dumped all over the floor. At least twenty pounds of crap had been crammed into a drawer only meant to hold a few hanging files. I laughed and went to the kitchen to search for a screwdriver and some pliers.

The fix was simple. Two screws had come loose that held in the bottom panel, and the drawer had been "wobbly" because one of the wheels that was supposed to roll along the track had come off. I put it all back together and started to pile the shit she had stored inside back in. There were some papers, manila folders, and a stack of notebooks. The top notebook had toppled off the stack and flipped over, landing with the back page open. Thinking nothing of it, I went to grab it, but one of the sentences on the page caught my attention.

He lies.

What the fuck was this now?

I should have just closed the notebook and kept my nose out of Layla's business. But I couldn't shut it after seeing the word *He*. I'm a man—a possessive and jealous one, no less. So, like an asshole, I kept reading.

He's not dependable.

My heart sank. *Fuck.*

I'd landed right on one of her pros and cons lists. That had to be what all of the notebooks were. This one was right at the top, and the last damn page. It had to be recent.

I reasoned with myself. *It's probably about something else. I'm jumping to conclusions.*

I'll never be his priority.

My hope dwindled as I continued.

I'll get hurt again.

Fuck.

Any hope that the list wasn't about me went out the window when I read the last two.

Never really wanted kids.

I deserve more.

Fuck. I stared at the paper and reread the last part again.

I deserve more.

She did. Layla deserved more than an ex-con with an ex-wife who'd just sprung a kid on him.

I looked once more at the list, and it hit me that it was the last page of a notebook, and everything had been written on the right side of the page. There was a line drawn down the middle, but the entire left side was empty.

No pros.

Being a glutton for punishment, I turned the page to look at the other side and saw the headings. Pros at the top of the left, cons at the top of the right. Only on this side of the page, the con side wasn't half full—it was filled to the fucking brim. And the pro side wasn't empty either. There was one entry on the right.

I love him, even though I don't want to.

"Gray?" Layla's voice called from her bedroom.

I hadn't even noticed the water had shut off. I fumbled to shut the book and stick it back in the drawer.

I shut my eyes. "Yeah?"

"Did you order yet?"

"No."

"What about sushi? Umi delivers pretty fast, and they have the best tuna sashimi. I don't think I have the menu, but they have all the standard stuff."

"Sure. That's fine."

I got up from where I'd been sitting to fix the drawer and snoop, wanting to give some thought to how to handle what I'd read before talking to Layla about it. The bottle of wine I'd opened was still on the counter, but I bypassed it and went to the few bottles of liquor I knew she kept in her closet. Pouring a double shot of Jack from a dusty bottle, I sucked it back in one gulp. It tasted like shit, but the burn felt good going down.

I had another and poured a glass of wine before Layla walked out of the bedroom. She flipped on the kitchen light.

"You're just standing here in the dark?"

I hadn't noticed the sun had gone down, taking away all the illumination from the window. It must've been pretty damn dark.

"Lost in thought, I guess."

Layla tilted her head. "Anything you want to talk about?"

"No. How about you?"

Her eyes looked away. "No. Just a big day for both of us, I guess."

I nodded.

She played with her phone and then walked to stand beside me. "I found the menu online."

Her hair was wet and her face free of makeup. I looked over at her while she scrolled through and read the menu. The freckles I loved so much were more pronounced from this angle. I wanted to memorize the pattern for some reason.

"Here." She passed me her phone. "I'm going to get the seared ahi tuna. If you like the Amazing roll, I'll split that with you, too."

My eyes could barely focus on the menu on her phone. They just kept wandering over to study her freckles. I couldn't ever pinpoint what it was that I loved about them, but looking at her right now, I decided it might've been their girlish quality, which contradicted the strong woman. Layla hid them like she didn't want anyone to see anything but the strength in her.

God, she's so fucking beautiful. So real, so intelligent, so...everything.

"What do you think?" she said. "Do you like the stuff in the Amazing roll?"

I hadn't read a word of the menu. "Yeah. That sounds good. I'll just get what you're having." I hit the telephone number on the screen of her phone and dug my wallet out of my pocket.

"Can I place an order for delivery?"

The woman asked what I wanted. But I'd already forgotten.

I covered the phone. "What did you want again?"

Layla's face crinkled. "Seared ahi and the Amazing roll. I thought you wanted the same thing?"

"Yeah. That's right."

The rest of the night didn't go much differently than my attempt at ordering. I couldn't keep up with our conversation or even my own train of thought. The damn pros and cons list kept coming back to haunt me, as did Max's words.

I just wanted to grab Layla and hold her, tell her that her list was wrong. But the more I thought about her list, the more I realized it wasn't so far off.

He lies.

There was no denying I'd fucked up with her by not telling her about Max right away. Trust took a long time to build and two seconds to tear down. I'd thought we were making progress, but...

"You see what you want to see in women, Gray." That's what Max had said.

I'll never be his priority.

While I'd like to think that she and Ella would be my top priorities, who was I kidding? Soon enough, I'd be a single dad to a devastated little girl. What would be my priority—taking Layla to dinner or staying home with my daughter?

Never really wanted kids.

We'd never even discussed a family. Stupidly, I'd assumed she wanted kids. But where was the basis for that assumption? She lacked respect for her own mother and father and the situation they'd raised her in.

"You see what you want to see in women, Gray."

Shut the fuck up, Max.

I deserve more.

I couldn't argue with that one. Layla deserved the world at her feet.

Oddly, the one that hurt the most wasn't even a con. It was the only thing she could come up with as a pro.

I love him, even though I don't want to.

By the time Layla and I were ready to turn in, I'd had too much to drink and wanted to sleep just so I could pretend tonight never happened. Slipping into bed behind her, I wrapped my entire body around hers. My arms clutched tight around her waist, while my body curved to envelop hers. It couldn't have been too comfortable for her, but I needed it.

I really fucking needed it.

Pressing my lips to her shoulder, I wanted to tell her everything she was concerned about was going to be fine. But I couldn't be that selfish.

Instead, I whispered. "I want you to be happy more than anything."

She turned in bed to face me. It was dark, but I could see her face.

"Gray...I—"

A cell phone ringing cut her off. It took a moment to realize it was coming from the end table on my side. My first reaction was to ignore it, let it go to voicemail. But then I remembered I had a daughter now.

Reaching over and grabbing the phone, I tensed at seeing Max's name on the screen. It was eleven o'clock at night. I sat up as I swiped to answer.

"What's up?"

Her voice was shaky. "I just called an ambulance. I'm having a lot of trouble breathing."

Chapter 32

Gray

"It's okay, sweetheart. Shhh..." I stroked Ella's hair and swayed back and forth with her until her cries began to slow. The front of her hair was soaked with the tears she'd shed. It killed me to see her so upset. And I didn't like having her in a germ-infested hospital waiting room while doctors finished with Max's tests. But what choice did I have at one in the morning?

Layla had come with me, even though I'd told her it wasn't necessary. Looking at her face, I wished I'd tried a little harder to get her to stay. She looked freaked out, and I couldn't blame her. I was fucking freaked out, too.

When we'd arrived at the Emergency Room, the ambulance had already brought Max in, and a woman from Social Services was sitting with Ella. Max had stopped breathing twice in the ambulance on the way over—completely flatlined. They were able to revive her, but the reality of the situation smacked me right in the face. *This is really happening.* Maybe not today, maybe not tomorrow. But soon enough. And I wasn't ready for it. Neither was the poor little girl in my arms.

"Mr. Westbrook?" a doctor in blue scrubs called from the doorway of the waiting room.

"That's me." I walked over, and Layla stood and joined me.

"I'm Dr. Cohen, one of the oncology surgeons on staff here. Your wife is stabilized now. We've inserted a tube down her throat to help her breathe. One of her tumors is located near the esophagus, which caused some food particles to get stuck. Over time they've built up and caused swelling, which further compromised her air passage."

"So she's going to be fine?"

The doctor frowned. "For today. We're hoping now that the passage has been cleared, her swelling will go down, and the tube can come out in a day or two. But I must make you aware that it's just a Band-Aid, Mr. Westbrook." His eyes drifted to Ella in my arms.

Her eyes were wide open, but she was just staring into space without blinking. I wasn't sure if she was listening, much less comprehending what we were talking about, but he obviously wanted to be frank and felt he couldn't.

I flashed my eyes to the doctor, then Ella, then back to him, acknowledging that we'd do our best to speak in code. "Can the blockage be cleared permanently?"

"She has an advanced directive. The typical methods we might try are not available to us."

Translation—Max had legally called it quits.

"Okay."

"We have had some success with PDT—photodynamic therapy. A light-activated drug is injected, which collects more cancer cells than normal ones. Then a scope is put down the throat and into the lungs, and a laser light kills the cells we've collected. A few days later, we go back in and collect those dead cells. It's an option, but as of now, not one we have consent for. Perhaps you can talk to her about it once she's off the ventilator. For now, we'll need to take it one day at a time. As I said, your wife is stable, so you should probably go home and get some rest. She has some personal belongings with her that you can take or have locked in the hospital safe before you go."

"Max is my *ex*-wife. But thank you for everything, Doctor."

After he left, Layla looked down at Ella in my arms. "She fell asleep during that."

"Oh good."

Layla kept staring at Ella while shaking her head. "I knew it would be tough on her. But seeing her today..." She paused. "She's going to be devastated. You're going to become her world, Gray."

The contents of that damn notebook flashed back to me.

Never really wanted kids.

I'll never be his priority.

I looked down. "I know."

I checked in on Max one more time and picked up the few personal items she had with her—house keys, a small wallet, and a necklace they had taken off of her neck. After the last few weeks, I didn't think anything could shock me anymore. But holding what Max wore around her neck left me speechless once again. *Her wedding band.* We'd bought matching ones from the guy who'd married us down in the DR.

After, we hailed a cab, and I managed to climb in without waking Ella. All three of us were quiet as we pulled away from the curb. The weight of everything was too much to fight my way through for any type of meaningful discussion.

"I'm thinking I should take her to her house to sleep. She's never been to my place, and it might help if she wakes up in her own room. Max's house keys were in the envelope with her other belongings."

"Oh. Yeah. That's a good idea."

The last thing I wanted to do was separate from Layla. I could feel the distance between us in the backseat of the cab, even. Physical separation would only make it worse—give her time to think about how fucked up her life would soon be if she stuck with me. But asking her to sleep at my ex-wife's house was a lot.

I treaded lightly. "Should we drop you off?"

"Yeah. Thanks."

The quiet stretched the rest of the drive to Layla's. Her hand was on the door handle before we even pulled to the curb.

"I have a meeting tomorrow in Connecticut. But let me know how things are."

"Will do."

She leaned over and kissed me on the cheek. It wasn't like I could move with a tiny human wrapped around me. "Goodnight."

Layla was halfway out the door when I started to panic. "Layla, wait…"

Turning back, she looked at me. If I'd had any doubt that I loved her before, I was damn certain in this moment. For some reason, it felt like I shouldn't let her get out of the car.

Remind her you love her.

Remind her you love her, you pussy.

"I...I...Thanks for today. And tonight. I appreciate you sticking around with me at the hospital."

She smiled sadly. "Of course."

"Good night, Freckles. Flick the bedroom light on so I know you're in okay."

I made the driver stick around until the light turned on, and then I did something I never dreamed I'd be doing.

I took my daughter home to sleep in my ex-wife's house that she'd bought with money she stole from me.

"Can I help you?" I'd run to the front door without a shirt on when the bell rang, not wanting it to wake Ella. Actually, *terrified* that it would. Whatever. Semantics.

"I'm Paula."

"Can I help you, Paula?"

"I take care of Ella."

I'd completely forgotten that Max said she had a nanny for the mornings when she worked.

"Nice to meet you. I'm Gray."

Paula's face dropped. "*Oh.* Is everything okay with Max?"

"Why don't you come in?"

I grabbed my T-shirt from the living room and threw it on, then spent ten minutes bringing Paula up to speed on Max's current health. Apparently, Max had filled Paula in on the situation with me already. She knew I was Ella's father and that Max had kept it from me. I wasn't sure how much further Max had gone into our history.

"So you watch Ella in the mornings? Even now that Max isn't working anymore?"

"I was watching her from seven until noon, but Max asked me to start staying until five last week. Afternoons get tough for her now."

I nodded. "Can you keep that schedule for me? I think it would do Ella a lot of good to have as much of her routine unchanged as possible while Max is in the hospital. That's why I stayed here last night with her."

"Of course. Max and I have already talked about me staying on…after…" Her face fell, and then she thought of something that sent the corners of her lips toward a smile. "I've been with Ella and Max since Ella was born. She jokes that I'll be left to you in her will."

It was a giant damn relief to know I had some help—at least until I figured things out. When Ella woke up and raced into Paula's arms, my neck unknotted for the first time in two days.

I rubbed the back of it and watched the two of them interact. It took a minute or two for Ella to even notice someone else was in the room. She crinkled up her little nose at me, but smiled. "Did you have a sleepover?"

"We did." I tapped a finger to her nose. "But you fell asleep for it."

She giggled. "Is Mommy still in the hospital?"

"She is, sweetheart."

"Is she getting fixed?"

My eyes flashed to Paula. "Yeah. She's getting fixed."

"Are you going to stay with me until Mommy comes home?"

"I was planning on it. I thought maybe you could come stay at my house one night." I leaned forward and whispered in her ear. "I have a dog."

Her eyes widened. "Can we go now? Can we go now? Please?"

"I need to do a few things. But we can go later. How does that sound?"

Paula took Ella into the kitchen to help her make breakfast, and I used the time to rearrange some meetings I had scheduled for the day. When I went to check on how things were going, Paula offered me coffee.

The two of us spoke quietly on the side while Ella was busy stirring the pancake batter.

"Max has had a few overnight stays in the last year. She doesn't usually let Ella visit her. She thought it was too hard to see her with all the needles and monitors attached. Of course, I'm not telling you what to do. But I figured you might want to know what Ella expects."

"Wow. Okay. That's great. Thank you. She took it pretty hard at the hospital last night. I assumed I should bring her up to visit today. But I *was* worried it would be tough again for her. Max is intubated." I looked over at Ella and sipped my coffee. "She seems a lot better this morning, but I'm probably better off not bringing her then."

"I'm here all day. You can just go about your regular day, if you'd like. If you stop up to see Max, please give her my best."

Breakfast with Paula and Ella set my mind even more at ease. They had a routine that included Ella standing on a stool and rinsing the plates. I could tell she was crazy about Paula. When the appointment I'd called earlier to cancel called me back, I decided to push it a little later in the afternoon rather than cancel it all together. Ella had her schedule, and I was going to need to learn how to balance shit at some point anyway. Plus, the hospital was near the appointment, so I could check on things with Max beforehand.

———

That night, I poured a glass of scotch and leaned back into the couch. Ella had finally fallen asleep, and I was wiped out. Single parenting was definitely not an easy fucking job.

I'd had two meetings today, stopped into my office to do a few hours of paperwork, visited Max and talked to her doctors, gone back to Brooklyn to pack up Ella's stuff and bring her to my place, then cooked us some dinner and played with her and Freckles until she started yawning.

At that point, my dog and his trusty shoe had abandoned me. I couldn't get him to leave the foot of the bed in the guest room where Ella was staying. Couldn't blame him, I guess. Lately he'd spent more time with the kid downstairs I'd hired to walk him than he spent with me. Plus, Ella was a hell of a lot more excited to roll around on the floor and let him lick her face than I felt by eight thirty.

I took a few gulps from my glass and picked up my cell. Layla and I had exchanged a few texts during the day, but I needed to hear her voice.

She answered on the third ring. "Hey. Can you give me just a second? I have someone in my office."

I looked at my watch. Nine o'clock. "You're still at work?"

"Yep. Give me a minute. I'll be right back."

I heard voices through the muffled receiver, and right before she came back on the line, she must've uncovered it, because I heard a woman's voice say, "If you change your mind, you know where we'll be."

"Thanks, Maryanne."

She came back on the line. "Sorry. Some of the associates are going out for drinks, and a friend of mine was trying to drag me along."

It reminded me yet again how different her life would be with me now. Even though I hated the thought of her beautiful ass sitting without me in a bar, I couldn't be a dick.

"Why don't you go? Whatever you haven't gotten done at the office by now can wait until tomorrow."

She sighed. "I suppose. But I'm tired, too. I was actually looking forward to going home and taking a bath. I didn't sleep so well when I got home last night, so I came into the office at the crack of dawn to catch up."

Another thing that was my fault. The life of a single parent was basically non-existent. Someone dating that person didn't get the wining and dining they deserved. And that was best-case scenario.

"Sorry," I said. "How was your day otherwise?"

"Not bad. How's everything going over there? Did Ella like Freckles?"

I closed my eyes, rested my head back against the couch, and propped my feet up on the coffee table. "The traitor is sleeping at the foot of her bed right now."

"Well, I'm sure she's more fun than you for him anyway, old man."

"Go easy on the old man. I'm only a few years older than you."

"Do you have your feet up on the coffee table and a drink in your hand at nine o'clock on a weeknight right now?"

I smiled. "Wise ass."

Toward the end of our call, I said, "I miss you. It's a fucked-up situation I'm in right now. I'm sorry I'm not able to take you to a nice dinner after work. Or sit behind you in the bath after a long day. You have no idea what I'd give for that."

Layla was quiet. "I know. I understand. You have to do what you need to do, Gray. You have a little girl now. When you love someone, you put their needs first, before your own. That's just how it is. Looking back, I think that's why I never forgave my dad when I got older. He didn't put what was best for us first, what was best for my mother. He put himself first. And I never got past that. You're going to be a great dad. I already know it."

After I hung up, I finished my drink and stared up at the ceiling for a long time. Layla was right. When you love someone, you put their needs first. It was cliché as fuck, but sometimes that meant letting them go. I think I'd known for a while what I needed to do; I just didn't want to admit it.

Admitting it meant I'd have to act on it. And acting on it was going to fucking kill me. But what else did I need thrown in my face to tell me I'd be doing the right thing?

The list I'd found—

Never wanted children.

I'll never be his priority.

Max's comments—

"She's not ready for a family yet."

"You see what you want to see in women, Gray."

Layla's own words—

"When you love someone, you put their needs first, before your own."

"That's why I never forgave my dad..."

Chapter 33

Gray

I stood in front of Layla's building and stared up at her bedroom window. The light was on, and I'd seen her shadow pass by a little while ago, so I knew she was home. I just didn't have the balls to go in yet.

Layla had no idea I was coming. I'd spent the last forty-eight hours thinking of what I would say to her. If I told her I'd read her list and wanted to put her needs first, it would only make her feel bad. I knew her—she'd feel guilty that she wasn't there to support me when I needed her. It was just the type of woman she was.

And I wasn't strong enough to fight her if she said she wanted to stick it out. Because I wanted nothing more in this world than to fight tooth and nail for us.

So, I decided to absolve her of any guilt and let her think it's what I really wanted. It would break my vow never to lie to her again, but she'd already wasted enough time on me—more than a year of Saturday trips, not moving on for a long time after she'd stopped visiting, and then the last few months. It wouldn't be fair to keep her any more. Quick and over—that's what it had to be. *She'll probably be pissed.* But it's easier to move on when you're angry than when you have guilt over wanting different things than someone you care about.

I took a last look up at the window, tucked my own heart away, and headed for the door. I rang the buzzer and started to sweat, waiting for her to answer.

"Hello?"

"Hey. It's me. Sorry I didn't call first."

"Hey. That's okay. Come on up." The door buzzed, and the deadbolt unlocked.

I thought about changing my mind ten fucking times on the short elevator ride up. And then I hesitated before I stepped off.

Layla was waiting at the door to her apartment as I stepped off. "This is a nice surprise," she said.

Say that again in ten minutes.

I found it difficult to speak and had to cough to clear my throat. "I need to talk to you."

Her face turned to concern. "Is everything okay? Did Max..."

I shook my head. "No. Nothing like that."

She hesitated before opening the door and stepping aside. Normally, I'd grab her the minute I got close, wrap her in my arms, and plant my lips on hers. As much as I wanted that one last time, it would only make it worse.

"Is Ella okay? Where is she?"

"She's fine. Sleeping. I asked Paula to work a few hours tonight instead of today so I could stop over."

Layla wrapped her arms around my neck. "So this is a booty call then?"

Fuck. I wanted her booty, all right. My damn body reacted the minute she touched me. How the fuck was I going to get the words out when everything in me wanted her? I looked down.

Don't be a pussy, Gray.

Get it done. Over with.

Put your wagging tongue away. They'll be plenty of time to lick shit at home—like your wounds.

I took a deep breath, swallowed, and looked up into her eyes. God, she was gorgeous. So beautiful and full of everything that was good.

She pressed her breasts against me. I could feel her hard nipples through our shirts. "Cat got your tongue?"

I even fucking loved her sarcasm.

I put my hands on her arms and lifted them off of me. The look on her face was as if I'd physically slapped her. She took a cautious step back and folded her arms across her chest in a self-protective stance.

"What's going on, Gray?"

"I have a lot on my plate right now."

"I know you do." Her voice had a touch of anger in it. She was always two steps ahead of her clients and knew how to read a situation better than anyone I'd ever met. The rest of the conversation we were about to have was a formality. She knew what was coming.

"Between the new business, dealing with Max, connecting with Ella—it's just too much."

"Well, it's not like you can do anything about any of those. This is what you were dealt. You'll deal with it."

I looked away. "Yeah. I will. And that's my point. I have a lot I need to take care of. So I won't have much extra time. I had to shuffle around my day and work things out with the babysitter just to find the time to get here tonight."

Her arms at her chest unfolded, and her hands went to her hips. Layla was *pissed*. "Spit it out, Gray."

"I don't have time for anything else. I need to end things between us."

"My father had time for a wife and daughter *and* a side piece and bastard child. When you want something bad enough, you *make* time for it."

Like a coward, I looked down. "I'm sorry."

She wasn't going to let me off that easy. "Look at me."

I raised my head, but left my eyes closed for a few seconds before opening them.

"You don't even want to try? I get that we won't have much time for now. But things will settle down eventually."

Her voice cracked a miniscule amount, but I caught it. Not thinking, I reached out to comfort her. She stepped back.

"Answer me."

I looked her in the eyes and broke both our hearts. "No. I don't even want to try."

She looked back and forth between my eyes, searching for something. Then she walked to the door and opened it. "Get out."

I walked toward the door and stopped in front of her. "Layla...I'm—"

She cut me off and pointed toward the hall. "Just get the hell out!"

The hardest steps I've ever had to take were walking out of her place. She'd given me a second chance when I hadn't deserved it. There was no way I was ever getting a third. This was it.

My legs felt like lead taking the last few steps. I turned around for one last look at her, but I didn't get a chance. She slammed the door in my face.

———

If anyone could cheer me up, it was my old bunkmate, Rip. It was the only thing I'd looked forward to since I'd walked out of Layla's apartment four nights ago.

Paula had Ella. Max no longer had the tube down her throat and had improved so much the doctors were talking about releasing her in a few days, and Rip was about to be a free man. What more could I ask for today?

Layla, that's what.

The guards greeted me like I was an old friend, instead of a former prisoner.

"Look at you, Pretty Boy." Officer Kirkland whistled. "What's that suit cost? More than I make in a month, I bet."

"Pipe down, Kirkland." I smiled. "You're just jealous because I've been released. How much time you got left? Twenty, twenty-five years until you can retire?"

He shook his head. "Don't remind me."

"How's Rip? He excited for today?"

"Must be. Heard he stayed awake for the entire morning news."

From behind Kirkland, a door opened and O'Halloran, another decent guard, escorted Rip down the long hall.

O'Halloran raised his chin to me. "You keeping out of trouble, Westbrook?"

"I haven't murdered my ex-wife yet. If I can manage that shit, I can keep outta this place."

He smiled. "Take care of yourself. And Rip here, too."

Rip shook hands with both guards and then opened his arms wide, with the hugest smile on his face. The moment was more emotional than any I'd had with my own father. We hugged it out with a lot of backslapping.

"How's it going, old man?" I asked him. "Miss me?"

"Sure did. Guy that took your bunk snored like a banshee and is a damn slob."

My smile felt good. "Not sure you get to complain about anyone's sleeping habits there, Van Winkle." I nodded toward the door. "Let's get the hell out of here before they decide to keep one of us."

Rip had me make three stops in the first hour of our drive back to the city. The first time he wanted McDonald's for lunch, the second time he needed to use the bathroom, and the third time he wanted to hit Walmart to pick up a cell phone. I took him to a Verizon store instead.

While he perused the flip phones, I grabbed a salesperson and told him to set me up with the latest iPhone and add it to my monthly plan.

"Here you go. Happy freedom day." I held out the bag.

Rip looked down at my offering. "What's this?"

"It's a cell phone—a real one." I lifted my chin to the flip phones he'd been browsing. "Unlike those things."

"I can't afford that."

"You don't have to. It's on me. Added it to my monthly bill. Once you're on your feet again, you can take it back over."

"I can't take that from you. Those things are expensive. That had to be over a hundred bucks."

I managed to contain my smirk. *Try a grand.* "It was on sale. Plus, I owe you."

He took the bag. "What do you owe me for?"

"Three years of listening to my crap."

"Your crap was more interesting than *my* crap. In fact, I don't have any crap," he laughed.

"Come on. Let's get back on the road."

There wasn't much traffic, so we relaxed as we drove and shot the shit. It didn't take long to catch up on Rip's life. All he had left was his one daughter who lived in Seattle.

"How's your lawyer lady doing?" he asked. "You tie that one up yet?"

My last letter to Rip had been a few days before everything went down with Ella and Max. Obviously, I had a ton to catch him up on. I didn't really feel like talking about it, but there was no hiding from it when it was just the two of us in the car.

"That's a long story," I warned him.

He leaned back in his seat. "Got a few more hours to kill. Start at the beginning."

So I did. Poor Rip spent the next hour shaking his head. He mostly stayed quiet, with a few "you got to be *shittin'* me" responses thrown in—until I got to the part where I'd broken it off with Layla.

"I never told you why my Laura doesn't talk to me anymore."

Laura was Rip's daughter. My eyes flashed to him and back to the road. "No. You never mentioned it."

I knew the story about why he'd gotten sent to prison—how he'd wanted to help with his granddaughter's medical bills, so he'd used his old-school printing shop to make fake Social Security cards. For a hundred dollars apiece, he'd cranked out more than a thousand phonies, all the while sending his daughter the cash anonymously. When he'd gotten arrested, his daughter had figured it out and stopped speaking to him. He'd never mentioned why, and I didn't push.

"Sweet Daniella, God rest her soul, was sixteen when her heart started to fail. Eighteen when she became too critical to get out of bed anymore. She'd had a dozen surgeries since she was born, and they just couldn't fix it. She needed a transplant. Most people think there's one big waiting list for organs. There is, but there isn't. You register with your transplant center. But you can register with more than one transplant center to try to increase your odds of getting an organ—it's called multiple listing. But the insurance company only pays for one set of tests, and then there's travel and hotels and everything that comes along with transporting a sick kid to a different facility. You need money."

"I had no idea."

"Yeah. Me neither. I knew my daughter wouldn't take the money if she knew how I'd gotten it. So I sent it to her anonymously. Rich people do that sometimes. Hospitals call them medical angels."

"Did she use the money?"

Rip looked down and shook his head. "Daniella had started to get real involved with her church group the last year of her life. And she'd made a lot of friends at the children's hospital, kids who were also on organ lists. She didn't want her mother to take the money because she thought money shouldn't give one person an advantage over another. She had friends on the same list as she was who couldn't afford to be on multiple lists. So my daughter wound up donating the money to the hospital's uninsured children's fund."

"Shit."

"Yeah. Laura had to go through losing Daniella alone while I was in prison for a crime I didn't need to commit. She'll come around eventually, I hope. But she's mad that I didn't communicate with her—never even asked how Daniella felt about being added to other lists. She says I just made the decision for her, as if I knew what she'd want." He paused. "*Sound familiar*?"

I sighed. "I get your point. But it's different. I'm trying to do what's best for Layla."

"And I was trying to do what was best for Daniella and Laura. But we don't get to decide what's best for other adults, son. They get to decide for themselves."

I understood what he was saying. I really did. But sometimes people you love won't do what's best for them if it means hurting someone they care about.

"Let me ask you something. Would you do it all over again?"

"What? Get myself in trouble to save my granddaughter? Of course. I'd spend the rest of my life in that shithole you just picked me up from if it meant she could've lived longer. But...I'd talk to her before I did it this time. Maybe not tell her my plan, but I'd at least find out *her* wishes. Had I done that, I'd have saved us all a lot of heartache."

We were quiet for a while after that. Rip stared out the window, lost in thought and no doubt enjoying his new freedom. I did what I'd been doing for a solid week— ruminated over my decision to end things with Layla.

When we got close to the city, Rip said, "I couldn't get a space at the Y in Queens. They were filled up. So I got one at the Bronx Y. You can just drop me wherever you're going. I'll grab a train up to the Bronx."

I'd almost forgotten that I hadn't told Rip about the arrangements I'd made. "I got you a place."

"Thanks. But I can't stay with you. I need to get back on my feet. I have enough money to last me a month or two."

"Wasn't inviting you to stay with me," I teased. "I got you your own place. In Queens. Bottom floor of a two-family house, not too far from where you used to live. First month is free. If you like the place, we can work it out so you do some work around the house and help the other tenant out here and there in exchange for rent."

"That sounds too good to be true."

"You haven't met the other tenant yet…"

Chapter 34

Layla

"*Law & Order* is much more interesting," Etta said. "No offense."

I laughed. "None taken. Not much goes on in traffic court that's too exciting."

The cashier called *next*, and Etta and I went to the window to pay her fines. The ADA had agreed to drop the driving without a license tickets in exchange for Etta pleading guilty to an unsafe door opening and broken taillight ticket—both hefty fines but not moving violations.

Etta had laid her confused old lady act on so thick, the ADA actually apologized for having to hit her with something. The judge, on the other hand, saw through Etta's charade and gave her a twenty-minute lecture. I was pretty sure Judge Peterson might be a year or two older than Etta. But it was taken care of, at least.

On our way out of the courthouse, we ran into Travis Burns, an attorney I hadn't seen in a few years. We stopped to talk, and I introduced Etta.

"You look great," he said.

"Thanks. So do you. What are you doing in traffic court?"

"Son of a VIP client got a DWI. You?"

I looked to Etta and smiled. "Etta's a VIP, too."

After a few minutes of chatting, Travis tilted his head. "Let's get together soon. Catch up over drinks?"

"Sure. I'd like that."

Etta wasted no time commenting when we walked away. "He's a real looker."

"Travis is a nice guy. Good attorney, too."

"Damn, Gray is an idiot."

When I'd picked Etta up this morning, she'd told me Gray had visited the other day and told her about us. She'd said it was none of her business, but thought it was a shame. I'd thought maybe I'd evaded a longer conversation about what had transpired between Gray and me. But it seemed that thought had been premature.

Even though I thought his reason for breaking things off was bullshit, I tried to pretend I understood. "Our timing was just bad," I said to Etta. "He's got a lot going on."

"Excuse my language, but that's big bullshit. The man has his head up his ass. Life threw him a curveball. I get it. But you don't stop swinging. You firm up your grip and smack it out of the park."

We walked down the courthouse steps and headed over to the parking garage. I usually took the train to court in Queens, but I'd wanted to pick Etta up, so I drove.

"You have to want to be with someone enough to overcome any obstacles," I said. "Gray didn't."

Etta stopped walking. "Is that what you think? That he didn't love you enough?"

"I think it's clear from his choice, Etta."

She shook her head. "Dear, you know I've known that boy since he was in diapers. He's loved three women in his life—his mother, God rest her soul, me, and *you*. He took three years in jail for a wife he cared about but never loved and married out of convenience. The man sacrifices for the people in his life like no other I've ever seen. That's what breaking things off with you was, sweetheart. He has it in his head that keeping you is not fair to *you*, for some reason."

We finished walking to the parking garage, found my car, and started on our way back to Etta's. What she'd said kept running through my mind. I'd been so shocked and pissed over what Gray had pulled that I'd never really stopped to think that maybe he was doing it to set me free. A selfless act like that did seem like more of a Gray thing to do than a dump-and-run because he was "too busy."

I drove the entire way to Etta's house lost in thought. She must've known I needed to mull over what she'd said, because she gave me space. I pulled into her driveway just as a man walked out of her house. He seemed to be about her age and wore a pair of slippers to carry out a bag of garbage.

Oh wow. Etta has a boyfriend.

I smiled. "Looks like you have better luck with men than I do."

Etta furrowed her brows and then realized what I'd thought. "That's Rip," she said with a laugh. "He's renting the apartment downstairs."

"Rip? As in Gray's old bunkmate?"

"The one and only."

Rip waved and walked to the passenger side of my car, opening the door for Etta.

He extended a hand to help her out, and I exited the car to say goodbye.

"Rip, this is…." Etta said.

He walked around the car and captured me in a bear hug. "I know who you are. Had to hear about you every day for long enough."

I smiled. Gray had shared Rip's story with me. The two men had a lot in common—both punished for things they did for other people. "I've heard a lot about you, too. Gray had said you were getting released soon. I didn't realize it had happened."

"Yep. Pretty Boy picked me up a few days ago. Set me up with a nice apartment to stay in, too."

"Oh. Wow. Well, welcome home."

Rip told Etta he was going to weed her garden and gave me another hug. "It was nice to finally meet you, Layla. I guess I'll be seeing you around soon."

I nodded, not wanting to explain that he probably wouldn't be. Once he was out of earshot, I said to Etta, "I guess he doesn't know."

She smiled. "Oh, he knows. We had dinner with Gray the other night."

I shook my head, confused.

Etta took my hand. "Let me tell you a little story. I think I already told you how me and my husband met—walked right into each other in the lobby of The Plaza Hotel—and how I once gave him the boot for a lie I'd caught him in. Well, he's a man, so of course that wasn't the only time he screwed up.

"In 1967, Henry was drafted into the Vietnam War. A few weeks before he was set to leave, he broke it off with me—told me he'd fallen for another woman and didn't love me anymore. I was heartbroken. It took me about a year before I started to move on. Back then, women were old maids if they were single at twenty-five, and my mother had started to pressure me to get back out into the dating world. Eventually, I met Fred." Etta looked down and smiled like she remembered him fondly. "Fred was a wonderful man. He treated me like a queen and made me smile at a time when I didn't want to. I adored him. But...I never really loved him like I had Henry."

"You married Henry, though, not Fred, right?"

Etta nodded. "Two years after I started dating Fred, he asked me to go to a fancy restaurant for dinner on my birthday. I had a feeling he might propose. I really cared for him. I knew he would make a wonderful husband. But it didn't feel right, because I didn't love Fred like I'd loved Henry."

"Did Fred ask you to marry him?"

"He didn't get the chance to. The night before my birthday, I went to The Plaza Hotel. It's where I'd met Henry the very first time. His father was a doorman there, and I'd gone for lunch when my grandmother was in town. I'd always thought the place was magical. Just being in the lobby gave me goosebumps; it was so beautiful. So, I got all dressed up like I was going on a date, and I went and sat in the lobby for a few hours, thinking about what I'd do if Fred proposed the next night. I decided in that lobby that I couldn't marry him, no matter how good of a catch he was. I would've been settling for Fred, and neither of us deserved that. After a few hours, I figured I'd go home. But you know what happened?"

"What?"

"I walked out the door at the exact same minute a certain man in uniform was walking in."

My eyes widened. "Henry was walking in when you were walking out?"

"He most certainly was. He'd gotten discharged, and just that day he'd arrived back home. His dad didn't work the door anymore. His knees had gone bad. Turned out, he'd become the hotel's elevator operator. He spent his evenings sitting on a chair, so I hadn't seen him, but Henry was coming to see his dad."

"Wow. That's so crazy."

"It is, isn't it? Eight million people in the city, and we were both at the same place right at that moment. Henry asked what I was doing there. And I explained I came to do some serious thinking about a man I'd been seeing for a while. I'll skip the part where I made him grovel and just tell you Henry had broken things off with me because he was going to war and didn't want me to waste years waiting for him when he didn't know what he could offer me if and when he came home. Men were coming back not right back then—or worse, not coming back at all."

"So you married Henry."

"Eventually. I forgave him because he did have my best interests at heart—even though he acted like a jackass making that decision for both of us like he did. Next week would have been forty-five years. We couldn't afford to get married at The Plaza, of course. But we went for drinks every year on our anniversary."

I smiled. "Thank you for sharing that, Etta. But the situation with Gray isn't quite the same, even though I know what you're getting at."

"I really hope it works out for you two, because once you've had true love, anything else feels like settling, and no one should ever settle when it comes to love." She squeezed my hand. "Thank you for today, sweetheart."

"Take care of yourself, Etta. You have my number if you need anything at all."

Chapter 35

Gray

Everything was finally starting to smooth out, yet the calm only made me more miserable. Max came home from the hospital today, Ella and I had developed a routine, and two of my company's first investments were doing great.

Of course it was a temporary step forward into smooth waters, because when Max was gone, the rocky waves would be back. I'd had a trial run at being a father, yet one that didn't involve the death of the only parent my daughter had ever known. At some point I'd be the replacement twenty-four seven, no matter what.

But for now, the lull of smooth sailing had me second-guessing what I'd done with Layla. Or nine hundred and ninety-seventh-guessing might be more accurate. I'd looked at Ella like a burden to Layla—but the truth was, as I got to know my daughter and got the hang of things, I had started to wonder if maybe, over time, Layla would come not to see Ella as a burden either.

Ella was a blessing. Sure, there were plenty of tough times ahead. But yesterday we'd spent the entire day together, and somehow my little angel kept the miserableness inside of me at bay. Today I was alone, and I wanted to fucking kill someone. I hadn't considered that she could make my life better—make mine *and* Layla's lives better.

I was in no mood for company tonight, but Etta had invited me for dinner with her and Rip three times in the last week. I didn't want to insult them both.

I let myself in with my key and stopped on the stairs, overhearing the two of them talking.

"She's a real looker," Rip said. "Probably has a line around the block of men wanting to take her out now that she's back on the market."

"Smart, too. I didn't see any other women in the courthouse looking like her. The man was very handsome. Had good posture. There's nothing like a man who can carry himself well."

I took the stairs two at a time. "I have a pretty good idea who the two of you are talking about from *smart*, *a real looker*, and *courthouse*, but I'd like to know who the *asshole* with good posture is."

Etta and Rip looked at each other like they'd been caught in the middle of a robbery. Wide-eyed, Etta tried to sweep what I'd heard under the table.

"Zippy." She walked over and kissed my cheek as I stood rigid, waiting for an answer. "I'm so happy the three of us were finally able to find time for another dinner."

I shook Rip's hand, looking him in the eye. "What's the story here, Rip?"

He looked at Etta and shrugged apologetically before turning back to me. "Etta went to court with your girl last week. Some suit was trying to make time with her in the hall of the courthouse, asked her to go out for drinks."

I clenched my teeth so hard, a headache immediately came on. "Who?"

Etta shook her head. "I don't remember his name. But he was handsome. Sounded like they were friendly. He was a lawyer."

"And she made plans to go out with him?"

"She was noncommittal at the courthouse."

The muscles in my shoulders loosened marginally. But then some sort of a strange, silent communication took place between Etta and Rip.

"What?" I said.

"Nothing." Etta pointed to the kitchen. "I think I smell the bread burning."

After she rushed to the kitchen, I looked at Rip again. "What else is there that the two of you aren't telling me?"

He blew out a deep breath. "Etta got a statement in the mail from your girl's firm yesterday. The fees were zeroed out. Layla had taken care of her stuff pro bono. Etta called the office to argue about getting a real bill, and when Layla wouldn't agree to give her one, Etta told her she wanted to at least make her a nice dinner to say thank you."

"Okay. So?"

Rip frowned. "Layla had plans...with the guy from the courthouse, apparently. A real big spender, too. Taking her to The Plaza tomorrow night for dinner."

The miserable feeling I'd had all day suddenly sprouted through my body. My head pounded, my stomach became knotted, and it felt like an elephant had sat his ass on my chest, making it difficult to breathe. I went to the kitchen, grabbed whatever alcohol Etta had in her cabinet, and filled half a glass. The urge to crush it in my hand was overwhelming.

Rip sat down in the living room. "I'm sorry, Gray. I didn't want to give you that news."

I drank half the bitter-tasting fluid in one gulp, hoping for something to help me feel calmer, something to numb me.

"I know she deserves a good life. I just hate that I can't be the one to give it to her. The thought of her being with anyone else makes me want to bash every fucking lawyer's head into a wall."

Rip chuckled. "Well, that wouldn't necessarily be a bad thing." He shook his head. "*Fucking lawyers*. No offense to your lady."

"How do you move on?" Rip's wife had been gone for four or five years now. "Does it get easier?"

"Did a single day go by that you didn't hear my Eileen's name when we were locked up?"

I thought about it. I was pretty sure I knew more about Eileen than Rip. My head fell into my hands. "Fuck."

Rip leaned forward, took the half-empty drink from my hand, and slugged the rest of it back. "Tell me about it."

I was miserable company during dinner and after. I'd have to send Etta some flowers to make up for it. At least Etta and Rip seemed to have hit it off. The two of them were actually pretty entertaining together. Between my sour mood and the additional drinks I kicked back, I left feeling ready to hit the sack.

I rested my head against the seat of the car for the entire drive home and closed my eyes. It wasn't like I'd expected Layla to stay celibate or anything. But what had it been? A whole two fucking weeks, and she was already moving on? And The Plaza Hotel? The fucker probably had a room for the night, too. I knew that move. A nice dinner, a couple of drinks—*you look gorgeous tonight... and, hey, my room is just upstairs.*

Fuck.

The car had stopped moving, so I opened my eyes to see where we were. I had to blink a few times to make sure I wasn't seeing things. We were stopped in traffic right in front of The Plaza Hotel. The same damned place the woman I loved would be out on a fucking date tomorrow night.

The next morning, I woke with my teeth still clenched, a blaring headache, and my palms sweating. The feeling of impending doom reminded me of how I'd felt the day before I'd started my damn prison sentence. But in my mind, the thought of Layla moving on had much longer-term ramifications. This loss wouldn't be over in a few years—because when you meet the love of your life, and lose her, what do you have left? Just life without the love. Before I met Layla, I hadn't even realized something was missing. Yet now, without her, I felt totally incomplete.

I'd experienced jealousy before, but it had come from a very different place—the green-eyed monster rearing its ugly head, an archaic sort of possessiveness over a woman that stemmed from some alpha-male, hormonal shit that bred on immaturity. But what I felt today was totally different. Sure, I wanted to beat the living piss out of the guy Layla had plans with tonight. But I also felt other emotions that were new to me—*fear*, *grief, loss.* As crazy as it seemed, it likely wasn't all that different than struggling with the death of someone you loved.

Luckily, I had a reason to drag my ass out of bed today. Otherwise I could have stayed put the entire day, wallowing in my pussified thoughts—which I was too chickenshit to act on. But I had responsibilities that took precedence over my self-pity. My daughter expected me.

I arrived at Max and Ella's house for my visit a little early. Paula was already there and helping Ella get dressed—*foo-sha* because it was Friday.

"How you feeling?"

I'd somehow come to terms with being civil to Max. While I would never understand the shit she put me through, or probably ever forgive her for it, I'd seen during her hospital stay that she had no one. And humanity made it impossible to torture her during the little time she had left.

"Good. Weak, but glad to be home."

I stuffed my hands into my pockets and nodded.

"How are things going with you and Ella?" Max asked. "She hasn't stopped talking about you since I got home."

"She's a great kid." I paused and thought about not saying what was on the tip of my tongue. But then I thought maybe it would offer Max peace. "You did a great job raising her. She's smart, happy, polite, and very settled for a little girl who's going through her mom being in and out of the hospital."

Max smiled. "Thank you. I regret lots of things in my life. But the thing I regret most is that you lost years with her because of my actions. She deserves you. And you deserve her. Time is a gift, and I hope you have many years with her, Gray. I truly mean that."

"Thank you."

Max took a deep breath. "I think we should tell her."

My eyes jumped to meet hers.

"I don't have much time left, and it might make the transition easier if she knows she still has one parent, that she's not alone in this world."

I suddenly got nervous. "You think she's ready for that?"

"I do."

I nodded. "All right, then. Whenever you're ready."

Max's smile was sad. "Time isn't something I can afford to waste. 'Don't put off until tomorrow what can be done today' is pretty much my mantra now."

Ella came flying into the room, and I quickly knelt to catch her. *God, I needed that hug, beautiful girl.* I squeezed her as hard as she squeezed me. Her little arms didn't fit around me, and I found myself thinking I really hoped she still did this when they did.

"Can we go to look for Stuart again today?"

Max's brows drew down, so I explained. "Central Park. I took her to the lake where they filmed *Stuart Little.*" I looked to Ella. "Sure. Why don't we stop off and get Freckles. I'm sure he'd like to come to the park."

She jumped up and down. "Yes! Yes! Yes!"

Max bent. "Sweetheart, before you go, there is something Gray and I would like to talk to you about."

Ella looked at her mother and signed a bunch of things I didn't understand.

Max laughed. "Yes. You have to put your listening ears on."

Paula seemed to sense we needed some time alone. "I told your mom I'd come back tonight to help with dinner and bath time," she told Ella. "I'll see you later, munchkin. I can't wait to hear about the park." She kissed the top of Ella's head and said goodbye to Max and me.

"Why don't we go in the living room?" Max nodded her head toward it.

My heart started to race. What if finding out disappointed her? What if she thought I'd known all along that she was my daughter and chose not to stick around? How the hell did you break the news to a little girl that a man she just met was really her father? I sure as shit hoped that Max had a plan, because I certainly didn't.

Max and Ella sat on the couch together. I sat on the chair diagonally across from them. Max looked at me, her eyes seeking approval to start. Only instead of confirmation we should begin, I must've offered a look like a deer in the headlights.

"It's going to be fine," Max whispered to me before shifting to face our daughter.

"Ella, do you remember when I told you that you were smart like your daddy?"

Ella pointed to her head. "I get my brain from my daddy."

Max smiled. "That's right. Well, I have some news for you."

I held my breath.

Ella signed something that made Max laugh. I really needed to learn the language fast.

"I don't think that Gray understood that, Ella. Tell him with your words *and* hands."

Ella went slow, showing me each word with her hands. "Gray." She moved her hands in a circular motion. "Smart." She tapped her forehead with one finger and then held up her hand, palm facing me.

I looked at Max in shock. *Is she asking what I think she's asking?*

Seeing my face, Max laughed. "Ella, are you saying Gray's smart like your daddy because you want him to *be* your daddy?"

Ella smiled and slapped both her hands over her face, covering it like she was shy. She spread two fingers to expose one eye and looked up at me, nodding.

I swallowed a few times to fight back a rush of unexpected tears. "Come here, you." Hooking an arm around her little waist, I lifted Ella up from the floor and onto my lap. I nudged her hands away from her face and smiled.

"I'm glad you want that, Ella. Because *I am* your daddy. I'm sorry I couldn't be here when you were a baby, but I promise I'm always going to be around from now on."

Ella stared at me, then looked to her mother for some sort of affirmation. Max nodded.

"Can I call you..."

She lifted her hand, extended her five fingers, and tapped her thumb to her forehead twice. It reminded me of a turkey. My signing ability was shit, but I'd stumbled across the word for *daddy* on my first night trying to learn it online. That one had stuck with me.

"I'd be honored if you'd call me..." I mimicked the sign and added the word with a crack in my voice. "Daddy."

Her smile choked me up. But then her pointer finger went to her lip, and she seemed to be pondering something. I glanced up at Max, who shrugged, and we waited.

"Does that mean I'm going to live with you and not Mommy?"

I shook my head, but then realized someday soon that would be the case, and I didn't want my first act as her official father to be a lie. I looked at Max and gave her the nonverbal cue for *how do I answer this one?*

Max took Ella's hand. "You get to have two places to call home. One with Mommy, and one with Daddy. And that's kinda cool because if one of us ever needs to...go away...you'll always have a place to call home."

Ella turned to me. "Are you going away again?"

"Nothing in the world could make me leave you now that I get to be your daddy."

Ella smiled. "Okay."

"And you know what else?" I said.

"What?"

"You know the room you slept in at my house?"

She nodded.

"That's going to be your room from now on. So you always have a place to call home when we're together. And, I'll tell you what, you can pick out your own paint color, and we can buy some decorations for it so it feels like your room."

Ella's eyes widened. "Can I paint it my favorite color?"

"We can paint it whatever you want."

She smiled. "My favorite color is rainbow, just like Layla's."

Chapter 36

Gray

The day went along like any other day with Ella after that. We stopped and picked up Freckles, who carried his old shoe with him the entire way to Central Park, and then the three of us spent the afternoon watching the model boats. While Ella searched for Stuart Little, I quietly obsessed over Layla's date tonight and remembered what a nice afternoon we'd had last time we were all here together.

Ella and I even bought ice cream from the same cart guy and sat on the same bench where the three of us had eaten it last time. It must've made Ella think about Layla, too.

She licked her cone while chocolate ice cream dripped down her fingers on the other side. "Can Layla come to the park with us next time?"

I didn't think I should explain that we'd broken up. Today was already info overload. "I don't know, sweetheart."

She licked some more. "Are you and Mommy married?"

I coughed as I swallowed my ice cream. "No, Mommy and I aren't married anymore."

"So, does that mean you can marry Layla?"

I wish. "It means I could get married again. So could your mom, technically."

"What's *tech-lick-ly* mean?"

"It means it could happen, but it's not necessarily going to."

She turned her hand, examined her fingers covered in melted ice cream, and dipped her head to lick them off.

"Like finding Stuart Little out there."

I chuckled. "I suppose so, yes."

"Why do people get married?"

Good question. I've been trying to figure out why I married your mother for years now.

"They get married because they love each other."

"Do you love Layla?"

Shit.

Well, that was at least one question I could answer wholeheartedly. "Yeah, sweetheart, I love Layla."

Ella was quiet for a long time after that. I glanced over a bunch of times while she licked her cone in silence, just knowing the wheels in her little head were spinning fast.

"What does love feel like?"

Jesus, she asked tough questions. "It feels like you would do anything in the world for that person to make them happy. It makes you happy and sort of warm inside."

She giggled. "My ice cream is making me feel cold inside. But I *love* ice cream."

Ella finished off her cone, and I bought a bottle of water to wet the napkins so she could clean off her hands, even though Freckles looked more than willing to take care of it for us. I'd thought our little heart-to-heart was over.

"Do I make you feel happy and warm inside?" she asked.

My heart swelled. "You do. And I'd do anything in the world to make you happy."

She smiled that toothy grin. "That means you love me."

I rubbed my nose against hers. "I certainly do. I love you very much, sweetheart."

Her face got very serious. "Are you staying here?"

"I'm going to stay forever, Ella."

***

I kept thinking about my conversation with Ella, even hours after I'd dropped her off. I'd meant every word I said to her. I loved her and would do anything in this world to make her happy. A month ago, if someone had asked me if I even wanted kids, I probably would've said no. My life experiences had made me sour on family life. I'd thought I knew the path I wanted to walk. Yet today, I didn't just accept that this was my fate—I *wanted* Ella in my life. Sometimes the most unexpected things redirect our course, and we realize we had no idea where we were even going before.

Which made me think...if I hadn't wanted a family not too long ago, and now I couldn't imagine my life without Ella, couldn't Layla feel the same way? Love changes everything.

If Ella didn't want me as her father, wouldn't I fight for her love? Wasn't that what I'd essentially told her today?

What does love feel like?

It feels like you would do anything in the world for that person to make them happy.

How could I decide what might make Layla happy when I hadn't even known what made *me* happy a month ago?

Fuck.

I'd screwed up. Big time. Again.

Layla might not want to be with me, but Rip, Etta, *everyone* was right—that wasn't my choice to make. It was hers.

I picked up my cell and glanced at the time on the phone. Seven fifteen. Scrolling with shaky hands, I got up and grabbed my wallet and keys. I found the number I needed and pressed *call*.

"Etta, what time is Layla's date?"

Chapter 37

Gray

Traffic. I jumped out of the cab two blocks from The Plaza and tossed a fifty at the driver. *Quicker to walk.* Which is what I started to do, until my walk turned into a jog, and the jog quickly turned into a full damn sprint.

The doorman wasn't sure whether to put his hand up to stop me or open the door.

"Where's the restaurant?" I demanded.

"Which one, sir?"

Shit. "All of them."

I started at the bottom. Palm Court was packed with people, but none of them was Layla. Next I hit The Champagne Bar, although that came up empty, too. I waited for the elevator to The Rose Club, but became impatient and went in search of stairs. Taking them two at a time, I made my way up and brushed past the maître d' as he attempted to help me.

No sign of her at the bar.

I headed to an interior flight of stairs, which led to an oversized living room-like setup. Scanning the large room, I was just about to move to my next stop when I saw the top of a woman's head over a tall red chair in a private corner of the room. She was sitting alone.

My heart raced out of control. It had to be her. As I got closer, I realized I had no idea what the hell I was going to say. Weaving my way through the furniture, I caught sight of a set of legs. Gorgeous, sexy, spectacular legs. I'd know them anywhere.

I stopped behind her chair and took a few deep breaths before taking the plunge.

Layla had her head down and was texting on her phone as I approached. It took her a few seconds to realize someone was standing in front of her. When she looked up, she blinked a few times.

"Gray? What are you doing here?"

"I need to talk to you."

The surprise on her face morphed into anger. "Here? Now? You didn't seem too concerned when I wanted to talk to you." She stood and folded her arms across her chest. "Make an appointment with my secretary on Monday for whatever you need."

"No."

Her brows shot up. "No?"

"It can't wait."

She shook her head and stepped closer. The fire in her eyes should have made me back up, but instead it fucking turned me on. It reminded me of the first time we'd met. Her blunt mouth had attracted me to her even before I'd noticed how perfect her lips were. That had been our thing—straight-up, no-bullshit honesty.

Her hands flew to her hips. "You have some balls, you know that? You dump me, write me off as if I never existed, then show up here while I'm waiting to have dinner and expect me to drop everything and talk to you?"

"Don't talk. Just listen."

The fire in her eyes flared. She opened her mouth to say something, then shut it and lifted her arm to look at her watch. "You've got one minute."

I couldn't resist the urge to touch her any longer. Reaching out, I cupped her face in my hands. She didn't smack them away, which I thought was a good sign.

"I fucked up. I know. I ended things because I thought it was best for you. Today I realized I didn't even know what was best for me, so how the hell could I have known what was best for you?"

Her face softened.

"I know you don't want children. A month ago I might've said the same thing. We both come from screwed-up families. But sometimes the unexpected comes along and makes us realize we never really knew what we wanted."

"You never even asked me if I wanted children."

I'd forgotten she didn't know I'd read her list. I looked down at my feet. "When I was looking for takeout menus, you were in the shower. I saw what you wrote."

Her eyes narrowed. "What I wrote? What are you talking about?"

I had the fucking thing memorized after so many times of playing it back in my mind. "I'll never be his priority... I'll get hurt again.... Never really wanted kids.... I deserve more."

I looked at her and nodded. "I know you deserve more. You deserve exactly what you want. But maybe there's a chance that what you want could change."

Layla's eyes seemed to go unfocused for a minute, as if she was searching for something. Then a look of recognition formed.

"You read one of my notebooks?"

"It wasn't intentional. But yeah, I did."

"And that's why you broke up with me? Because of the list?"

I shook my head. "I should've spoken to you about it."

"Yeah. You should've. You know why?"

I nodded. "Because I didn't have the right to make a choice for you."

"That's true. But it also would have given me a chance to tell you what you read wasn't about you."

"What?"

"That's right. I'd like to have kids someday. If you had *asked me*, I would have told you that. What you read was a list I made probably fifteen years ago—about whether I should *forgive my father*."

I stared at her in disbelief.

She ticked off the list on her fingers. "I'll never be his priority. I'll get hurt again. Never really wanted kids. I deserve more. I believe that was written when he didn't show up for my middle school graduation ceremony after he'd promised he'd be there. If I remember correctly, there was also *he's not dependable*. Because he wasn't. Ever."

I ran a hand through my hair. "Jesus Christ. Are you serious?"

"Based on that alone, you walked away from me. Without a fight?"

"Max said when you spoke to her—"

Layla held up a hand. "Don't even finish that sentence."

Shit.

She lifted her wrist and glanced at her watch. "Five seconds. Anything else?"

Shit.

It was now or never. I missed everything about this woman. From the way she smelled to the attitude she gave me to the warm feeling I had in my chest being near her again. My eyes dropped to her nose, and I realized she hadn't covered her freckles. It gave me the courage I needed to lay my heart on the line.

"I love you. I've never been surer of anything in my life. I fucking love you, Layla. We were meant to be together. We both knew it from that very first day. Loving you is like breathing; I can't stop."

Her pursed lips tilted upward, but then fell again. "You hurt me, Gray. *Twice.* I can't go through that again."

"I know. And if you let me have another chance, I promise I'll make it up to you. I won't doubt things between us again. I can't. Because I want to grow old with you, Freckles. We both grew up looking at our parents' relationships and not wanting to repeat what we saw. Ella will grow up wanting what she sees we have. We can break the cycle and do it right."

Tears filled her eyes. "I'm scared, Gray."

"Do you love me?"

She nodded. "I couldn't move on after we split the first time because I didn't know how to let go. I still don't."

"So don't, babe. Just hold on. And I'll do the same." My thumb caught a tear that spilled over.

"I miss Ella," she said.

It was my turn to get choked up. The only thing that made me happier than hearing she loved me was hearing she loved my daughter, too.

"She wants to paint her room in my house rainbow."

Layla smiled. "We can do that. When I was a kid, I always wanted white walls with a big rainbow painted on it."

She said *we*. I brushed my lips against hers. When she didn't stop me, I kept going. I licked her lips, urging her to open for me, and she moaned into my mouth. The kiss was more passionate than anything we'd ever shared. So much pent-up emotion zapped between us that it was impossible not to feel the burn. I wrapped her in my arms, holding her flush against me. The smell of her perfume and taste of her sweet kiss had me lost to where I even was. When I lifted her in the air, wanting to wrap her legs around me and back her against the nearest wall, Layla came to her senses.

"Gray..."

"Mmmm?" I tugged her hair, and my mouth began to explore her neck.

"We're in a public place."

I nibbled her ear. "Bathroom. Where's the nearest bathroom?"

She giggled. The sound was better than any melody to my ears. "I don't think we should go into a bathroom. But...we *are* in a hotel."

"Fuck, yeah." Reluctantly, I let her go, but only to race her out of the bar and toward the front desk. She had to practically run in her heels to keep up with me. Those things were definitely staying on.

Thank God, the hotel had a room.

Once we were in the elevator, I finally got to press her against the wall. I grabbed her ass and guided her legs around my waist, neither of us giving a shit that she was wearing a dress. Then I sucked on her collarbone and told her all of the things I couldn't wait to do to her.

"I can't wait to come inside of you. I don't even give a fuck that it's primal and chauvinistic. I want to mark every part of your body as mine. I'm going to leave bite marks on your thighs before I suck your pussy and you come in my mouth. I'm going to come in your sweet cunt and then your mouth. When I'm done, I'm going to bend you over the bed and fuck your ass with my fingers until you beg for my cock there, too."

"*God, Gray.*"

The doors slid open, and a startled-looking couple forced us to separate. Luckily, it was our floor.

Our only pause was stumbling into our hotel room like horny teenagers. And that was just because I couldn't decide where I wanted to fuck her first—up against the door, on the expensive desk in the corner of the room, or on the plush, king-size bed. Then again, the arm of the couch looked the perfect height for bending her over.... *Bed. The bed has to be first.*

Somehow I managed to strip us both out of our clothes while keeping our tongues entwined. I pulled back to look at her when she was naked. Her raven hair spread out over the white bedding, and her naturally tan body had a sheen of sweat I wanted to lick off from head to toe. But her beauty kept me standing there, staring.

"You are..." I was truly at a loss for words. "I want to say beautiful, but it doesn't seem like enough. You are... the love of my life."

She reached up, extending her hand to me. I kissed the top and the palm before threading our fingers together and climbing on top of her. Pulling our joined hands over her head, I lined up my cock with her slick entrance. Rubbing up and down, the feel of her wet heat was almost enough to make me come.

I took her mouth in a kiss as I pushed inside. My arms trembled as I steadied myself. "I love you, Layla."

"I love you, too, Gray." She smiled and wrapped her legs around my hips.

I'd wanted to stay put, tell her more about how I felt about her, but the urge to move was too great. I glided in and out, sucking on every part of her body as I went— her tits, her throat, her luscious lips. But when our eyes locked, we began to make love. Real, true, raw, painfully beautiful love. Like nothing I'd ever experienced.

I wanted to keep going slow, cherish this moment in time and never leave it, but when your woman utters the words, "Come inside of me. *Please* come inside of me," any chance of slow and steady gets tossed out the window.

My pace ratcheted up, and when she tightened her legs around my waist, I sank deep, rubbing against the spot she loved so much. Her eyes rolled back in her head, and she moaned.

"That's it. Come for me, babe. I'm going to fill your pussy.... I'm going to come so hard..."

Her body clenched down, and she began to spasm all around me. She called my name in a mix of a moan and scream as together we rode out her wave. When she started to come down, I sped up and fucked her even harder. Our bodies slapping against each other was the most erotic sound I'd ever heard. I was buried so deep, and she was so open for me, that my balls started to smack between her ass cheeks. Unable to hold back any more, I let go, coming long and hard inside of her.

It took a long time for us to catch our breath. Rolling off, I took her with me, settling on my back with her on top. Her head rested above my heart.

"Your heart is beating so fast."

"That's what you do to me."

I felt her smile against my chest while I stroked her damp hair.

A few minutes later, she turned her head and rested her chin on her hand to look up at me. "Shoot. I need to make a call."

My body stiffened. The only person she could possibly have to call at this moment would be her date. My arms locked around her, and I firmed up my grip. Logical or not, I was jealous of the man she'd stood up tonight for the mere fact that she'd *almost* gone out with him.

"Could we at least wait until my cock deflates before you get up to call another man?"

Her brows furrowed. "Another man? What are you talking about?"

"Weren't you going to call your date and apologize for standing him up?"

She lifted her head. "Wait. How did you know I was even here tonight?"

"Etta told me."

Layla started to laugh.

"What's so funny?"

"Etta. She played both of us. I'm supposed to be meeting *her* for dinner here tonight. She told me a story about how she ran into her husband here and said they came back every year on their anniversary—how when she was a little girl she always thought the place was magical, and then when she ran into the man she eventually married here, it confirmed it."

"I vaguely remember that from years ago. They'd both get all dressed up and come here every year."

"So it wasn't that you suddenly figured out you loved me and couldn't live without me, it was more like jealousy that got you off your ass to try to win me back."

"Does it matter what it took?"

"You're a jealous person normally, aren't you?"

"I'm only jealous when people touch what's mine, sweetheart."

"But I wasn't yours when you thought I had made plans for a date with a man tonight."

I reached down and pulled Layla up from my chest so we were eye to eye. "You've been mine since the day we met. We may not have always been together, but that didn't make you any less mine."

Epilogue

Layla

2 years later

I came home to something rare—a quiet house.

When I'd left this morning to have breakfast with my dad and half-sister, the house was already chaotic. Gray and Ella were out in the yard by 8AM, working on the garden from hell. Freckles had rolled in the pile of manure they'd planned to spread on one side of the yard today and then dashed through the sprinkler on the other.

Nothing like having coffee with the smell of wet dog and cow shit right before going to share a meal with two people who still made me jittery.

A few months ago, I'd been out with Ella and run into my half-sister, Kristen, again. She'd invited herself to join us for lunch, and when we were done, I realized I'd actually had a good time. It had opened a door I'd thought was permanently closed, and we'd been taking things slowly ever since.

I dropped my purse on the living room coffee table and went out back. No one was in the yard either, but I couldn't help laughing at the craziness I saw.

The house we'd bought in Brooklyn six months ago was a few blocks from where Ella had lived with her mother. I'd fallen in love with the neighborhood over the year and a half we'd frequently visited when picking up Ella. Max had surprised everyone, including the doctors, and lived for eighteen more months, rather than the three to six they'd told her was likely. Parts of that extended ride were paved with rough road—frequent hospital stays and heartache for Ella as she got older and really started to realize what was happening.

Ella had experienced so much change; it just seemed like one less thing she'd have to deal with if we stayed in the neighborhood she was already familiar with.

So, we bought a beautiful old brownstone with a small yard on a tree-lined street and decided to call Brooklyn home. Ella had shut down for a while after her mother passed, and Gray was desperate to connect with her. We both were. I'd suggested that maybe the two of them should come up with a project to work on, which would give them a reason to spend time together. Gray had broken out the blueprints for his mother's garden, the one they'd never had the chance to plant together, and that he'd flown out to California to plant around her burial plot.

I looked around our yard. In one corner was his mother's garden—complete to her specs with all of the trees, flowers, and plantings she'd designed twenty-five years ago. That project had drawn Ella back out, and Gray wanted to keep going. So, the two of them had decided to design their own garden—just like he'd done with his mother when he was little.

They'd spent most nights for more than a month designing it. On weekends, we'd walked around nurseries and garden shows, which frequently led to plan redesigns. Now they were on phase three of the planting. I didn't even want to know the value of everything planted in this crazy yard. I was pretty sure we had at least a car back here. But what it had given Gray and Ella, you couldn't put a price tag on. Her healing and their bonding was worth any amount of money.

I took one more look at the jungle and headed back inside. Where was everyone? I realized even Freckles wasn't around. His trusty shoe sat on his doggy bed— not his original one, of course. His former owner's worn loafer, which he'd carried around for the better part of two years, was now buried in our yard. About a week after Ella had moved in, Gray and I caught him putting his loafer to rest near the big tree in the middle of the yard. That night, he'd stolen one of Ella's light-up sneakers, and that was that. His old master had finally been replaced. These days he seldom traveled without Ella's little shoe.

I went upstairs to get changed and stopped at Ella's doorway to turn the light off. The white walls with a huge rainbow never ceased to make me smile. A few months ago, I'd been reading *Stuart Little* to her in bed for at least the hundredth time, and she'd asked me if her mom could see the rainbow from up above. I'd told her I thought she could. God only puts rainbows in the sky after a storm, and I'd always thought it was to remind us that things will get brighter again.

I flicked off the light in Ella's room and headed to our bedroom. The second floor of the house could get hot during the day, especially our room since my crazy boyfriend had double-insulated all four walls with soundproof insulation when we'd redone the upstairs. Just because we were full-time parents now didn't mean Gray took it easy in the bedroom at night.

I went into our walk-in closet and stripped off my clothes in favor of a tank top and shorts. On my way out, I noticed something in the middle of the bed.

A red spiral notebook. On the cover, in Gray's masculine, slashy handwriting, he'd written *Gray's Yeahway Notebook*. I laughed and sat down to see what he was up to.

Just like my books, the page was divided into pros and cons with a pen line down the middle. His list didn't have a heading at the top, so I tried to unravel the mystery.

The pros list was huge, and the first entry cracked me up.

Big dick.

I couldn't decipher what the next few were about.

Remote control

Programmed coffee

Fresh cherry tomatoes

Rip and Etta. Really?

What the hell was this crazy man up to? I kept scanning the list.

Magic tongue

Love of my life

Rainbows

The list went on and on and took up nearly the entire front and back of a page. The last entry made my heart sigh.

Because she has the other half of my heart, and together our souls beat as one.

I'd been so engrossed in figuring out the list that I hadn't heard anyone come in. Gray's deep voice made me leap from the bed, and the notebook went flying into the air.

"Snooping?"

"God, Gray." I held my hand across my heart, which felt like it might beat out of my chest. "You scared the living crap out of me."

He stayed in the doorway, filling it with his imposing frame. His arms reached over his head, holding onto the top. All it took was one look at the sexy half-smirk on his face, and I knew he was up to no good. The throb between my legs hoped whatever it was, it happened in this room.

His eyes pointed to the notebook on the floor. "Figure it out?"

"Yes, I think so. The title of the list is *Gray is insane*."

His lip twitched, and he stepped into the room. He picked up the notebook and handed it to me.

"Why don't we go through it together?"

I realized Ella hadn't run into the room. "Where's Ella?"

"Grandma and Grandpa's for the night."

Translation: *Etta and Rip's*.

Ella had started to call them Grandma and Grandpa about a year ago. They'd taken her overnight a few times for us—once when we had to go out of town for a business meeting together, and again on the night Gray had asked me to move in with him.

"Did you tell me they were taking her and I forgot?"

He shook his head. "Nope. Thought we could talk without interruptions. They have Freckles, too."

My body really loved the thought of an entire night alone with Gray. "What do you want to talk about?"

His eyes pointed to the list again. "Start reading."

I was intrigued, to say the least. Looking down, I read the first one. "Big dick?"

"I'd say it was above average, wouldn't you?"

"So this refers to your anatomy then?"

"Of course."

I chuckled. "Remote control?"

He sat down on the bed. "Do you know how to work it?"

"No."

"Well, I do."

My brows furrowed. "Okay...."

He eyed the list again. "Keep going."

"Programmed coffee?"

"How important is coffee to you when you wake up?"

"How important is number one on your list to you?" I said.

That sexy lip twitched again. "Keep going."

I looked down. "Fresh cherry tomatoes?"

"They're good from the garden from hell, aren't they?"

"Mmmm. Like eating balls of sugar."

Continuing with the puzzle. "Rip and Etta?"

"How long have they been married now?"

"I don't know. A few months?"

Rip and Etta had secretly gotten together as a couple within a few weeks of Rip moving in. That part hadn't shocked us. They were two peas in a pod. But we *had* been surprised when Rip proposed. He stood to lose some of the survivor benefits he received from his deceased wife's pension if he got remarried. When we'd mentioned that, he'd said he was fully aware, and he'd rather be broke and make an honest woman out of Etta than have some cash in his pocket—although they didn't have to worry about cash anymore.

Gray had gifted them the house they lived in as a wedding gift. Well, that and the other surprise gift he'd arranged. Somehow Gray had talked Rip's daughter into coming to their wedding. Rip had cried like a baby when he saw her walk in. And the rest of us couldn't help but follow suit.

Gray peeked at the list. "The next one better be self-explanatory."

Magic tongue

I shifted in my seat and smiled.

Next up was *Love of my life*.

"Do you love me?" he said.

"Of course. More than anything."

"Keep going."

"Rainbow?"

"What did you say to me after we finished painting Ella's room with that giant rainbow as a surprise?"

I remembered. "I said you were the rainbow of my life. You cleared the way for the rain to stop."

He took my hand and squeezed it. Together we ran through the remainder of the pro list.

"Figure it out yet?" he asked.

"Maybe I need to read the cons."

There was only one thing listed on the con list. I read it out loud.

"Stuck with me forever."

Gray stood. And then he got down on one knee and took my hand.

"I wanted to be prepared in case you needed to debate it before answering me. Knowledge of how to use the remote and program the coffeemaker, magic tongue, Rip and Etta beating us to the altar...they're just some of a never-ending list of reasons you should marry me."

He reached into his pocket and took out a beautiful box. Opening it, he revealed the most amazing engagement ring I'd ever seen. The center stone had to be three or four carats, and there were two stones on either side, each big enough to be an engagement ring on its own.

"When I told Etta I planned on asking you to marry me, and that I wanted to incorporate the stone from my mother's ring into the setting, she insisted I also take her original wedding ring and use that stone in the design, too. So this ring is made of three stones from the most amazing women from my life. The big stone in the center is just for you. And the ones on the sides are my mother's and Etta's. While I was working with the jeweler on designing it, I realized it was also symbolic to have three stones— because you're getting two of us, me and Ella."

Tears streamed down my face. I looked down at our joined hands and noticed Gray's were shaking. The man never showed his nerves.

"It's beautiful, Gray. I don't even know what to say."

"I might have padded the pro list in my favor a little. And the one con, being stuck with me forever, might outweigh the two pages of pros. But if you agree to be my wife, I promise that every day I'll work on adding a new thing to that pro list. I could say that you restored my faith in love, but you did more than that, Layla. You brought me back to *life*. So please marry me. Please tell me you'll spend the rest of your life as my wife."

I was so choked up, I could barely get out the words. "Yes. Yes. *God, yes.*"

Gray took my face in his hands, cupped my cheeks, and kissed me gently on the lips. "I almost forgot. I told Ella I was going to ask you to be my wife today, and she told me to tell you something."

"What?"

Gray leaned back and placed his thumb against his hand, spreading his fingers wide. "Mommy," he said. "She's going to stop calling you Layla and call you Mommy, if that's okay with you."

Tears of happiness flooded after that. I grabbed Gray in a hug and didn't let him go for the longest time. It was a good thing he'd made the list for me, because listing all the reasons I should marry this man could have taken years and many notebooks. But in the end, I only needed one truth on the pro list: Every piece of me loved every piece of him.

I sniffled back tears. "You made one mistake on your yeahway list, Mr. Westbrook."

He pushed a piece of hair off my cheek and smiled. "Oh yeah? What's that, Freckles?"

"*Stuck with you forever* is on the wrong side of the page."

Acknowledgements

To you – The *readers*. Thank you continuing to allow me to be part of your escape. Sometimes we can't leave, but need to go somewhere else for a while. I'm honored to have my stories keep you company there.

To Penelope – The last few months have been tough. From our crazy schedule to personal loss, you've been there to put up with me. I save a fortune in therapy because you're by my side. Thank you.

To Julie – Thank you for your friendship, support, and my perfect New York morning coffee.

To Luna – Thank you for your beautiful graphics, unwavering support, friendship, and honesty. I always know I can come to you for a frank opinion.

To Sommer – I'm pretty sure you figure out what I want before I do these days. You bring my books to life with your beautiful covers! Thank you!

To my agent and friend, Kimberly Brower – Thank you for always having your eyes open for new opportunities and being my sounding board.

To Jessica, Elaine, and Eda – Thank you for making me sound smarter than I am with all of your editing! You make all of my stories and *me* better.

To Mindy – I couldn't be more excited to have you join us! Thank you for working with me on this release from start to finish. I hope this was the first of many!

To all of the bloggers – Social media visibility is gone, affiliate programs have been decimated, and new laws and privacy policies are challenging. Yet you're still here day after day, posting tirelessly, and sharing your passion for books. Your enthusiasm is contagious and launches a book despite all that it has to overcome. Thank you for taking your time to read my stories, write reviews, make videos, and share teasers that bring my books to life.

Much love
Vi

Other Books by
Vi Keeland

Standalone novels
Sex, Not Love
Beautiful Mistake
EgoManiac
Bossman
The Baller
Dear Bridget, I Want You (Co-written with Penelope Ward)
Mister Moneybags (Co-written with Penelope Ward)
Playboy Pilot (Co-written with Penelope Ward)
Stuck-Up Suit (Co-written with Penelope Ward)
Cocky Bastard (Co-written with Penelope Ward)
Left Behind (A Young Adult Novel)
First Thing I See

The Rush Series
Rebel Heir (Co-written with Penelope Ward)
Rebel Heart (Co-written with Penelope Ward)

Life on Stage series (2 standalone books)
Beat
Throb

MMA Fighter series (3 standalone books)
Worth the Fight
Worth the Chance
Worth Forgiving

The Cole Series (2 book serial)
Belong to You
Made for You

CPSIA information can be obtained
at www.ICGtesting.com
Printed in the USA
LVHW011537260420
654464LV00001B/174